raise for

FOX
CREEK

"This genuinely thrilling and atmospheric novel brims with characters who are easy to root for."

—*The New York Times Book Review*

"As usual in a Krueger novel, the prose is elegant, the landscape of Minnesota's northeastern triangle is vividly portrayed, the character development is superb, and Henry's Native American mysticism is treated with understanding and respect."

—*The Washington Post*

"From *Iron Lake*—the first in the Cork O'Connor series—to *Fox Creek*, Krueger has exhibited a mastery and control that can't be denied. Maybe he should start calling himself an alchemist, because he has the formula down to an art."

—*St. Louis Post Dispatch*

"With its quick pacing and multi-layered plot, William Kent Krueger's *Fox Creek* dazzles early, sucking readers in, before giving way to a heart-thumping final act that delivers one hell of a reading experience."

—*The Real Book Spy*

ALSO BY WILLIAM KENT KRUEGER

FOX CREEK

A Novel

William Kent Krueger

ATRIA PAPERBACK

New York   London   Toronto   Sydney   New Delhi

ATRIA
PAPERBACK

An Imprint of Simon & Schuster, Inc.
1230 Avenue of the Americas
New York, NY 10020

First Atria Paperback edition May 2023

ATRIA PAPERBACK and colophon are trademarks of Simon & Schuster, Inc.

For information about special discounts for bulk purchases, please contact Simon & Schuster Special Sales at 1-866-506-1949 or business@simonandschuster.com.

The Simon & Schuster Speakers Bureau can bring authors to your live event. For more information or to book an event, contact the Simon & Schuster Speakers Bureau at 1-866-248-3049 or visit our website at www.simonspeakers.com.

Interior design by Yvonne Taylor

Manufactured in the United States of America

1   3   5   7   9   10   8   6   4   2

Library of Congress Cataloging-in-Publication Data is available.

ISBN 978-1-9821-2871-5
ISBN 978-1-9821-2872-2 (pbk)
ISBN 978-1-9821-2873-9 (ebook)

To the congregation of Hamline Church United Methodist,
who have been my faithful companions on
the spiritual journey we walk together.

ACKNOWLEDGMENTS

I have many friends in the Native community whose help and guidance have been significant in my understanding of these cultures not my own. But two of my friends deserve a special note of thanks. To Monte Fronk, officer for the Mille Lacs Band of Ojibwe Tribal Police, and Deb Foster, former director of the Ain Dah Yung Center in Saint Paul, I offer my heartfelt gratitude for your advice and counsel and for opening my eyes to so many issues important to Native people everywhere.

Also, my continuing thanks to my stellar agent, Danielle Egan-Miller, and to all the fine folks at Browne and Miller Literary Associates for their astute editorial eyes, savvy business counsel, and general all-around helpfulness across the many years of our friendship.

A huge thank-you to Peter Borland and Sean Delone, the finest editorial duo in the business, who, time and again, have helped shape my wayward manuscripts into more compelling and far more polished offerings.

And finally, to readers everywhere who have embraced my

work and let me know that my stories have found a place in their hearts, I offer my deepest and sincerest thanks for your continuing support and encouragement.

PROLOGUE

He's an old man, with more than a century of living behind him. When he rises each morning, there is no part of his body that doesn't feel the weight, the ache, the wear of all those years. Although he moves more slowly now, he still unceasingly walks the forests with which he has been in intimate communion since he was a boy, spends full days alone in the great North Woods. His disappearances have become a cause for concern among those who care about him, and there are many, not only on the Iron Lake Reservation but also in the town of Aurora and across much of Tamarack County, Minnesota. When he returns from a long absence and sees the worry on their faces, he smiles and asks, "What are you afraid of?" Their answers are vague fears for his safety. "If I lie down somewhere on a soft bed of pine needles and begin my journey into the next world without a chance for you to say goodbye, you can always burn tobacco and send me your prayers. I will hear," he promises.

His body is a thin wall between this world and that which awaits him beyond, but sometimes his spirit travels between these two worlds. He has occasionally flown like an eagle and seen from a high place his own body lying as if lifeless under a canopy of pine boughs. He understands his death is an experience neither to fear nor to welcome. It is simply a place toward which he has been walking since the moment of his birth.

The world around him is one that has both showered him in delight and presented him with enormous challenge. The delight has always been in nature, in the beauty it has offered, the solace, the lessons, the wisdom, the healing, the communion of spirits. The challenge has been of the human kind. At the hands of human beings, he has experienced cruelty, pain, deceit, avarice, jealousy, hate. Most of his life he has been a healer, working in the ways of the natural world to help guide others to a place of harmony, what his people, the Anishinaabeg, call *mino-bimaadiziwin*, the way of the good life. It is the purpose to which he was born.

But he feels the pull of another calling now, one that despite his age and knowledge and wisdom he doesn't understand. It is a dark calling, melancholy and unsettling. As he walks the woods in the communion of spirits, he asks for answers, which have not come. Patience has always been his grounding, but he feels himself growing restless and uncertain. He feels he is being followed, but not by anything human. Death is his shadow. The prospect of his own death isn't what troubles him. It is the sense that death will come to others, come far too early in their journey through this world. What the old man, this ancient soul, is trying to understand is this: Am I the one who stands between death and the others, or am I the one who leads death to them?

- PART ONE -

CORK

CHAPTER 1

It's after the lunch rush, and the man at the window orders a Sam's Special, large fries, and a chocolate shake, a pretty standard request. But while he waits, alone now that the line has dwindled to nothing, he jabbers on about this and that, then finally asks the question as if he hasn't been working up to it all along: "You're a private investigator, right?"

The man is a stranger, a face Cork O'Connor can't recall ever having seen in Tamarack County before, and Cork is good at remembering faces.

"I have a license. But mostly, I flip burgers. On the whole, I find it safer." Cork slides the bag containing the burger and fries across the window counter, then hands the man the shake. "That'll be nine seventy-five."

The man takes a ten from his shiny wallet, gives it to Cork, and says, "Keep the change." He stands looking at the bag and the shake, shifting a little on his feet, and finally comes out with it. "I need your help."

"The kind that requires a PI license?"

"Yeah. That kind."

"I'll meet you at the door."

Cork turns to his son, Stephen, who is scraping the charred grease from the lunch rush off the grill. Cork's son is twenty-one, average height and build, but his Ojibwe heritage is evident in the dark brown of his eyes, the near black of his hair, and the prominence of his cheekbones. More than any of Cork's children, he displays his Anishinaabe ancestry.

"Watch the window," Cork says.

Stephen nods, and Cork leaves the prep area and walks to the rear of Sam's Place.

It's an old Quonset hut, circa World War Two, which an Ojibwe man named Sam Winter Moon, long deceased, converted into a burger joint at the edge of Iron Lake, on the outskirts of Aurora, a small town deep in the great Northwoods of Minnesota, a stone's throw from the Canadian border. The front of the Quonset hut is the food operation. The rear is a sometime living area with a kitchen and a sometime office with filing cabinets. In the center is a table with four chairs for meeting the occasional client or, more often, simply eating a meal.

Cork opens the door, letting in the early May sunshine and the stranger. "Have a seat."

The man sits and puts his food on the table. That morning, when he arrived to open Sam's Place, Cork had taken off his jean jacket and draped it over a chairback. Now he sits in that chair, crosses his legs, and waits. Through the door to the prep area comes the rhythmic *scrape, scrape, scrape* as Stephen cleans the grill. The man stares at Cork as if waiting for him to begin. Cork stares back.

The man finally fumbles it out. "I heard you're . . . part Indian."

"My grandmother was true-blood Iron Lake Anishinaabe. Is that important?"

"Yeah." The man frowns a moment. "Or maybe. I'm not sure."

"That burger's getting cold, and the shake is getting warm."

The man stares at his packaged meal. "I'm not really hungry. But I could use a cup of coffee."

"Black?"

"Whatever," the man says.

Cork gets up and returns to the food prep area.

"What's it all about?" Tiny beads of sweat stand out on Stephen's forehead, the result of the heat from the grill and his work cleaning its surface.

"Don't know yet," Cork replies.

He fills two disposable cups from the coffee urn and heads back. He places one cup on the table in front of his guest, then sits down, sips from his own cup, and waits.

"My wife's gone missing," the man finally says without touching his coffee.

"You're not from around here, Mr. —?"

"Morriseau. Louis Morriseau. I go by Lou."

He offers his hand as an afterthought. When Cork takes it, he feels the damp and the fleshiness of the palm, which together remind him of a kitchen sponge.

"From Edina, down in the Twin Cities. I'm in real estate." Morriseau is in his late forties or early fifties, dressed in a long-sleeve blue shirt with some kind of logo stitched into the fabric over the area of his left pec. Cork doesn't recognize the logo but guesses that it's a brand you wouldn't find at Target. A place like Saks Fifth Avenue, maybe. Cork's never been there, but he can imagine. The loafers on the man's feet are shiny and as out of place in the North Country as his cologne. Earlier, during the rush, Cork had watched as Morriseau parked his shiny Escalade in the gravel lot in front of Sam's Place, well away from the dusty pickups and mud-spattered Jeeps, as if afraid the dirt and grit might migrate. "I do pretty damn well," Morriseau adds. Which lowers him yet another notch in Cork's estimation.

"Why is it important that I have Native heritage?" Cork asks.

"Dolores—that's my wife—has become fascinated with Indian stuff lately."

"Indian stuff?"

"You know, dreamcatchers, sage bundles, beadwork, sweat lodges, visions."

"And you have a problem with that?"

"She claims to be part Indian, but she's got no proof. It's just another one of her fancies. Last year she was into Transcendental Meditation. The year before it was Scientology. Every year something different. This year it's Indians."

"You say she's missing. How long?"

"Nearly a week."

"Have you reported this to the police?"

Morriseau shakes his head. "It's not like I don't know where she's gone."

"You believe she's in Aurora?"

"Around here somewhere, yeah."

"Why?"

"Because the man she's in love with lives up here and he's Indian."

"So that's what this is about. Another man."

"It's a passing fancy. Dolores is always wrapped up in one fad or another."

"You think she's what? Just into her Indian period?"

"Something like that, yeah."

"Why not simply wait it out?"

"Because this isn't like when she was into yoga or marching for PETA. This is another guy."

"An Indian from around here."

"Yeah."

"And you know this how?"

"She left me a note, told me she was leaving me. And she keeps a journal, writes in it every day. I read it. She talks about this guy a lot in the last few months. It's clear she's bonkers over him."

"Bonkers? Are they lovers?"

"God, I hate that word. It's so . . . delicate. But yeah, from what I read they must be screwing like a couple of rabbits. Me and Dolores, we don't share a bedroom anymore. She claims my snoring keeps her awake."

"What is it you want from me?"

"Find her. Take me to her."

"So you can do what?"

"Talk her into coming home."

Cork thinks about the Escalade and the distance the man put between his precious set of wheels and any taint from the local vehicles in the lot.

"You're sure that's all? Just to talk to her?"

"I swear."

"What if she doesn't want to listen?"

"I'll cross that bridge when I come to it."

"Do you have a photo of Dolores?"

Lou Morriseau takes a snapshot from the wallet where he pulled out the ten, lays it on the table, and slides it across to Cork. She's a stunning woman, a redhead. Her eyes are green, her smile like one you'd see on a billboard for a successful dental plan. It's a static photograph and Cork doesn't want to read too much into it, but he thinks the woman looks a good deal smarter, or maybe just deeper, than her husband.

"This Native paramour who's stolen your wife's heart, do you have a name?"

"Yeah. It was in her journal. Now it's burned into my brain." The man's face goes taut, as if, in fact, a red-hot brand has just seared his soul. His lips curl into a snarl, and he spits out, "Henry Meloux."

CHAPTER 2

Stephen stands at the serving window, watching as Louis Morriseau drives away. "Henry?" he says. "You've got to be kidding me."

Cork stands beside him, watching the Escalade disappear. "I don't know what was in her journal. Can you imagine Henry and Dolores Morriseau doing it like a couple of rabbits?"

"Fifty years ago, maybe," Stephen says. "Did you agree to take him on as a client?"

"Only as a favor to Henry, just to keep that guy off his back."

Cork had used his cell phone to snap a photograph of Morriseau as the man crossed the gravel lot to his Escalade, and he studies the shot now, with Stephen looking over his shoulder.

"The guy's soft," Stephen notes. "Henry could take him in a heartbeat."

"Henry is a hundred and five years old. At least."

"I'd still lay odds on him."

"As soon as your sister gets here, I'm heading out to Crow Point to clear this up." Cork shakes his head. "Henry the homewrecker. Imagine that."

An hour later, Jenny, Cork's oldest child, arrives in her Forester. She's brought Waaboo, Cork's grandson, with her. Cork steps from the Quonset hut and watches the two of them as they stand together for a moment, eyes to the sky. Cork sees it, too, a bald eagle circling above a grove of birch trees down the shoreline of Iron Lake. The great wingspan seems to press against the spring sky as if the bird is gliding along an azure wall, searching for an opening. The eagle finally settles on a limb of the tallest tree, where it perches awhile, eyeing the glittering afternoon blue of the lake. Jenny and Waaboo turn, and when he sees his grandfather, the little boy cries, "Baa-baa," and runs across the gravel. Cork lifts him, swings him around in the air, and Waaboo squeals with delight. His real name is Aaron Smalldog O'Connor. He is five years old and of mixed heritage. He's become the small jewel of the O'Connor household, the delight at the center of so much of their lives. Stephen long ago gave him the nickname Waaboo, which means "little rabbit" in the language of the Ojibwe, and it has stuck.

"I'm gonna help make Waaboo burgers," the little boy declares after Cork has set him back on his feet. There's a menu item at Sam's Place named after him, a bison burger that has become quite popular.

"No," his mother says. She has a satchel over her shoulder, from which she pulls a couple of books—*Horton Hatches the Egg* and a *Sesame Street* coloring book. "He's going to do some reading and some coloring until his father picks him up."

"He could help for a while," Cork tells her.

"Child labor laws," Jenny says with a stern look.

"Not if he's just working for the fun of it."

"Don't go, Baa-baa," Waaboo pleads.

"I have to, little guy. I need to talk to Henry Meloux."

Cork explains to Jenny what's going on, and when she hears the story, she laughs until tears roll down her cheeks.

"Cuckold?" young Waaboo asks. "Is that what comes out of a cuckoo clock?"

"Not quite," Cork says. "And in Henry's case, completely ridiculous. I'm hoping to be back in time to close tonight. But if not—"

"Don't worry about it," Jenny says. "We'll make sure it's covered."

It's midafternoon in early May, a day aromatic with spring. The scent of pine seems especially strong to Cork as he drives his Expedition north along the edge of Iron Lake. Partially hidden among the trees, cabins that have been closed up much of the winter are being reopened, and soon Aurora will be alive once again with summer residents and tourists. Which is good for Tamarack County, whose economy has never quite recovered from the closing of the iron mines that once meant great wealth for the region. On the other hand, it will bring an end to the blessed quiet that always descends with winter. Except for a brief few years when he was a cop on the South Side of Chicago, this far-north outpost has been Cork's home his entire life and, despite the mosquitoes and blackflies of summer and the Arctic blasts of winter, he loves this place with his whole heart.

He pulls the Expedition to a stop behind a dusty pickup truck parked at the side of the graveled county road near the double-trunk birch that marks the trail through the Superior National Forest to Crow Point. The truck belongs to Rainy, Cork's wife. He hasn't seen her in a couple of days. She's been helping Meloux on Crow Point, while Leah Duling, who usually sees to the old man's needs, is gone to the Lac Courte Oreilles Reservation in Wisconsin to visit family. He locks his vehicle and begins the two-mile hike to the isolated cabin of Henry Meloux.

The great Northwoods has awakened from a long winter slumber. Pink lady's slippers, red columbines, and pale nodding chickweed dot the trail's edge like strewn jewels. Flycatchers, chickadees, mourning warblers, and blue jays flit among the pines and groves of aspens and birches, their calls like the voice of the forest itself. The smell of the still-wet, newly thawed earth gives the air a fecund, musky scent that is perfume to Cork's nose.

He crosses Wine Creek and, not far beyond that, enters land on the reservation of the Iron Lake Ojibwe. Soon after, he breaks from the trees and stands at the edge of a meadow. On the far side is Meloux's cabin, a single-room structure built nine decades earlier. Near it is another cabin, only a few years old, which Cork helped to build. It's where Leah Duling sleeps. There's no electricity on Crow Point, no running water, and between the two cabins stands an outhouse. Cut wood lies stacked against the sides of both cabins, and woodsmoke rises from the stovepipe that juts from each roof. Meloux is sitting on a long bench made from a split log, which is set against his front wall. His hair is white, and he wears a white shirt. His overalls are so faded they're nearly the same color as the shirt. Against the dark logs of the cabin and with the bright afternoon sunlight full upon him, Meloux seems to glow.

Cork crosses the meadow and greets the old man. "*Boozhoo*, Henry."

"*Boozhoo*, Corcoran O'Connor."

Meloux isn't just old, he is ancient. His face is like the shell of a map turtle, etched with so many lines there could be one for every year of his existence. Despite his great age, something young and vital remains in the glint of his dark eyes. He is a Mide, a member of the Grand Medicine Society, a healer. At the moment, he is holding a hatchet, which he is slowly sharpening with a whetstone.

The old man pauses in his work. "You came for my niece?"

"That's one reason. Where is she?"

"Guiding a sweat."

The old man nods toward the west, where a thread of white

smoke rises near the small sweat lodge on the shoreline of Iron Lake. He sets the hatchet and whetstone on the bench and the two men enter his little cabin. Inside, Cork catches the aromatic scent of burned sage.

"You've smudged," he says.

"There has been much cleansing of spirits today. Smoke with me and I will explain."

From a shelf, the old man pulls a canister and a long-stemmed pipe wrapped in beaded cloth, then leads the way back into the sunshine. Meloux settles himself next to the hatchet and whetstone on the split-log bench. Cork sits beside him. Meloux removes the canister lid, takes a pinch of tobacco from inside, offers it to the spirits of the four directions, then fills the pipe.

The sun is blazing, and though the day began with a chill, the air has warmed significantly. Cork removes the jean jacket he's been wearing and lays it on the ground. Meloux strikes a kitchen match on the surface of the bench, lights the tobacco in his pipe, and the two men spend several minutes smoking in silence. When the tobacco is burned to ash, Meloux speaks.

"She came to me yesterday."

"Who?" Cork asks.

Meloux looks at him as if it's a ridiculous question.

"Dolores Morriseau? She's here?"

"You are like a blind fox, Corcoran O'Connor. You have a swift mind, but you cannot see what is right in front of you."

Meloux nods toward a pair of women's shoes placed on the ground next to the cabin door. The shoes are expensive looking, with spiky high heels, nothing like the footwear Cork's wife, Rainy, would have chosen for a hike to Crow Point.

"She came yesterday, with blisters on her feet from those torture devices. My niece gave her a pair of moccasins."

"How did she find you?"

"I received word that she was in Allouette, asking about me. I sent Rainy to bring her. When she stood before me, it was clear that not just her feet were in misery. Her spirit was being tortured, too."

"Her husband is looking for her."

In the mysterious way the old Mide knows so much, he seems to know this, too. "The woman he is looking for he will not find here."

Cork isn't sure what that means, but at the moment it doesn't matter. He spots two women approaching across the meadow. One he knows well. The other he's seen in a photograph. When Rainy Bisonette is near enough to be heard she calls, "Henry told me you'd be coming."

Rainy has been Cork's wife for nearly two years but still, whenever he sees her like this, her face radiant in the sun, his heart does a small leap of gladness and gratitude. Like her great-uncle Henry Meloux, Rainy is Mide, a healer. And like Meloux, she understands the world in a more generous way than Cork believes he ever will.

Dolores Morriseau doesn't look like the attractive woman in the photograph Cork was given. She wears no makeup, and her hair, soaked from the sweat and probably from her brief dip in the cold water of Iron Lake, which often follows a sweat, hangs down in wet-mop strings. She looks drained and tired, and Cork thinks Meloux probably insisted that she fast before the sweat. Cork stands and offers his place on the bench, which she accepts with a grateful sigh.

"I feel empty," she says.

"That is a good beginning," Meloux tells her.

She looks up and seems to take Cork in fully at last. "Who are you?"

"Cork O'Connor," Rainy says. "My husband."

"And a private investigator," Cork adds. "Your husband came to me today, Mrs. Morriseau. He's looking for you."

"He followed me?" She says this with hope, and some life seems to come back into her eyes.

"He says he wants to talk to you."

"I can't imagine what he has to say that he hasn't said before."

Rainy says, "Maybe you'll hear him differently now. He came for you. That's a start."

"Maybe." Again there's hope on the face of Dolores Morriseau. "When did you see him?"

"This afternoon." Cork takes out his cell phone and finds the photograph he took of Louis Morriseau. He hands the phone to Dolores, who holds it close to her face and squints.

"Who is this?" she says.

"Your husband."

She lifts her eyes to Cork, and they're filled with bewilderment. "I've never seen this man before in my life."

CHAPTER 3

Cork says, "That's not Louis Morriseau?"

"Don't you think I'd know my own husband?"

"Just take a moment. It's not the best photo I've ever shot."

"This guy is blond and as white as cottage cheese. My husband is three-quarters Ojibwe. And look at that gut. Soft as bread dough. My husband works out every day." She hands the phone back. "What kind of private investigator are you?"

Cork hears a little rumble of laughter escape from Henry Meloux. "Blind fox," the old man says, then lifts the hatchet and whetstone and begins again to sharpen the blade.

"All right. From the beginning," Cork says. "What brought you to Henry and how did you get here?"

The woman looks tired again, but not just from the drain of the sweat. "Things have been rough for a long time. Things between me and Lou. Everything in general. I thought I needed to pull myself together if there was going to be any hope for us. I met Henry several months ago when he did a burial ceremony for my husband's uncle."

Cork glances at Meloux, who says, "The mother's family is Makwa Clan. Leech Lake Anishinaabe. I have done two burial ceremonies for them and helped in other ways."

"Henry and I talked after the ceremony," Dolores continues. "Really talked. Connected." She looks to Henry for validation, and the old man offers her a smile and a nod. "He told me if I ever needed him, he would be here for me. I didn't know how to find him, so Lou's brother brought me here yesterday."

"This morning, I received word from the reservation that a stranger was asking about me," Meloux says. "He claimed to be one of The People, but something about him was not right. I had him sent to you, Corcoran O'Connor."

Although this explains the mysterious way Meloux seemed to have known he was coming, Cork still understands that the old Mide has a gift for such forewarnings. Meloux once explained it as a communication with nature that Cork himself could nurture if he was so inclined. "It is not a secret language," the Mide had said. "You need to quiet all the other voices in your head and listen."

Which is a discipline Cork has never quite been able to master. So, nature sings to him the beautiful music that many others also hear, but it has never spoken to him as it does to Meloux.

"Like Mrs. Morriseau says, the man who wanted to hire me clearly wasn't Native," Cork says.

Meloux shrugs. "Then it would seem there are at least a pair of weasels."

"Your husband's brother?" Cork asks. "Where is he?"

"Anton has a good friend in Yellow Lake. He's staying there. He said he'd check on me tomorrow and take me back if I was ready."

"Okay. You mentioned that you and your husband have been going through a rough patch, Mrs. Morriseau," Cork says.

"Call me Dolores."

"Can you tell me about that, Dolores?"

The woman sits back against the smooth logs of the cabin. "Doesn't every marriage take work?"

Rainy glances at Cork and smiles. "Even good marriages."

"And we have a good marriage, Lou and me. Or we did. I'm not sure anymore."

"What happened?" Cork asked.

"About six months ago, after Lou's uncle died, he began acting different. Distant. Afraid. Uncertain. Which isn't like him. One of the reasons I fell in love with him was that he was always so sure of himself. Not in an obnoxious way. He just knew who he was and what he wanted. He told me that the first time he saw me he knew I was what he wanted. And he went after me with a vengeance. I couldn't say no to him. But in a good way." She smiles, a little dreamily. "It's always been like that."

"The man I spoke with today claiming to be your husband said he was in real estate."

"He's a real estate attorney. Lou handles property transfers and disputes, easements, that kind of thing, mostly in the Twin Cities, but also some in outstate Minnesota, and even in Canada. He's very successful, not because he's pushy. Like I said, just sure of himself. It's a very attractive quality."

"Do you know what caused the change in him?" Cork says.

She shakes her head. "Whenever I try to talk to him about it, he just pushes me away. Not literally. He closes up. Something's broken in him. In us. In me. That's why I came. I needed to find a way to feel whole again."

"There are still wounds that need healing, Dolores," Rainy says. "If you stay awhile, I know we can help."

"What about Lou?"

"I can't help him if he's not here," Rainy says.

"And apparently, he's not," Cork says. "What I'm going to do is this. I'll go back to Aurora and talk to our impostor, see what his story is. I'll check back with you, Dolores, and we can decide what you want me to do. If that's to go fetch your real husband and bring him here, I'll do what I can."

"Why would someone pretend to be my husband?"

"That's one of the things I need to find out."

"Thank you, Mr. O'Connor."

"It's Cork."

"What do you charge for your services?"

Cork and Rainy exchange a look, and Cork reads her face. "Consider this one a favor." He gives Rainy a kiss and turns to go.

"I'll drop by the house later to get a few things, then come back to Crow Point," Rainy tells him and gives him a quick kiss goodbye.

Cork starts away, but before he's taken two steps, Meloux says, "You're forgetting this." The old man sets the hatchet down and lifts the jean jacket from the ground where Cork laid it on his arrival. "Blind fox," Meloux says with a grin that wrinkles his face even more.

Cork offers the Mide a grudging Ojibwe thank-you: "*Migwech.*"

Cell phone service on the rez is often spotty, and on Crow Point particularly it can be an issue. Cork isn't able to try the number the phony Mr. Morriseau gave him until he's back in his Expedition. In response, he gets only a message saying the user is unavailable, which is the same message he receives every time he tries the number thereafter.

He drives straight to Sam's Place. Jenny's still there, along with two kids who work shifts around their classes at the local junior college. Waaboo and Stephen have gone home.

"What did Henry have to say?" Jenny asks after Cork reports

that he found Dolores Morriseau on Crow Point. She stands in the doorway to the food prep area, wiping her hands on a clean towel.

"Mostly insults," Cork says. "He called me a blind fox."

She smiles broadly. "I'm not sure what that means, but it sounds pretty funny."

"Has Mr. Morriseau been back?" Cork asks. He shows Jenny the photo on his cell phone.

"We haven't seen him."

"He's not answering my calls."

"Which means what?"

"He could be somewhere out of cell service. He could have turned off his phone. He could simply be ignoring me."

"Why would he ignore you?"

"For starters, he's not the real Mr. Morriseau."

"Who is he?"

"Remains to be seen."

"Why is he pretending to be Morriseau?"

"Another part of the mystery. Are you doing okay here? I'd like to talk to Marsha Dross."

Jenny glances over her shoulder at the two customers standing before the serving windows. "We're fine until the dinner rush."

"If it looks like I'm going to be held up, I'll send Stephen to give you a hand."

He drives over the rise where the Burlington Northern tracks run and enters Aurora's small downtown. In the latter part of the previous century, when the mines in the area began to close, Aurora, like many of the towns on Minnesota's Iron Range, took a downward slide. In the wake of massive job losses, families abandoned the Range and many of the businesses that had served them were forced to close. For a long time, those who stayed in that part of the North Country survived, but few prospered. Tourism has become one of the saving graces and a major economic foundation for much of Minnesota's Arrowhead. In summer, the resorts on Iron Lake, old and new, flourish, and the streets bustle with unfamiliar faces. Fall brings the leaf peepers. Miles of snowmobile trails and groomed cross-country ski trails attract the hearty in winter. The town has slowly made a comeback. New shops fill once-empty storefronts. New homes are being built at the edges of town. Property values are climbing. And the permanent population is on the rise. Aurora, Minnesota, the seat of Tamarack County, Gateway to the Boundary Waters, has blossomed anew in the wilderness.

The Sheriff's Office sits a block off the main street. It's a no-nonsense structure of tan brick that includes a wing for the county jail. Cork leaves his Expedition in the parking lot, checks in at the contact window. George Azevedo, the deputy on duty, tells him the sheriff is ten-seven, having an early dinner at Johnny's Pinewood Broiler.

"Go easy on her," Azevedo says. "She's had a rough day."

The Broiler is only a couple of blocks away and Cork walks there. The mouthwatering aroma of fried fish reaches his nostrils long before his feet reach the Broiler. The place is an institution in Tamarack County, an eatery whose Friday Fish Fry, Saturday Night BBQ, and Sunday Prime Rib Fest are legendary. Inside, he finds the sheriff alone in a booth next to a front window. Although the fried fish is what most patrons come for on Fridays, Marsha Dross has a plate of half-eaten wild rice meat loaf—another renowned staple on the Broiler's menu—in front of her while she stares at a stenographer's notepad on which she's written a list of some kind, a sharpened pencil in her hand.

She looks up. "Want the badge back?"

In her late forties, she's sturdy-looking, never married, her hair just beginning to fringe with gray. Fifteen years earlier, Cork wore the sheriff's badge that she wears now. From the look on her face, it's clear that the little metal shield weighs on her every bit as heavily as it weighed on him.

"Heard you've had a bad day." Without being invited, he takes the empty seat on the other side of the booth. "What's going on?"

"Budget cuts."

Cork holds up his hands. "Say no more. Maybe you should think about coming to work for me. Flipping burgers is a lot less worrisome."

"Why are you here, Cork?"

"A man came to see me today. Tried to hire me to find his wife."

She's clearly irritated at his interruption. "What about it? That's what you do. Besides flipping burgers."

"This man isn't who he claimed to be."

"Who is he?"

"My question exactly."

"And why is he claiming to be someone he isn't?" Her voice and demeanor have changed. Cork sees the spark of intrigue in her eyes. She sets her pencil down.

He plucks his cell phone from the pocket of his jean jacket and pulls up the photo he snapped in the lot of Sam's Place. "That's him."

"How do you know he's not who he says he is?"

"His wife told me, after I showed her that photo."

"So, you've tracked her down?"

"Wasn't hard. Whoever that guy is, he knew that the woman he was looking for had come here to see Henry Meloux."

"And she found him?"

"She's with Henry right now, out on Crow Point. I tried to call the man claiming to be her husband, but he's not answering his phone. I thought I might check in with you, see if you'd be willing to have your guys keep an eye out for him."

Dross picks up her pencil and flips to a clean page of the notepad. "What's her name? And his—or the one he's using?"

Cork tells her.

"What's he driving?"

"An Escalade. Black."

"Have the plate number?"

Cork shakes his head. "But how many black Escalades are there in Tamarack County?"

"Send me that photo you took. I'll get copies printed and out to my guys. This Dolores Morriseau, what's your take on her?"

"Hard to read. Clearly in distress. But there's a man hunting her who's not who he says he is, and she's asked for my help. For the moment, that's all I need to know."

CHAPTER 4

The house on Gooseberry Lane has been home to Cork since his birth. Within its walls, he's grown from infancy to adulthood, as have his children, and now his grandson is being raised there. The house is two stories, painted white, with a covered porch that runs the full length of the front, and a stately elm in the front yard, planted when Cork was an infant. Some things in a person's life are often taken for granted, but for Cork, the comfort this house has provided him and his family is a blessing for which he never fails to feel a deep sense of gratitude.

He finds his son-in-law, Daniel Bisonette, and Waaboo in the kitchen, where they've set up a complicated Hot Wheels racetrack on the linoleum. There are ramps and tunnels, and Daniel and Waaboo are so deeply involved in their play and making so much engine noise between them that they don't notice Cork standing in the doorway, watching. Daniel is Rainy's nephew, and like her, a member of the Lac Courte Oreilles Band of Lake Superior Chippewa out of Wisconsin. He's employed as a natural resources officer by the Iron Lake Band of Ojibwe. With Jenny, he shares a passion for the written word. Cork's daughter has published two novels based on true events in the lives of the O'Connors; Daniel is an accomplished poet. Cork knows little about poetry, and although he likes what he's read by Daniel, he has to admit that sometimes the deeper meanings escape him.

"Hey, Baa-baa!" Waaboo cries when he finally notices his grandfather, but he doesn't stop his play.

Daniel looks up and grins. "We'll dismantle everything before we start fixing supper."

He rises from the floor. "Let me talk to your grandpa awhile, Waaboo." He and Cork sit at the kitchen table while the little boy continues with his racing and racing noises. "When I picked up Waaboo at Sam's Place, Jenny told me about the guy who asked you to look for his wife."

"I found the woman with Henry. Rainy had just guided her in a sweat."

"And did you convince Mrs. Morriseau that she should talk to her husband?"

"Turns out the man who's looking for her isn't who he claims to be."

"Not her husband? Who is he?"

"I don't know yet. I've been trying to call him but getting nothing. I just came from talking with Marsha Dross. She's going to have her guys keep an eye out. He shouldn't be too hard to spot. He's driving a black Escalade."

Cork hears fast steps coming down the stairway in the other room. A moment later, Stephen sweeps into the kitchen, carefully dances around the racetrack on the floor, and makes for the cookie jar on the counter, which is shaped like Ernie from *Sesame Street*. "Hey, Dad." He pulls out a chocolate chip cookie and reaches into the refrigerator for milk. "Did you talk to Henry?"

Once again, Cork relates the events of the afternoon.

"The guy's an impostor? No kidding? Why?"

"Good question."

Waaboo finally notices Stephen and the cookie. "Can I have one?"

Stephen says, "Ask your dad."

Daniel shakes his head. "You had one when we got home."

"Please."

"How about I give him half of mine?" Stephen offers.

"A reasonable compromise," Cork puts in.

Daniel throws his hands up in surrender. "I'm outnumbered. But nothing more till dinner, Waaboo."

Stephen breaks the cookie, gives half to the little boy, and says to Cork, "Can I be there when you ask the phony Morriseau what's going on?"

"I've got to find him first. And I need you to do me a favor."

"Sure."

"Rainy's coming by in a while. I'm going back to Crow Point with her to talk some more with Dolores Morriseau. A few more details to nail down. Would you mind closing Sam's Place for me tonight?"

Stephen pauses with what's left of his cookie halfway to his mouth. "Maybe I have a date."

Cork gives his son a skeptical look. "When was the last time you asked a girl out?"

Stephen eyes the half cookie in his hand and sighs. "I'll cover for you."

By the time Daniel clears the Hot Wheels track from the kitchen floor and begins putting supper together, Rainy still isn't home. Cork has tried calling her cell phone but hasn't been able to connect.

"I'm heading out," he tells Daniel.

"Maybe she's on her way," Daniel says.

"Then I'll run into her," Cork says. "And we'll be back for supper together."

When he takes off in his Expedition, the sun is low on the horizon. Cork reckons he has just enough daylight left for his purpose. He arrives at the double-trunk birch and finds Rainy's dusty pickup still parked there. As he sets out for Crow Point, the trail before him is sunk deep in the long shadows of early evening. He's brought a flashlight for the return journey, just in case he ends up lingering at Henry's cabin. The air is cooling rapidly, and he wears his jean jacket. He has no concrete reason to be concerned, but a sense of uneasiness has settled on him and he can't shake it. He thinks about what Meloux has told him, that if he stills all the voices in his head and listens, the woods will speak to him. But that evening all he hears is the quiet after the birds have gone to roost and the swoosh of the wild grass brushing against his boots and pant legs.

When he breaks from the trees, he pauses. The sun has been below the horizon for a while, but the soft blue afterglow lights Crow Point. Although suppertime has passed, Rainy or Meloux would have prepared a meal, and the good aromas that always permeate the air at mealtime should still be lingering. But there's no such smell in the air, and on the far side of the meadow, no hint of woodsmoke rising from the stovepipe of either cabin. He can see that Meloux's door stands open. By now, the old Mide should have been aware of his presence in the mysterious way he always seems to know. Cork doesn't need the woods to tell him that something isn't right.

He approaches cautiously. When he steps into the open doorway of Meloux's cabin, he sees that nothing is amiss. The place looks just as he left it. He goes to Leah Duling's cabin, where Rainy has been staying, and opens the door. Here, too, all seems normal.

Parked next to this cabin is a side-by-side ATV that Leah typically uses when she goes into Allouette. Generally, Meloux refuses to ride in the machine; despite his age, he still prefers to walk the several miles to the reservation community.

An outcropping of rock stands on the west side of the meadow. Cork follows a well-worn path through the outcrop to a ring of stones where for decades Meloux has built fires, often for sacred purposes. There's no fire in the circle of stones, and when Cork feels the ash and char, it's cold. Finally, he checks the sweat lodge. There's residual warmth from the sweat that afternoon, but nothing else.

He stands looking beyond the birches and aspens that line the shore of Iron Lake, stares at the dark water, concerned by the emptiness on Crow Point. He knows that Meloux often takes to the woods for rambles that can last a day or sometimes more. The old man prefers to go alone, something that worries Leah and Rainy no end. Cork has been less concerned. Meloux knows these woods better than any human being, knows how to survive under any circumstance of weather. He wonders if maybe Meloux has gone for an evening stroll and the women have insisted on accompanying him. That's the most reasonable speculation. Still, it doesn't sit well with him.

He returns to Meloux's cabin and once again inspects the place. This time he notices something he missed before. There has always been an ancient Winchester rifle resting on a rack on Meloux's cabin wall. The rifle is gone. Cork goes to a shelf where he knows Meloux keeps the cartridges for the Winchester in an old tin can. The can is empty.

He steps into the evening air, where the light in the sky is fading rapidly, and spends several minutes trying to clear his head of all other voices so that he might hear what the woods have to tell him. Then he says, "God damn it all to hell," and searches the ground for any signs that may indicate which direction Meloux and Rainy and Dolores Morriseau must have gone. In doing so, he discovers a circumstance he can't quite interpret. Over the years, the ground between the cabins has been worn bare of grass and is usually covered with a layer of soft dirt. There are always footprints left by those who live on the point and those who visit. But the dirt that evening has been swept clean, not a print left to read. Cork stares at the blank slate of the ground, bewildered.

Finally, he stands alone in the shadow of approaching night with the darkening Northwoods before him, the abandoned cabins at his back and, beyond them, the shiny blue-black mercury surface of Iron Lake. In the still, oppressive air of that emptied place, he asks himself the same question Dolores Morriseau put to him earlier that day: "What kind of private investigator are you?"

At that moment, the answer is painfully obvious.

CHAPTER 5

Stephen and Daniel stand with Cork in front of Meloux's cabin. Back home, Jenny is holding down the fort home with Waaboo, awaiting any word that might come from Rainy. The men carry flashlights, whose beams cut across the scene in long, straight sticks of white, illuminating spots here and there, but are maddeningly inadequate in the vast dark of the night that has descended.

"No sign of struggle," Daniel points out. "That's good."

"But no prints either," Stephen says, scanning the bare dirt with the beam of his flashlight. "It's been swept clean. That's not like Henry or Rainy. Must've been whoever came for the woman. But why?"

"To obscure numbers, directions, get rid of as much evidence of their visit as possible," Cork says.

"Your bogus Mr. Morriseau?" Daniel says.

"Him and maybe more. Without any tracks in the dirt, it's impossible to say."

"How would they find Crow Point?" Stephen says.

"Maybe just kept checking around until someone told them. It's not exactly a secret," Daniel replies.

"The more you ask, the more you expose yourself," Cork says. "People remember you. Easy to give a description if the law comes knocking. If you want to skirt the law, you find other ways."

"Like what?"

"Maybe they put a tracker on my Expedition and followed me."

"Not many vehicles on the road out here from Aurora," Daniel says. "You'd probably have known if you were being followed. Any chance they planted something on you? Got the GPS coordinates while you were out here earlier?"

"I don't know how they would have done that."

A half minute of quiet follows in which the only sound is the haunting cry of a loon out on Iron Lake.

"At Sam's Place," Stephen finally says. "Remember? You came into the prep area and got coffee for you and the bogus Morriseau."

Cork plays it over in his mind. "And I left my jean jacket on the chair back."

He takes off his jacket and holds it up in the beam of Stephen's flashlight, checking all the pockets, then the outside. The little device is pinned under the collar in back.

"Damn, I led them right to Henry."

"These guys are sophisticated," Daniel says. "But who the hell are they, besides our fake Morriseau?"

"They must've been after Dolores," Stephen says. "Did they take Rainy and Henry, too?"

"Henry's Winchester is gone," Cork says. "Maybe everyone got away before these people came."

"Got away where?" Daniel asks. "Allouette?"

Allouette is the larger of the two communities on the reservation and only a few miles to the east of Crow Point. There's a trail along the shoreline that opens onto an old forest service road, which Meloux or Leah takes whenever they head to Allouette.

"Maybe." Cork looks toward the vast dark of the north, where the meadow is walled by the great Northwoods. "Or maybe there."

"Why not take the trail to the double-trunk birch?" Stephen asks.

"That's the way I came, so whoever was tracking me probably came that way, too," Cork replies. "And whoever they are, if I were them, I'd have someone watching the path toward Allouette."

"Closing off any escape route," Daniel says.

"Exactly," Cork says. "So if I were Henry, I'd take to the woods. Even in the dark, no one knows it better than he does."

"If we're interpreting all this correctly, where are the bad guys now?" Stephen asks, eyeing the impenetrable curtain of night beyond the reach of their beams.

"I'm hoping we're wrong and there's an explanation we're not thinking of. But if we're right, they've probably gone after Henry," Cork said.

"What about Rainy and Dolores? Could they have split off or something?"

"These guys have been thorough. Like Daniel said, they probably covered all the easy escape routes. So, I hope the women are with Henry."

"What do we do?" Stephen says.

Cork considers. He's had time to digest the possibilities, calm his own panic, and wrap his head around a plan. "You two go back to Aurora. Daniel, you stay with Jenny in case word comes. Stephen, you head out to the rez, see if anyone knows anything there. Maybe we're all wrong and that's where they've gone."

"What about you, Dad?"

"I'm staying here."

"And if the guys who swept the ground clean come back?" Daniel asks.

"I don't intend to make myself a target. But I want to be here if it's our people who come."

Daniel has brought the service weapon he carries when he's on duty as a natural resources officer, a Glock 19. He takes it from his holster and hands it to Cork. "In case," he says.

In his long history with law enforcement and in the years since, Cork has killed men. It has taken a toll on his soul. He once vowed never again to hold a handgun, but it has proven to be a promise impossible to keep. He has accepted that he is *ogichidaa*, which is a word in the language of the Anishinaabeg that means "one who stands between evil and his people." Still, he waves off the Glock. "Whoever was here might be watching. They may try something with the two of you on your way back."

"I don't like leaving you alone without a gun," Stephen says.

"I'll be fine. But before you go, turn off your flashlights."

"Why?"

"Just do it."

All the beams are cut off. It's the time of the new moon. Except for the vast blanketing of stars there's no light in the sky. They stand in the dark a few moments, until Stephen asks, "What are we doing?"

"You've been here so many times you can find your way back blindfolded," Cork explains. "Unless you absolutely have to, don't turn on your flashlights. And don't say a word as you're going. If someone's watching, I don't want them to know you've left. Better all the way around."

"Should we let the sheriff know?" Stephen asks.

"Let's wait until morning, when we can see better. Maybe we'll know more then. And maybe," Cork says hopefully, "Henry will have brought them all back. When you get home, let me know you've made it safely. And let me know if you find out anything.

I'll have my cell on mute. If something's shaking here, I'll try to let you know."

"Good luck with that," Daniel says.

Despite all the science and technology involved, all three understand that a successful call to or from Meloux's cabin is up to the whims of nature.

Stephen hesitates before leaving. "Dad?"

"Yes?"

"I can't help thinking about the dream Henry and I shared."

Cork understands. Since he was a child, Stephen has been visited with visions, always in dreams, always of dark things to come. Months earlier, Stephen had a vision of Meloux lying dead beneath pine trees. The old Mide shared with Stephen that he'd had the same vision.

"You didn't dream Rainy or Dolores Morriseau, did you?"

"No."

"Then let's not jump to any conclusions. Get going. And be careful."

He has taken a blanket from Leah's cabin and now lies on it in the tall meadow grass. He stares up at the stars, what so many people call the heavens. Heaven is a concept Cork still wrestles with. In the belief of the Ojibwe, the soul, when it leaves the body, follows a path to the west, toward a place called *Gaagige Minawaanigo-ziwining,* a place of everlasting peace and harmony. Raised in the Catholic Church, Cork knows about the Christian concept, pearly gates and all. Heaven, in his own thinking, is simply a complete letting go of all ills, all worries, all cares, a place that he believes doesn't exist on earth, but he's not able to let himself embrace the idea of an idyllic afterlife. To Cork, heaven is just a word.

He lies with a heavy weight on him, a deep concern for those he loves, Rainy especially. He lost his first wife to violence, and the grieving was a long, slow crawl to the place where he could finally let go. Then he met Rainy, and almost immediately her connection to him put her in jeopardy. He seems to attract danger like some people draw mosquitoes, as if danger comes to feed on him. *Ogichidaa*, he has thought of himself. But maybe the reason he has to stand between evil and those he loves is that there is something about him that evil needs, something evil desires. If he were alone, if he'd never loved, never married, never had children, would it have made a difference?

Too late for that now, he tells himself. What's done is done. The question is, what's ahead?

He tries to lay out a plan. If someone returns and it's not Henry or Rainy or Dolores Morriseau, what then? He has no firearm, nothing to defend himself or the others. Then he remembers the cautioning words Henry Meloux, a great hunter in his day, has offered him many times: *Patience is the father of the hunt.* So Cork waits and watches and listens to the loon on the lake, and finally, although he still questions everything he's ever been told about the afterlife and God and Kitchimanidoo, the Creator, he whispers a little prayer.

"Please watch over them. Please keep them safe."

CHAPTER 6

Cork wakes covered in dew, shivering because the night has been cold. The sun is a glaring golden eye that's just risen above the eastern horizon. He hears the song of warblers in the aspen trees that edge the meadow. On the far side, a white-tailed doe and her spotted fawn are feeding, their heads rising periodically to ensure that they're alone and safe. They suddenly freeze, then bolt for the cover of the trees. Cork lies back down on the blanket and waits.

From the direction of Allouette, against the glare of the rising sun, a figure steps into the meadow and, like the deer whom he's frightened away, pauses to check his surroundings. He's too distant for Cork to see him clearly. He stands eyeing the cabins, then his gaze sweeps the meadow. Cork lies still among the tall wild grasses. The figure begins walking again, making straight for Meloux's cabin.

He knocks when he arrives, waits, then knocks again. Receiving no answer, he moves to Leah's cabin and tries there. There are no locks, and he could open the door on either cabin. But he doesn't. He walks to the outhouse and knocks on the door there. He turns then and starts across the meadow toward the outcroppings that hide Meloux's fire ring. He disappears behind the rocks, and a minute later, Cork sees him heading to the sweat lodge. When he's assured himself that it, too, is empty he starts back across the meadow toward the cabins, passing only twenty yards from where Cork lies in the grass.

He's Native, a stranger. He's not tall, but despite the jacket he wears, it's obvious that he's sinewy. No weapon is visible, although there might be one concealed under the jacket. Cork feels the urge to leap up and challenge the stranger's presence on Crow Point, but patience is his guide.

The stranger stands at Meloux's door and seems to be considering the advisability of entering. Instead he calls out, "*Boozhoo, Mishomis.*"

When Cork hears him address Meloux respectfully as "Grandfather," he finally stands and says, "*Boozhoo.*"

The stranger turns, and when he discovers Cork only a stone's throw distant, looks as if a ghost or a wraith has materialized before him out of nowhere. "Oh," he says. "Sorry. I didn't see anyone."

"Who are you looking for?"

"Dolores Morriseau."

"Why do you want her?" Cork's gaze is steely.

The man returns Cork's hard look in kind. "That's really between her and me."

"Who are you?"

The man squares himself as if for a physical confrontation. "How about you tell me who you are first."

"The name's O'Connor."

"Cork O'Connor?"

"Yeah."

The man relaxes. "Heard of you. I'm Anton Morriseau. Dolores is my sister-in-law."

"If you don't mind, I'd appreciate seeing some identification."

The man pulls a wallet from his back pocket, dips into a fold, then holds out a card. Cork walks toward him slowly, carefully takes the driver's license, and confirms what the man has told him.

"Sorry if I seem edgy." Cork hands the license back. "There's been some trouble."

Anton Morriseau returns his wallet to his back pocket. "What kind?"

"Not sure exactly. But Henry's disappeared on us. Along with your sister-in-law, Dolores. She said you brought her here."

"Henry's done ceremonies for us on the Leech Lake Rez, and I've come here a couple of times for ceremonies. Dolores showed up saying that she's worried about my brother, about their marriage. Looking to pull together a lot of broken pieces, I guess. She's convinced Henry Meloux can help her. So I brought her here. I've been staying with a buddy in Yellow Lake. But what about this disappearance?"

Cork explains what occurred the night before and what he was doing in the meadow grass.

Morriseau eyes the ground. "We shouldn't be walking here. We might still be able to pick up a track or two."

"You a hunter?"

"Among other things." Morriseau squats for a better look at the swept-clean ground. His eyes slowly travel to where the bare dirt meets wild grass. He rises and walks to the edge of the meadow, then gradually moves to where the path leads to the double-trunk birch and the county road. He kneels and examines the packed earth of the path. He turns, strides to the trail that comes from the direction of Allouette, and examines the ground there, too. Finally, he returns to Cork. "Whoever they were, they didn't sweep the trails. We might be able to get prints there. There's also a line of flattened grass heading across the meadow in that direction." He points north where, not far beyond the distant wall of pines, lies the vast Boundary Waters Canoe Area Wilderness.

Cork has spent some time sizing him up. "You say you're a hunter, but there's a lot about you that makes me think you might also be a cop."

"Leech Lake Tribal Police." His eyes move away from Cork and become hard and fixed on something across the meadow. "Company," he says in a low voice.

Cork turns and sees Stephen and Daniel approaching in the early light. Sheriff Marsha Dross is with them. When they arrive, Cork makes the introductions.

"Nothing useful from anyone on the rez last night, Dad," Stephen reports. "Nobody I talked to has seen any of them."

"You think they've been abducted?" Dross directs this to Cork.

"It's a possibility, but I'm hoping they got away before the goons arrived."

"Okay, let's think about this for a minute before we all go off half-cocked," Dross says. "Is there any sign of violence?"

"No," Cork acknowledges.

"And Stephen tells me that Henry often takes off for long walks in the woods and is sometimes gone overnight, right?"

"True," Stephen says.

"So what makes you think it's something more than that, a long walk and Rainy and this Morriseau woman have accompanied him?"

"Why sweep the dirt clean of tracks?" Anton Morriseau asks.

"Maybe they were sweeping away something else and cleaning away the tracks was simply a by-product."

"Henry's rifle is gone," Cork points out.

"He's a hunter," Dross says. "Maybe he was planning to shoot a squirrel for supper while they're out there."

"Henry was a great hunter once, but his eyes aren't what they used to be," Cork replies, growing irritated with this delay. "As far as I know, he hasn't hunted in years."

"Rainy shoots," Dross says.

"Not for sport or food. She's only shot to protect herself. Come on, Marsha. I know you're going to tell me all this could just be coincidence, but I don't believe in coincidence, and in your heart, neither do you."

"There's a line of trampled grass across the meadow," Morriseau points out. "Hard to say who made it. Could have been Meloux and my sister-in-law and Rainy, but I'm leaning toward thinking that it's probably whoever came for them."

"So, the question is this," Cork says. "Are Henry and Rainy and Dolores prisoners now or are they still the prey?"

"And here's another one," Morriseau says. "Why are these guys so desperate to find my sister-in-law?"

Dross holds up her hands as if stopping traffic. "Look, Cork, I understand what you're saying, but before I can commit the resources of the Sheriff's Department to an all-out manhunt, I need actual proof that there's been an abduction or that an abduction is in the works. I can get some eyes in the sky, maybe locate Rainy and Henry and the Morriseau woman."

"That'll take time and there's no guarantee of anything. I'm going after them."

"I'm going, too," Anton Morriseau says.

"Count me in," Daniel says.

Cork shakes his head. "Not you. You need to stay and watch over Jenny and Waaboo. We still don't know exactly what we're dealing with here, and I don't want to have to be worrying about other people I love."

"Cork—" Daniel begins.

"No argument. You stay and protect what's here." He can see that Daniel is prepared to continue the discussion, and he says more gently, "Please, Daniel. Take care of my daughter and grand-son."

Daniel hesitates, then gives a reluctant nod.

"They shouldn't be hard to track," Morriseau says. "I just hope we get to our people before they do."

"They're with Henry," Cork tells him. "There's no one who knows those woods better. If anybody can keep them safe, it's Henry."

He says this as much to calm his own fear as to reassure Anton Morriseau. But he knows only too well the mind-set of human predators. If you get in their way, you're like a fly they'll swat without a second thought. If it is Dolores these predators are after, Rainy and Henry could easily become collateral damage.

"Let me get you a sat phone, and I'll arrange with the Forest Service to fly a search plane over the area."

"And we'll need to throw some gear together," Cork says. "No telling how long we might be in those woods."

"The longer we wait, the riskier it becomes for Dolores and the others," Morriseau says.

"Like I told you, they're with Henry. He'll do everything he can to keep them safe," Cork assures him.

Morriseau shakes his head. "I respect Meloux, but he's an old man. I doubt he's a match for the kind of people it looks like might be tracking him."

Stephen, who's been quiet, says, "You don't know Henry."

PART TWO

RAINY

CHAPTER 7

For a long while after Cork has left, heading back to Aurora to dig into the mystery of the man claiming to be Dolores's husband, Rainy sits with Henry in the sunshine on the bench next to his door. Henry is quiet, intent on the work of sharpening the blade of his hatchet. Rainy has taken Dolores to Leah's cabin, where the woman will lie down for a while to rest. Rainy is exhausted. Guiding a sweat is a serious responsibility, physically and emotionally demanding. This one was especially difficult, but not because of Dolores. Rainy found herself restless, distracted, and she's still uncertain why. Her own unsettled spirit didn't seem to affect the other woman's experience, and for that she's grateful.

"You remind me of a butterfly on a flower, Niece," Henry finally says, looking up from his work.

"What do you mean, Uncle?"

"Your wings never stop moving but you go nowhere. A sweat should calm the spirit."

"I wasn't able to focus."

"Something is troubling you?"

"Yes, but I can't put my finger on it."

"A sweat is usually a good way to do just that."

"Not this time."

Following the sweat, she and Dolores both dipped themselves in the icy water of Iron Lake, and her body has cooled. She lays her head back against the logs of the cabin wall, closes her eyes, and lets the late afternoon sun lay its warm hand fully on her face.

"Maybe your heart absorbed the troubles of the other woman's heart. That happens sometimes."

"Maybe." She opens her eyes and is blinded a moment by the sun. "I wonder what's going on. Why did someone pretend to be her husband?"

"Your husband will find this out I think."

Rainy smiles. "You called him a blind fox."

"He sees well enough when he needs to."

Henry grows still, his gaze set on the hard blue of the lake visible through the poplars and birches that edge the shoreline. Then his head shifts toward the wall of pines to the north. His face is like a sheet of paper that has been crumpled tightly then opened, full of a hundred wrinkles and creases. His dark eyes squint, but not from the glare of the sun. He seems to be looking intently at something. Or perhaps for something.

"What is it, Uncle?"

For nearly a minute, Henry doesn't answer, just stares. "Your restlessness in the sweat, Niece. Tell me about it."

Rainy closes her eyes again, thinking. "It wasn't like anything I've experienced before. In sweats, everything goes soft in me. My concerns melt away. My spirit finds a place of peace. But not this time. This time I seemed to be standing before a door that wouldn't open for me. And I was glad it wouldn't open, because on the other side was something terrible." She takes a deep breath. "That's never happened in a sweat before."

Henry is listening, but his eyes are on the woods across the meadow.

Rainy checks on Dolores, then rejoins Henry on the bench. "She's sleeping. The sweat was good for her."

Even if her own experience was unsettling, Rainy's relieved to know that the sweat was helpful to Dolores. She likes the woman, who is smart and open and who wants desperately to mend the cracks in her marriage. It's clear she loves her husband, and that's always a good beginning. Henry hasn't replied, and she sees that the old man's attention is distant. "Uncle?" she says.

"Talk. I hear." But he doesn't look at her.

"I'm going to begin making supper."

"Wait," Henry says. His voice is low and hard.

"What is it, Henry?" she asks.

"That door you stood before in your sweat. I think it is about to open."

He has not told them why as they roll and tie a blanket for each of them. Rainy has roused Dolores, who obeys without asking questions. Though the day has warmed, Henry has instructed each of them to bring a jacket. While Dolores prepares herself, Rainy helps Henry put items into a canvas knapsack—jerky, biscuits left from an earlier meal, a bag of dried cranberries and nuts. Henry puts in a box of kitchen matches and the flint and steel he sometimes uses in starting his fires inside the stone ring. He takes a sheathed hunting knife from a wall shelf and puts that in as well.

"Niece," he says to Rainy. "My hatchet is outside. Bring it."

Just before they leave his cabin, he lifts the old Winchester from the wall pegs that cradle it, scoops cartridges from the tin can where he stores them, and drops the rounds into a pocket of his coat.

Rainy is frightened, but she doesn't question Henry. She has seen him this way before, quiet but commanding, and she understands that whatever his purpose, it's for the safety of them all. The final thing Henry picks up to take with him is his beaded deer-hide medicine bag.

Dolores is waiting, her blanket rolled and tied and slung over her shoulder. When Rainy and Henry join her, she says, "I don't know what's going on, but I'm afraid."

"We are going into the woods," Henry says, quietly but firmly. "We are safer there."

"Safer from what?" Dolores asks.

"From a man who pretends to be your husband but is not. And others, I think. They are coming."

"How—" she begins.

Rainy cuts her off. "If Henry says someone's coming, then someone's coming. We need to go."

Before they leave, Rainy tries to call Cork on her cell phone, but the service fails her completely.

They head into the meadow.

"Niece, you and Dolores Morriseau go that way." Henry points toward the tallest pine along the distant tree line. "Walk ten feet apart."

"Why?" Dolores says.

She's a smart woman, Rainy understands, and her questions are not unreasonable, but Dolores doesn't know Henry. "Just do as he asks," Rainy says, trying to keep her voice even.

"Wait for me when you get there," Henry adds.

Rainy and Dolores split off and separate themselves. They move through the wild meadow grass quickly, while Henry moves along another line. Rainy can see that altogether they are making several lines of exodus, none very clear. A few minutes later, they all meet at the tall pine.

"What now, Uncle?" Rainy asks.

"We wait."

Henry sits. A low growth of sweet gale separates them from the meadow, providing a good blind. Dolores sits, too. Rainy lets the knapsack slide from her shoulders to the ground. She takes a leaf and crushes it between her fingers, releasing a sharp scent. She has often used the plant leaves as an insect repellent and also as a remedy in healing stomachaches and other internal ailments. Behind the shielding of these plants, she feels protected. She would love to question Henry, but it's clear that silence is what he expects of her now.

Dolores admitted to being afraid. Rainy is afraid, too. She's been in danger before, several times in fact since she fell in love with Cork. She knows that Cork is *ogichidaa*, one who stands between evil and his people. Although Henry was once a legendary hunter and certainly still has a warrior's spirit, she can't help wishing that Cork was with them behind that blind of sweet gale.

Like wolves on the hunt, just as the sun is about to set, they finally show themselves. Two men come from the direction of the trail that leads to the double-trunk birch. One comes from the east, the direction of Allouette. The last comes from the end of the point, from the lake. They're all dressed in hunter's camouflage and carry rifles. She can see that their intent in approaching this way is to prevent anyone from escaping. To pen them like sheep for the slaughter. Her stomach has drawn taut, not just with fear but with outrage. She would love to leap into the meadow and challenge their presence in this place that is dedicated to healing. But like Henry, she sits and watches from behind the blind.

They converge on the cabins, checking Leah's first, then Henry's. They check the outhouse, then one of them walks the path through the rock outcroppings to Henry's fire ring and then to the sweat lodge. They reconvene at the cabins and appear to hold a council. Among three of the men, there is some arguing. Rainy can see the gesticulations, and although they're too far away for her to discern words, she can hear raised voices. There's a bit of shoving, which one man, maybe the leader of the group, puts a quick halt to.

The fourth man has stood apart from the others. He has been studying the ground, kneeling here and there in the slanting orange rays of the setting sun. As the others argue, he walks slowly away from them, his attention glued to the ground as he approaches the meadow. He pauses at the edge of the tall wild grass, lifts his eyes, looks a bit to the left, then to the right. It occurs to Rainy that he may be trying to see the trails she and her companions have left. Then his gaze slowly tracks across the edge of the tree line and comes to rest on the blind of sweet gale.

Henry whispers, "It is time for us to go."

CHAPTER 8

It's twilight and they have walked half an hour without speaking. "How did they find us?" Dolores finally asks, her voice trembling.

"They found only our cabins," the old man reminds her. "But they have someone with them who understands these woods. They will come looking for us."

"How do you know?"

Rainy knows. She knew the moment the man gazed across the meadow at the blind of sweet gale that hid them.

"It is enough that I know," Henry says quietly. "But they will not find us. At least not tonight. Come." And he leads the way.

The woods are dim, the sky above moving toward the color of the char in Henry's fire ring. It will be a clear night, Rainy understands, a cold night, and she sees now the reason for her uncle's insistence on jackets and blankets. She understands, too, from the items Henry put into the knapsack, that he is prepared to spend many nights in the great Northwoods. She hopes that won't be necessary. She hopes the men who invaded Crow Point will give up quickly.

It's not clear that her uncle knows where they're going. They strike out in one direction, then shift to another. They come to an area of exposed rock. For more than a hundred yards in all directions, it's as if a great knife has scraped the earth away, leaving a few rounded crowns of bare and broken rock. The only living things among the rocks are thin fingers of lichen.

"Step only on stone," Henry cautions them as they make their way carefully across. "And do not disturb the lichen."

They cross the rocky hillocks, and from there, Henry meanders a bit more. At last, they arrive at the base of a steep rise, which is a wall of rock. Rainy calculates that despite all their walking, they've gone only a mile or so north of the meadow. By the time Henry bends and peers into a breach in the rock wall, it's almost too dark to see.

"Bear den?" Rainy asks.

"Many winters, I have seen the tracks of sows who have used this as shelter in their long sleep."

"There's not a bear in there now?" Dolores says.

"She ended her sleep weeks ago. She will not return."

The den is cramped when they enter, and smells rank. The floor is covered with desiccated leaves. Rainy uses the flashlight app on her cell phone, and they arrange themselves. Dolores and Henry roll out their blankets, but Rainy secures her blanket with some stones as a covering over the mouth of the den so no light will leak outside. In their musty shelter, they sit against the rock walls, exhausted.

"You were right to be unsettled in your sweat, Niece. These men are wolves."

"Thank you, Uncle Henry, for getting us away in time." Rainy says a silent prayer of thanks for the old Mide's uncanny prescience.

"Who are they?" Dolores finally asks, keeping her voice barely above a whisper.

"I do not know," Henry says. "But I believe they have come for you."

"I don't have anything anyone would want."

Rainy's back is against a sharp edge of rock, and she shifts herself. "What about your husband? Is it possible he has something? Maybe they want to use you to get at him? You said he's in real estate law."

"I don't know what he has." Tears roll down her cheeks, and she looks ready to collapse.

Rainy puts her arm around the woman. "They won't find us, will they, Uncle Henry?"

"Not tonight. We should eat and get some rest. We will leave this den at first light and circle back toward Allouette. That will take most of the day."

"Then we'll be safe," Rainy says as if it is a given.

They share jerky and some nuts and dried cranberries from the knapsack. It's not much, but it's better than nothing. When they settle in for the night, Rainy has no blanket, but she makes herself as comfortable as she can with her back against the wall. She doesn't sleep. She sits awake thinking about the men who invaded Crow Point, about the man pretending to be Lou Morriseau. She tries to make some sense of a mystery that has too few clues. She thinks about Cork and wonders when he will come looking for her, because she knows he will. At the moment, she's more worried about him than about her own circumstance. She's afraid that if he comes to Crow Point, he'll run smack into the invaders. She wishes she had been able to call, to warn him. She takes her cell phone from the pocket of her jacket, but here in the darkness of the cave, it's hopeless.

Her back is cramped, her concerns too many. She takes the hatchet from where it has hung from a loop on the knapsack and crawls from the den into the dark and chill of the night outside.

There's no moon. The vault of heaven is broken by the branches of the pines overhead, and the stars are scattered. The dark is profound, impenetrable. She can barely see her hand in front of her face, and she grips the hatchet for comfort. Far away, she spots flickers of light, like the periodic winking of fireflies. She focuses on them, straining to see.

She's so absorbed that she's surprised when Henry whispers in her ear, "It is a rare man who can track at night."

The old man settles himself next to her and stares where she stares.

"Can they track us here?"

"I have done my best to make sure they cannot."

Rainy thinks about the meandering route her great-uncle took when she wasn't at all certain that he knew where he was going. She understands now that his purpose was to mislead these trackers. Rainy's eyes have adjusted, and she can make out his face near her own. He is intently studying the distant points of light.

"I did not think they would follow us this far." It's the first note of doubt she has heard from him.

"Will they find us?"

"Not unless they can see a footprint on stone."

Now Rainy thinks about the large area of bared and broken rock they crossed, and Henry's admonition to step only on stone.

"Take this, Niece."

He places something long and heavy on her lap, and she realizes it's the Winchester.

"My eyes are not what they used to be. But I have seen you shoot. If you need to, can you do that?"

She is a healer. Her life is about mending the body and the spirit. Still, she doesn't hesitate. "If I have to." And she grips the rifle.

They watch together for another ten minutes, but the pin-points of light come no nearer.

"They cannot find our trail among the rocks," Henry says. "They have stopped for the night."

A few minutes later, the tiny periodic firefly glows are replaced by the more constant light from a campfire.

Henry says, "They are certain of themselves. They are not afraid to let us know they are coming." He turns his face to Rainy, and even in the inky black of that night, she can see a small smile play across his lips. "But they should be."

PART THREE

THE WOLF

CHAPTER 9

For most of the afternoon, LeLoup has waited on the lake in the inflatable kayak. The others, he knows, will approach by land. Kimball will call on the sat phone when they are all in place. LeLoup has only one responsibility in the operation ahead: Make certain no one tries to escape on the water.

He has never been on Iron Lake and he appreciates the beauty of it, though it's too populated for his taste. He prefers lakes where there's nothing on the shoreline but the rocks and trees put there by the hand of nature. Under the warming sun of early May, he imagines what the lake must have been like before the white people arrived and built their cabins, their town. He does this a lot, this daydreaming of a time before everything was ruined. Useless, he knows. But then so much of what a human being does every day is, in the end, useless. Or rather, he thinks idling in his kayak, pointless.

He was pleased when Kimball assigned him to cover the avenue of escape by water. It meant he would spend as little time as possible with the others and would afford him the opportunity to enjoy a long, solitary paddle. He has lately been too much in the company of men he despises. Too much in the company of human beings, period. Alone in the sanctuary of nature, that's where he belongs. But circumstances dictate otherwise. And so here he is in an inflatable kayak with the Weatherby MeatEater he uses in all his operations, a rifle he trusts. Trust has always been an issue with him. Which makes him think of Kimball just as the sat phone, silenced for this operation, vibrates.

"Execute" is the only word Kimball offers.

LeLoup lifts his paddle and makes for the birches and aspens that line the shore of the finger of land the locals call Crow Point. He's been told only what he needs to know. Kimball keeps everything close to his vest. And all Kimball has said is that no one leaves the point.

"How many are there?" Herring had asked as they prepared for the assault.

"I don't know," Kimball had answered. "At least two, but maybe more."

"Will they put up a fight?" McHugh had asked.

"What do you care, Leo? You're hired to fight if you have to."

"Itching for a fight, in fact," McHugh had said.

Except for Kimball, LeLoup knew none of the others before they gathered for this mission. He's worked with Kimball before. He doesn't like the man, but the operations he brings LeLoup in on always pay well.

Despite McHugh's desire for action, Kimball has cautioned them that the woman is not to be harmed.

"What about the Indian?" Herring asked before they split up. "This Meloux?"

Kimball said, "Expendable."

"And if there are others?" McHugh looked eager.

"No witnesses. But if you kill the woman, I'll gut you myself."

They know what the woman looks like. Kimball gave them all

a copy of her photograph—a pretty redhead with green eyes and a winning smile. But LeLoup has no idea of her importance in the operation as a whole. His job at the moment is to help seal this isolated point of land.

At the shore, he turns the kayak broadside and disembarks onto a flat rock, one of many that line the edge of the clear water. He lifts his rifle, slips the sling over his shoulder, and draws the inflatable onto the rock. When the mission is finished, he'll kayak back the way he came. It may be deep night by then, but he has often navigated by the stars and the dark doesn't bother him at all.

He glides among the trees, whose trunks are white and whose leaves, on this May afternoon as the sun is just about to set, are deep green. The color reminds LeLoup of the eyes of the woman in the photograph. He can see cabins, two of them. One is ancient but sturdy looking. The other is newer, yet still of a simple log design. There's also an outhouse. He sees no electric lines, nothing that suggests the modern world has encroached here and, despite the grim possibilities of the mission, the scene gives him a pleasant feeling.

He remains hidden among the trees, waiting until the others close in. Beyond the cabins is an open meadow and beyond that a line of pines where the deep woods begin. On the west side of the meadow rise two rock outcroppings. A well-worn path leads toward them from the cabins. He sees no people. There's no smoke coming from the stovepipe on the roof of either cabin. The scene looks deserted. A smile plays on his lips. Kimball, he thinks, has finally stumbled.

The others appear, moving cautiously toward the cabins. Kimball and Herring check the first cabin, the newer one. McHugh kicks open the door on the ancient-looking cabin. LeLoup joins them just as Herring is checking the outhouse.

"Nothing," McHugh says with disgust. "Where the hell are they?"

"There's a path to those rocks," LeLoup says. "I'll check there."

Kimball gives him a nod of approval, and LeLoup follows the path to the outcroppings. Beyond, he finds a stone ring filled with the ash and char of many fires. For pleasure? Council fires? Ceremonies? He spots a small, hut-like structure up the shoreline and heads there. Even before he reaches the sweat lodge, he knows exactly what it is. He's done many sweats. Near the lodge is the ash and char from a recent fire, which he knows was used to heat the Grandfathers, the stones that were placed in the center of the lodge. A blanket still drapes the door. He uses the barrel of his Weatherby to push it aside. The lodge is empty, but he can still feel residual heat.

He returns to the cabins where the other men are arguing.

"Someone tipped them off," McHugh is saying. "They knew we were coming."

"No one tipped them off," Kimball says. "No one knew we were coming."

"That fat ass Fredricks knew," Herring throws in. "I told you he was too soft for this mission."

"He's the best communications man I know," Kimball says. "We need his ears and eyes. He didn't give us away, Mike."

"Yeah? Well, somebody did." Mike Herring looks at McHugh. "You disappeared last night. Where the hell did you go?"

"To do your mama. She was good but not the best I've ever had."

Herring grabs for McHugh, but Kimball intervenes.

While the argument has gone on, LeLoup has knelt and has been studying the ground. The daily comings and goings at the cabins have worn the ground bare and mostly the area is loose dirt. LeLoup is trying to read the prints left there. He can see the tracks made by his cohorts, large boot prints. Among them are the smooth prints of moccasin soles. And also the prints from a boot too small to be one of the men. He rises, sorts the tracks in his thinking, carefully follows the moccasin prints and the small boot prints to the edge of the meadow. They don't lead onto the path that cuts through the tall wild grass, the path Kimball and Herring followed from a county road a couple of miles distant. Instead, the tracks separate and disappear into the meadow. He looks closely at the grass, which is waving slightly in an evening breeze that has come with sunset. He smiles, understanding what he sees. If they'd stayed together, they would have trampled enough grass to be easily followed. Separating, they have done their best to complicate things. Useless, because he will be able to find where they've bent and broken the grass stalks, but he admires the effort. He scans the distant tree line, looking for any sign that they might still be hiding, watching and hoping the men will simply leave.

"Three," he says, without turning back.

"What?" Kimball says.

"There were three here. They left just before we came."

"Can you tell where they went?" Kimball steps up beside Le-Loup and looks where he looks.

"Into the woods."

"To hide?"

"Maybe. Or maybe they plan on going deeper. You know what's out there, not far away?"

"What?"

"The Boundary Waters."

"Boundary Waters? What the hell is that?" Herring says. He's the only American in the group. He's built like a linebacker and even if he didn't boast about being born and raised in Mississippi, it's easy enough to tell from his accent.

"A million acres of trees and lakes and rivers and no people.

In the States, they call it the Boundary Waters. There's another million acres just like it on the other side of the border. In Canada, we call it the Quetico."

"You're a tracker, LeLoup," Kimball says. "One of the reasons you're here. Can you track them?"

Something in LeLoup warms and expands, the great anticipation of a hunt. He nods once and says, "It will be a pleasure."

CHAPTER 10

"I need a broom," LeLoup says.

"A broom?" Herring laughs. "Spring cleaning."

"Of a sort," LeLoup says. "Go check the cabins."

"Fuck you. You're not my boss."

"Check the cabins," Kimball says.

Herring's lips form a frown, but he does as he's been told.

Kimball says, "Any idea how long ago they left?"

"Not long," LeLoup replies. "But I'd say McHugh's right."

"Right?"

"They knew enough not to take the trail you were on or go toward the town on the reserve or risk the lake. They must have known the deep woods were their only option. I don't know how they'd have known that unless, as McHugh said, someone tipped them off."

Kimball eyes the cabin where Herring has just appeared, returning with a broom. Herring holds it out to LeLoup and says, "I ain't doing your cleaning for you."

Kimball says, "You make any calls on your sat phone on your way here?"

"No. Why?"

"Give it to me."

Each of the men carries an Iridium 9575, no larger than a cell phone. Herring pulls his from the inside pocket of his camo jacket and hands it to Kimball, who punches in some numbers, then hands it back.

"Let me see yours," he says to McHugh.

"Hell, I was with you the whole time."

Kimball holds out his hand and McHugh reluctantly delivers his sat phone. After Kimball has checked it, he turns to LeLoup. When he's checked all their phones, Kimball shakes his head. "Maybe somebody spotted us. Doesn't matter now. We just need to make sure they don't get away."

"Into the meadow," LeLoup says. "All of you."

"What for?" Herring snaps.

"Spring cleaning," LeLoup says.

"Come on." Kimball leads the way, leaving LeLoup alone on the bared ground between the cabins.

LeLoup slips the strap of his Weatherby over his shoulder and begins where the first of the men's prints appear, carefully sweeping the area clean of tracks, which includes those left by the three people who've fled. He makes his way to the edge of the meadow grass and joins the others standing there. He tosses the broom far out into the tall wild stalks, where it settles out of sight.

"What good will that do?" McHugh says. "Hell, they can see you've swept it clean."

"But they can't see anything else. Like how many of us there are. And maybe it'll confuse them for a while, give us time to do what we're here for."

Kimball says, "McHugh, you're going back the way we came, then return to town."

"What for?"

"You need to move our vehicle. I don't want it anywhere near here."

"I thought we hid it pretty good."

"I don't want to take any chances. I want it gone. Go back to town." He looks to Herring. "You hid the ATV you came on?"

The man nods. "Nobody'll find it."

"So, what do I do?" McHugh says, clearly disgusted. "Just wait around while you have all the fun?"

"Get back to Fredricks. Have him monitor all local communications. If anyone comes looking for these people, we'll need to know, especially if the hayseed authorities around here get pulled into this. Keep us apprised of their movements and anything else we need to know. If things go south, we may need you as backup. Understood?"

McHugh nods, but it's clear he's not happy being left out.

"Go on. Double-time it," Kimball orders.

McHugh turns and lopes toward the path that leads through the woods to the road two miles away.

"I need to take care of the kayak," LeLoup says. "Then we'll get started."

He makes a wide circle of the cabins, staying in the tall grass. On the shoreline, he draws the knife from the sheath on his belt and makes a long cut in the polypropylene hull in order to deflate the craft quickly. He rolls up the flattened kayak and hides it and the paddle among a clump of sumac. Then he returns to where the others are waiting.

The sun has set, but the treetops still burn orange with the last of the light. The men stand facing north, the deep woods there. LeLoup smiles at what's ahead. For him, it's a test, the kind he's good at. The kind he's been hired for.

"Well?" Kimball says. "Lead the way."

"Wait here. I'll call you when I find what I'm looking for."

"Hell, I'm tired of waiting," Herring says.

"You'll wait," Kimball says and nods for LeLoup to proceed.

He makes his way across the meadow. The trail is faint, a broken or crushed stalk here and there, nothing more. They've been careful, his prey. When he reaches the tree line, he sees a clearer trail, the prints of a small moccasin among the soft dirt and needles beneath the pines. He follows the trail to a place where other prints converge. One is from a pair of moccasins and the other from a pair of small boots. He steps to the edge of the meadow and signals for Kimball and Herring. Just as they've rendezvoused in the pines, LeLoup spots a stranger entering the meadow from the trail McHugh took. They hide themselves and watch as the man crosses the meadow and checks the cabins.

Herring has his rifle snugged against his shoulder, his sights on the man. "I can ice him."

"Lower your weapon," Kimball says.

"Why didn't McHugh take care of him?" Herring sounds disgusted.

"Because unlike you, McHugh understands that until we have the woman, the more quietly we go about this, the better. If he's smart, he kept out of sight and let the man pass."

"We need to move before he spots us," LeLoup says.

He turns and leads the way deeper into the woods, moving in the direction of the few tracks left by the three who've fled. If he were tracking alone, he'd be careful of the trail he himself leaves, but he's with two men who know nothing and who leave a trail an idiot could follow. It won't matter. He'll find the people he's been hired to find and Kimball will deal with this business, whatever it is, before anyone has a chance to catch up to them. In and out of the woods in a few hours, he believes. The looming dark doesn't concern him. He's tracked before by artificial light and by torchlight. He even relishes the additional challenge.

Within fifteen minutes, he's lost the trail. It's been heading almost due north, then it vanishes. He turns around to backtrack.

"What is it?" Kimball says.

"They shifted direction somewhere behind us."

"And you didn't see it?" Herring says, grinning with obvious pleasure.

LeLoup doesn't respond, just turns around. Fifty yards back he finds his mistake. Or rather the clever misdirection. He understands that his prey doubled back and changed their route. They knew, or at least suspected, that even in the deep woods they would be followed. He moves west, where their trail leads him, trying to be more cautious as the twilight deepens and the woods grow dark.

His prey change directions several times. Eventually, LeLoup must rely on the flashlight clipped to his belt to follow the trail. It's a LingsFire tactical, small and powerful, with the option of a red beam. In the dark, the red helps him see the contours of ground prints more easily. He understands now that it won't be a quick in-and-out operation. In all likelihood, they'll have to spend the night in the woods.

"Any idea where they're going?" Kimball asks.

"They've wandered a bit, but basically they're headed north. Into the Boundary Waters."

"Not toward the reservation or Aurora?"

"Not yet. But sooner or later they will. Once I get a sense of which option they've chosen, we'll move to cut them off."

"You're saying we won't catch up with them anytime soon?"

LeLoup can hear the censure in Kimball's voice. "We'll keep moving," LeLoup says. "If they stop for the night, we'll find them."

"They'll see your light coming long before we reach them."

"Maybe so. But if they use a light to keep going, we'll spot them, too. My guess is that they'll hole up somewhere. That's when we get them."

Kimball makes a noise in his throat. Agreement? Disgruntlement? Whatever, it's clear he's not happy. Which doesn't bother LeLoup much. For him, this isn't about pleasing the man who's hired him. This is becoming about something far more important. He hides his smile from Kimball.

They come at last to an area at least a hundred yards wide and composed of several small hillocks of exposed and broken rock. LeLoup starts across, moving carefully because it would be easy to turn an ankle. The other two men follow. They've brought out flashlights as well, bright white beams. LeLoup spends half an hour trying to pick up the trail again, but even as he searches, he knows it's useless. The vast moonless dark that has descended and the expanse of rock have conspired to hide the trail of his prey. He will have to wait until morning. But patience is something he's good at.

"What now?" Kimball asks, his disappointment obvious.

"We rest for the night."

"We'll be in this damn forest all night?" Herring says. "It's already getting cold."

"Build a fire," LeLoup says.

"You crazy? They'll know we're here."

"If they're close enough to see your fire, they're close enough to have seen our flashlights. They know we're here."

"And they can hit us if they want."

"Their prints have told me that there are probably two women and one man. Are you afraid of a couple of women?"

"We'll rest here," Kimball says. "But we'll post watches. Go ahead, Herring. Build your fire. Maybe it'll even draw them to us."

"Moths to the flame?" Herring says. "If so, we'll burn them."

Kimball nods once, then adds as a reminder, "But not the Morriseau woman."

LeLoup settles down for the night. He knows there will be no moths coming to this flame. Out there in the dark is someone who understands these woods, for whom this vast wilderness is home, who believes this place offers sanctuary. Whoever that person is, in the morning, LeLoup will find him. Or her. In the comfort of this knowledge, he quickly yields to sleep.

- PART FOUR -

CORK

CHAPTER 11

By the time they've gathered their gear and reconvened back at Crow Point, it's midmorning. Cork and Anton Morriseau each have a small pack with a few provisions inside and a rolled blanket atop. They both carry scoped rifles. The sun has been dulled by a high gray haze and dark clouds have begun to mount in the west. The weather report is for snow. This isn't unheard of in early spring in the North Country, where Cork has seen snow fall in every month except July. How much snow depends upon the track the storm will follow, and the report is uncertain. He stands with Anton Morriseau and Stephen near Meloux's cabin, where they've rendezvoused. Stephen won't be going with them, a great disappointment to him, Cork knows. But he has another job for Stephen, an important one: Find Lou Morriseau.

Anton Morriseau has already tried calling his brother several times, on both his cell phone and his office phone. No answer, but he's left messages. He's told Cork and Stephen all he knows that might be helpful. His brother has been distant from the family for a long time now. Vastly different values. He lives in Edina, a wealthy suburb of Minneapolis. The rest of the Morriseaus live in the small town of Bena, on the Leech Lake Reservation. Not just a couple of hundred miles apart. A world apart. Lou has been traveling to Canada a good deal recently, real estate dealings there. When Dolores came asking how to find Meloux, she said Lou had gone to Canada once again. She hadn't heard from him and didn't know when he might be back.

"Lou always wanted money. Money and the things money can buy. I guess I understand. Life on the rez isn't easy. We lose our young people all the time to dreams of something better in the Cities. Not a lot of them find it. But Lou did."

"So no indication of any problems?" Cork asks.

"Nothing he talked to me about."

"Any idea why someone would be interested enough in Dolores to go to all this trouble to find her?"

Morriseau rolls this over in his thinking, then gives his head a shake. "No idea. She's a good woman. Best choice Lou made. Kept him grounded. But from what Dolores told us, sounds like things haven't been easy for a while."

"Any specifics?" Cork asks.

"Nothing you could lay a finger on."

"Business troubles?"

"Lou never talks business. At least not with me."

"What about the rest of your family?"

"Maybe."

"Have you spoken with them today?"

"Couple of times. They're in the dark, just like us."

"Still, we should talk to them. They may know more than they think." Cork looks to Stephen, who nods.

Morriseau has already supplied the home address for his brother, and the number there, his brother's cell phone number, and the phone numbers of family members on the Leech Lake

Reservation. As they prepare to separate, he gives Stephen a skeptical look.

"Awfully young for this kind of work. Sure you can handle it?"

Cork can see that his son is irritated, but Stephen says simply, "Don't worry about me. You just find our people." His dark, serious eyes settle on Cork, and he adds, "Be careful, okay, Dad?" At last, he turns and begins along the path back to the double-trunk birch.

"Let's go," Cork says and leads the way across the meadow, following the line of trampled grass left the night before.

All his life, Cork has been a hunter. He has still-stalked game, read their fragile trails through the woods, brought them down with both rifle and bow. This trail through the woods is incredibly easy to follow. Fairly quickly, he can see from the varying prints that there are three individuals tracking the people he cares about. The boot prints are large, so he assumes they were left by men. Their carelessness tells him that they're not worried about being followed. Which means that either they believe they'll accomplish their mission quickly and be gone before they're caught, or they don't care about being caught. Which means two additional things to Cork: They don't know Henry—he will not be easily found—and they don't mind the prospect of a firefight.

"Easy to read their trail," Morriseau says at his back. "They're either stupid or they're not worried that we might catch up with them."

We're on the same page, Cork thinks, and he's glad to have this man with him.

After a while, Morriseau says quietly, "Meloux is doing his best to misdirect, but these guys have a good tracker with them. I'm guessing he did some of this tracking last night in the dark. Hope Meloux knew that."

"I wouldn't worry about Henry," Cork says. "I'm pretty sure he grabbed his Winchester before he left. He's not helpless."

"But I'm guessing his eyesight's not what it used to be."

"Rainy's a fine shot, if it comes to that." Which, Cork hopes, won't be the case.

They reach an expanse of hillocks composed mostly of bare and broken rock. Cork knows this place. He's heard the Ojibwe call it the Hungry Hills because tracking game here is impossible.

"I should have guessed this is where Henry's meanderings would bring them," he says. "No man alive could follow him through this."

They separate and move among the rocks, looking for anything.

"Here!" Morriseau calls out.

When Cork reaches him, he can see the char of a recent fire. Morriseau is bent with his hand over the ash. "Cold," he says.

"This wasn't Meloux," Cork says. "He'd never risk a fire."

Morriseau eyes the Hungry Hills. "These guys didn't care that they were giving themselves away. So where did they all go?"

They search along the edges where the rock gives way again to forest. It doesn't take long to pick up the trail left by the nameless men.

"They've destroyed any signs our people might have left. But they continue to head into the Boundary Waters," Cork points out.

"Why doesn't Meloux just circle east to Allouette?" Morriseau says. "The town's not that far. It's what I'd do."

"I don't ever pretend to know what's in Henry's head," Cork replies. "I just know we should trust him. Let's go."

Once again, they follow the trail left by the three men, which any idiot can see.

*   *   *

The sun has been eaten by clouds. The wind is cold, and whenever they have a clear view, Cork can see the darkness of the approaching storm. Ordinarily, this would mean rain, but it's still early May and the sweep of the air out of Canada is cold enough to deliver snow. He wonders about Rainy and the others. Did they have enough time before they fled Crow Point to prepare for snow? To prepare for any of the unthinkable possibilities that have come with the strangers who are after them? But Henry is with them, and despite all the other circumstances, Cork knows that's the essential one.

Midafternoon, they come to a marshy area of tamaracks and stunted black spruce. There's a large pond at the center, which is a mirror of the darkening sky. The tracks of the three men split there. Two go east around the pond, the other west.

"Maybe these guys lost the trail," Morriseau says. "They split up to try to find it."

"But look there." Cork points toward an obvious print in the soft earth. "Way too small to be one of the men. That's got to be Rainy's boot print."

"I don't see any moccasin prints," Morriseau says. "Henry and Dolores must have gone the other way."

"Let's split up," Cork says.

"I'll go west," Morriseau tells him. "Holler if you find anything."

Cork turns east and follows the edge of the marsh. He moves quickly because both Rainy's boot prints and the trail left by those who are after her are very clear. He comes to the rotting trunk of a tamarack brought down by a long-ago storm. The trunk is covered in green-gray lichen. Cork can see where a boot has scraped away some of the lichen. He's about to step over the fallen tree but stops and studies the ground.

There's a splashing of blood on the far side of the fallen tamarack. For a moment, Cork feels as if his heart has stopped beating. It can't be Rainy, he tells himself. It can't.

He calls to Morriseau, who joins him, and they both step carefully over the downed trunk.

"What the hell?" Morriseau says.

They stand bewildered. There are clear signs that someone has lain in the undergrowth. The area is spotted with spilled blood. Cork walks away a bit, trying to find more of Rainy's boot prints, but sees nothing except the trampling of the men who are tracking her.

Fear nests deep in Cork's heart. Something has happened to Rainy.

Morriseau says, "Let's spread out, see if they left anything behind." By *anything*, Cork knows he means *anyone*.

They spend a few minutes searching the area but find nothing, only the blood near the rotting trunk.

Finally, Cork grits his teeth and says, "Go back and circle the other way. I'll meet you on the other side."

They rendezvous on the far side of the marsh at a place where the men's tracks head north again.

"Anything?" Cork asks.

"One set of moccasin prints. Small. A woman's."

"Dolores," Cork says. "They split up, maybe to confuse whoever's after them."

Morriseau studies the ground, where the trail the hunters have left to the north is abundantly clear. "Meloux's still leading the women into the Boundary Waters."

Cork thinks about the blood and wonders grimly, *Both of them?*

- PART FIVE -

RAINY

CHAPTER 12

Henry wakes her early. Rainy is surprised she's slept. He signals her to follow him outside the bear den. They sit in the cold morning, where the light is barely enough to make out the separation of shapes. Henry points, and Rainy sees the distant beams sweeping the Hungry Hills.

"It is time for us to go, Niece."

They wake Dolores and use the light of Rainy's cell phone to gather themselves. When they're ready to leave, Rainy pulls the blanket from the entrance and rolls and ties it. One by one, they crawl into the cold, gray morning. Wordless, the two women follow Henry.

As the day slowly breaks, he leads them north. They move in a single line. Henry has cautioned them about leaving as little sign as possible. Avoid soft soil and try to leave no tracks. Step over the underbrush, not through it. Be careful not to break any of the foliage as you pass. If you snap a fallen branch underfoot, pick it up and throw it far to the side. If you step on rocks, don't displace them. Even with all this caution, Rainy knows they won't be completely invisible. But it will slow the men who are tracking them. Despite his age, Henry keeps them all moving quickly.

The land through which they travel was shaped aeons ago by both massive volcanic upheavals and the relentless scrape of glaciers. What's left exposed is some of the oldest rock on earth. It is a varied landscape of lakes, streams, marshes, sudden rock outcrops, and sheer cliffs. Rainy has often thought there could be no more beautiful place in the world. But now she sees mostly how difficult it is to traverse and wishes it were flatter and less populated by bramble.

After an hour, they come to a scattering of boulders and Henry signals them to stop. They sit among the rocks, careful, as Henry has advised them, not to scrape loose any of the lichen growing there. They haven't eaten since the light meal the night before, and Rainy breaks out more jerky and divides the biscuits.

"I thought you were going to work your way east, Henry, back to Allouette," Rainy says. "But we just keep going north."

"If these vultures who follow us have half a brain, Niece, that is exactly what they will expect us to do, to seek the shortest route to safety. As soon as they see that we have turned east, they will move swiftly to cut us off. Maybe they could succeed in this, maybe not. But I would rather be cautious. North, I feel safe."

"Maybe they've given up," Dolores says hopefully. "We've come a long way."

"They are hungry, and I think they will not stop until they have tasted blood," Henry says.

Dolores's eyes go wide with fear. "Ours?"

"Or enough of their own," the old man says.

"What do they want?" Dolores asks, more of herself than the others.

Rainy can see how drawn the woman's face is. Dolores is tired, of course, because none of them slept well. And before that there was the deep concern she brought with her into the sweat, which she said was about her marriage. But Rainy wonders now if there is more to it than that.

"Maybe it has something to do with your husband," she suggests. "You said he's been acting distant lately."

"A midlife crisis, I thought. Maybe a little tired of being married." Dolores stares down at her hands. "Or maybe just tired of me."

"Do you believe that?"

"I don't know what to believe. I can hardly believe I'm here right now with a bunch of wolves at our heels. And I swear to you, Rainy, I have no idea why. But it's got to be because of Lou, right? I mean me, I'm nobody."

"The why can wait," Henry says. "To stay ahead of the wolves, that is what is important now."

Dolores takes a deep breath and looks at the sky. "Storm coming."

Rainy has seen the clouds mounting and felt the lingering cold in the air. Dolores is right. A storm is coming, and what it will bring is worrisome.

"*Goonikadin,*" Henry says.

"What?" Dolores asks.

"Snow," Rainy translates.

Dolores slumps. "Oh, God, just what we don't need."

"Snow can be a good thing," Henry says.

Dolores gives him a tired, irritated look. "How?"

Henry's dark eyes settle on her for a long while. "Like a beautiful face, snow can hide much beneath it."

"I need to relieve myself," Rainy says.

"I could tinkle, too," Dolores says.

"The other side of the rocks," Henry says. "Disturb nothing."

They have walked all morning under a threatening sky. At noon, they come to a marsh with a small pond at its center. The area is filled with tamaracks and stunted black spruce.

"Rest," Henry says.

An hour earlier, he'd asked for the hatchet Rainy brought from the cabin, and he had cut a sturdy branch from a hard maple. He'd taken the knife from the knapsack, trimmed the twigs and leaves so that only a bare stick remained, three feet in length. Remembering that they were supposed to leave no trace, Rainy had asked him what the stick was for. The old man said only "You will see." After that, as he walked, he'd used the knife to shave a sharp point on the end of the stick.

Now, as they pause, Rainy sees him searching the edges of the marsh. When they have rested, he gestures to Dolores. "You go that way." He points west. "Walk as I have shown you, carefully. Leave no trail. We will meet on the other side of this pond."

"What about you?" Dolores asks.

"My niece and I will go this way." He nods toward the east.

"Why?" Dolores asks.

"Just go," Rainy says. "Henry knows what he's doing."

The woman starts left, and Rainy turns with Henry to circle the pond in the other direction.

"Niece," Henry says. "Leave boot prints."

"What? But, Uncle Henry . . ." she begins.

The old man lifts his white eyebrows, and Rainy silences herself and does as he has asked.

They walk for a hundred yards until they come to a fallen, rotting tamarack trunk. When Rainy lifts her foot to step over, Henry says, "Use your heel to scrape the lichen from the bark."

Another clear sign of their passing. But it's what Henry has asked and so she complies. The moment her foot hits the ground on the other side of the fallen tamarack, Henry says, "Stop, Niece." He steps over the trunk and holds up the knife with which he's sharpened the stick. "Now step away."

As Rainy watches, Meloux digs a narrow hole where her foot

landed, and he plants the stick with the sharpened point jutting four inches above the ground.

"Bring me leaves and old brush," he says.

She brings him what she's gathered, and carefully Henry covers the sharpened point. When he's finished, Rainy can't tell that there is anything beneath. She looks across the pond and can see that Dolores is waiting for them. Henry's trap has taken precious time, and Rainy isn't sure it has any chance of working.

As if sensing her concern, Henry says, "If we are lucky, Niece, they will see that even rabbits have sharp teeth. It will make them step more carefully, slow them in their coming."

She prays that Henry is right.

PART SIX

THE WOLF

CHAPTER 13

The other men rise slowly in the cold dawn. It's still more night than day, but for the last hour, LeLoup has been using the red beam of his flashlight to look for signs of the prey they're after. As a tracker, he appreciates the zigzag of the trail they followed leading to these rocks, where he hasn't been able to find a single indication of their passing. A little flame of respect has been lit inside LeLoup. These women, this one man, they will be more of a challenge than Kimball led them all to believe.

Herring stirs the ashes from the fire he lit the night before. "Damn, I'd sell my grandmother for a cup of hot coffee. We should have packed in some supplies."

"We didn't know we'd be on a chase," Kimball says. "We were supposed to surprise them at the cabins."

Herring spits on the ground. "That's what you said about Louis Morriseau."

Kimball gives Herring a killing look. "LeLoup tracked him perfectly. If you hadn't screwed that up, we wouldn't need his wife."

"Not me. Was McHugh got gun-happy first."

"Clock's ticking on this," Kimball says. "We don't have time to waste. We need to catch up with them today. You better make sure that happens, LeLoup."

"It's going to take some time to find their trail. From here, they could have gone anywhere."

"We'll look southeast first, the direction of the reservation town," Kimball says. "If I was running scared, that's where I'd go."

"They tried to throw us off yesterday with all that twisting and turning," LeLoup says. "They may be scared, but they're not exactly running."

Herring unzips the fly on his camo pants and begins to pee against a rock. "You got a better idea?"

"Not at the moment," LeLoup confesses.

Kimball's sat phone vibrates. "Yeah," he answers, then listens. "Roger that." He turns to the other men. "They're predicting snow this afternoon." He levels a hard look at LeLoup. "And word is that this man we're chasing is a hundred years old. If you let a man with one foot already in the grave outrun us, LeLoup, I'll shoot you myself."

"I'll get them." It's no empty boast. LeLoup knows what he's capable of.

"All right. Flashlights on. Let's start looking," Kimball says.

Kimball and Herring move to the southeast edge of the rocky hillocks and begin looking there. LeLoup has already covered that area. He begins at the western edge, where, if their prey were going to circle back toward Aurora, he might spot some sign. But he finds nothing. As the gray of dawn gives way to the stronger light of day, he works his way north and finally finds what he's been searching for—a single, small boot print pressed into a thin covering of pine needles over a soft patch of earth. From the orientation of the heel and toe, the direction they've headed is obvious to him. He calls to the others, who join him.

"This way," he says, and he nods toward the northeast.

"Circling back to the reservation," Kimball says. "Just like I thought."

"Not a circle yet," LeLoup says. "Maybe just more misdirection. We'll know soon enough." He starts off, tracking carefully, and the others follow.

In fifteen minutes, they come to a ridge that runs for a couple of hundred yards. The thin, rocky soil is dominated by aspens. LeLoup holds up his hand, signaling them to stop. They stand before a section of the ridge that is mostly exposed rock. LeLoup points a finger toward a cleft in the stone. Herring moves to the left of the opening. Kimball takes the right and nods for LeLoup to check out what's inside.

LeLoup flips on the high, white beam of his LingsFire flashlight and bends into the opening. Even before he enters, he can smell the powerful odor of the sow that used the den during the long winter months. It's a good space for a black bear, he discovers, but it would have been cramped with three people inside. Still, he can see from the recent disturbance of the leaves and twigs littering the floor and from a few crumbs dropped from a biscuit that this is where their prey spent the night. He backs out.

"They were here," he reports.

"How long ago?" Kimball asks.

"They had to wait until there was enough light to see by, so maybe an hour."

"Which way?"

LeLoup scours the ground. Within minutes, he's found a sign, the snapped branch of a moose maple. "This way," he says and starts northeast once again.

He feels at home in this arboreal landscape, but it's a sense of having been adopted by it rather than born to it. He grew up a city kid, no father he ever knew and a mother who died when he was so young that he has no real memory of her. His memories begin with the residential school, the cold faces of the nuns, the sobs in the night from other Native kids afraid or homesick or in pain. At sixteen, he left school and made his way to the Northwest Territories, a place as far from the grit and noise of the city as he could get. As luck would have it, a man who was half Scotch and half Denendeh, a hunting guide out of Yellowknife, took him under his wing. From Bill McCrory he learned the art of tracking. McCrory told him he was the most natural tracker he'd ever seen, that despite his upbringing among concrete towers, he understood the woods in a way few people ever did. McCrory died in a hunting accident, shot by a stockbroker from Montreal who didn't know a rifle barrel from his own dick. LeLoup enlisted in the military after that, served in Afghanistan, and on discharge had gone back to Yellowknife. Which is where Kimball, who'd once been his commanding officer, tracked him down and recruited him.

The sat phone vibrates and Kimball answers, listens, signs off. "Fredricks says we've got people following us. The cavalry to the rescue."

"How many?" Herring asks.

"Only two. They left from the old man's cabin this morning."

"We're hours ahead of them," LeLoup says. "No worries." And he turns back to his tracking.

The trail is difficult to follow but far from impossible. Kimball and Herring are his biggest concern. Herring is impatient and impulsive, and Kimball is nervous. Kimball's responsible for this mission, and he's already made significant errors in judgment. He let Lou Morriseau slip through his fingers at the cabin north of Winnipeg. By the time he went after the man's wife, she was gone, and it had taken Kimball too long to follow her trail to Tamarack County. Kimball did the initial poking around in Aurora, but because LeLoup is obviously Native, Kimball sent him to do the asking on the reservation. Like most white people, Kimball assumes all

Natives feel a kinship with one another. But LeLoup was a stranger to the people on the Iron Lake Reservation, and he knew his questions about Meloux would raise suspicions. When they directed him back to O'Connor, the PI in Aurora, Kimball sent Fredricks to do the talking. Fredricks, a buffoon if ever there was one. Still, it had been Fredricks's idea to plant the tracking device on O'Connor on the off chance that he would lead them to Meloux. Which worked. But Kimball screwed up, maybe his biggest screwup yet, because he failed to understand the situation on Crow Point. It's obvious to LeLoup that this Meloux is a good deal more than just an old medicine man.

LeLoup didn't need the weather report Kimball received over the sat phone to know that snow is coming. He sensed it in the dark hours of the morning, when he took the last watch, felt the front moving in, could smell the moisture carried in the clouds it was bringing. While he'd searched for signs before dawn, he was thinking about the difficulty the snow would create if they didn't find their prey quickly. He has begun to suspect this might be a greater challenge than he'd anticipated.

Even on rock, the unwary can leave their mark. A turned stone. The scuff of a heel across a strip of lichen. Blood where a fall has caused a scraped hand or knee or ankle. Yet LeLoup, in the dark of that morning, could find nothing. Which might have been pure luck on the part of his prey, but he's begun to suspect otherwise. The zigzag of the trail the night before, which at first had seemed to indicate that these people might be lost and wandering, led eventually to those difficult, rocky acres. And the trail this morning led to good shelter for the night. LeLoup has come to understand that there is nothing haphazard in the movements of those he's tracking. He understands, too, that he and Kimball and Herring have entered ground eminently familiar to their prey. Despite their firepower, their sat phones, their ruthlessness, they are the ones at a disadvantage now. And the coming snow will only make matters worse.

After several hours of enduring Herring's snipes about their too slow progress and Kimball's constant reminders that snow is imminent, LeLoup leads them to a bog pond, where he pauses. Heading east is a clear set of the small boot prints he's certain belong to a woman.

While LeLoup considers this, Herring blurts out, "Jesus Christ, a blind man can see where they've gone."

Kimball says with irritation, "He's right, LeLoup. What's the holdup now?"

LeLoup turns to the west and begins to walk in that direction.

"Where the hell are you going?" Herring says.

LeLoup ignores them and walks fifty yards before he sees the first sign, a broken stem of bog laurel. The break is recent. He walks back to where the others are waiting and tells them what he's found.

"Well, hell's bells," Herring says. "They split up."

"And the smart ones went east, back toward the reservation like I said." Kimball grins in a gloating way.

"Maybe," LeLoup says. "But maybe that trail's clear because they want us to go east."

"All right," Kimball says, using the voice he hauls up when it's time to play commander. "We split up, too. Herring and me'll go east, you go west. Ten minutes, just to see where each trail leads, then we rendezvous back here."

"Be careful," LeLoup says.

"Why?" Herring says.

"The old man is smart."

"The old man is already next door to dead," Herring throws back. "I'm going to make sure he finishes the trip."

"Go," Kimball says and gives Herring a push.

LeLoup turns his back to them and retraces his path to the broken twig. He finds the next sign twenty yards farther along, where the soft moss that carpets the edge of the marsh has been pressed down by moccasins. He speculates that they've divided into two groups, skirting the lake on either side, maybe in an attempt to confuse their trackers. He believes that the trail he's following will join eventually with the one Kimball and Herring have followed and they'll find that their prey have continued north, deeper into the wilderness.

He's a quarter of the way around the bog pond when he hears Herring scream.

CHAPTER 14

"Christ! Oh, Jesus! Oh, God! Oh, God!"

Herring is on the ground. A stick sharpened into a spike has gone completely through his boot and foot, and the bloody point protrudes through the laces. His contortions have pulled the stick from where it was anchored in the ground.

"Hold still, goddamn it," Kimball says. He's kneeling, trying to grasp Herring's leg.

LeLoup presses Herring firmly to the ground so that Kimball can extract the spike. When it's out, Kimball flings it away angrily. The spike lands on the surface of the bog pond with a small splash. It has left a hole in Herring's boot sole that a little mole could easily scurry through. Blood is spilling all over the ground.

Herring's eyes are squeezed shut in pain, but his mouth is open and he's letting loose a stream of curses.

"Hold him down while I get his boot off," Kimball orders Le-Loup.

The process takes a while because they get no help from Herring, who continues to writhe. When the foot is free, Kimball strips off the bloody sock.

"Went between your bones," he tells Herring. "Looks like nothing's broke but it'll take a shitload of stitches to close this thing up."

"We have to leave him," LeLoup says.

"No," Herring says. "I can walk."

"The hell you can," Kimball says.

"You're not leaving me behind." Herring looks at the bloody hole in his foot, grimaces and looks away. "Wrap it up somehow and put my boot back on."

"Wrap it up with what?" Kimball says.

LeLoup stands. "I've got an idea."

He walks to a patch of the sphagnum moss that carpets the edge of the bog, takes his knife from its sheath, and cuts out two small squares. He brings the moss squares to where Herring lies on the ground with his foot in Kimball's hands.

"What the hell!" Herring cries when LeLoup places a patch of moss over the wound on the top of his foot.

"In the First World War, they used moss just like this as field dressings because it kept the wounds sterile. Also helped staunch the bleeding. Give me that bloody sock."

LeLoup cuts the sock into strips, places the second patch of moss over the wound in the sole of Herring's foot and wraps the strips tightly around both patches to secure them. "See if you can get his boot on," he tells Kimball.

Herring complains bitterly, but in the end, the boot is fitted and loosely laced. Kimball puts his hands under Herring's arm. "Let's get you on your feet and see if you can travel."

Together, LeLoup and Kimball lift their comrade and stand him upright.

"Walk," Kimball says.

Herring takes a tentative step. "Ah, Jesus!"

"You want us to leave you?" Kimball snaps.

"All right, all right." Herring takes another step and another. He limps forward a dozen yards. "I can do this."

LeLoup finds a long stick of dead wood and hands it to Herring as a staff.

"Your rifle," Kimball says, handing the weapon to Herring. "Let's get going. We've wasted too much time as it is."

Just as LeLoup suspected, the two trails circle the bog pond, meet on the far side, and continue north. Kimball's speculation that they would head east and work their way back to the reservation town of Allouette was reasonable. That's what most people might have done. But both the ghost of a trail they've left and the booby trap that has hobbled Herring confirm for LeLoup that their prey aren't like most people.

When he was in uniform and tracking in Afghanistan, he'd read the enemy from the signs they left behind. He could predict the ease with which a resulting firefight might be conducted or advise on an approach to the enemy that would avoid ambush. He'd been able to construct accurate profiles of the men he tracked just from the way they handled themselves in their flights.

At the bog pond, he'd read the signs correctly and had warned Kimball and Herring. Their stupidity—Herring's anyway—was his undoing. The people they track aren't stupid or careless or overwhelmed by fear, although under the circumstances, they probably should be very afraid because, except for the Morriseau woman, if they're caught, they're dead. He wonders if they have any idea why they're being pursued. He's not certain himself, except that it's connected to the failed operation north of Winnipeg, the man he tracked to the remote cabin there. He's not paid to know why he's been hired. He's paid to do what he does best. Track and kill.

It's an hour before Kimball says, "Enough."

LeLoup has been waiting for this. He's been reading the signs more easily. Their prey are tiring, leaving greater evidence of their passage. LeLoup feels the driving urge to press forward quickly, to move in for the kill. But Herring's fallen farther and farther behind, and Kimball has slowed to accommodate him. The pace they've been keeping will never allow them to catch up with their prey.

"We're cutting you loose, Herring," Kimball finally says.

"I'm keeping up," Herring insists.

"We're moving like turtles now. I can't afford to lose the Morriseau woman. You on the other hand . . ."

"Expendable," Herring says, as if it's a verdict. He brings his rifle off his shoulder and aims it at Kimball's chest.

"Relax, Herring. I have no intention of killing you. In fact, you can do some good here." Kimball points to a small rise crowned with an outcrop of rock. "I want you to take up a position there. We know we're being tracked and I'm pretty sure that damaged foot of yours is helping cut the distance between us and them. Your job is to hold them up."

"Eliminate them?"

"If you can."

"And in return?"

"When we've got the Morriseau woman, we'll come back for you."

"If I'm still alive."

"Make sure you are."

"And if I'm caught?"

"I guarantee that we have the resources and the influence to help free you."

"And if I say no to this plan of yours?"

"There's no saying no. The situation is unfortunate but clear."

LeLoup, who is quite a bit ahead of the other two, has been prepared to move swiftly to put Herring down if Kimball's negotiation fails. He wouldn't hesitate for a moment to blow the man's heart out of his chest. Not only because he doesn't like Herring, but it's the kind of thing he's been paid to do. Here and before.

Herring chews on his options, which are limited to two: accept Kimball's suggestion or die where he stands. Kimball has offered the possibility of an out that has a future to it, and if Herring is smart, he'll take it. But LeLoup has no faith in Herring's brain.

"All right," Herring says. He looks beyond Kimball to LeLoup. "You can find your way back here?"

"Blindfolded," LeLoup says.

Herring looks to Kimball. "How long?"

"Within twenty-four hours, you'll be back in civilization. We'll get that foot seen to and I'll buy you a bottle of Johnnie Walker Blue to kick off your recovery."

Herring eyes both his companions carefully, as if trying to read the thoughts in their heads. Finally, he gives a nod.

"Your sat phone," Kimball says and holds out his hand.

"Hell, that's the only connection I have with civilization."

"If you get caught, I don't want you to have that or anything else that might be traceable."

"I know where you are," LeLoup assures him. "When Kimball says so, I'll be back to extract you."

A few flakes of snow have begun to drift down from the low, dark clouds. Herring looks at the sky. "Snow, you said."

"It'll give you cover," Kimball tells him. "They'll walk right into your sights. You can't miss. And if you eliminate them, there will be a bonus in it, I promise. That sat phone," he says with his hand still extended.

Herring hands over the device, then begins to limp his way up the slope to the crown of rocks. LeLoup agrees with Kimball that it's a good, strategic position. If the man is patient and his aim is true, Herring might just be able to eliminate the trackers who are following. At the very least, he will delay them.

When Herring's in place, Kimball turns to LeLoup. "Lead on. We need to catch them before this damn snow comes down in earnest."

PART SEVEN

CORK

CHAPTER 15

In the late afternoon, snow begins to fall. The flakes are large and float down, and they melt as soon as they hit the ground.

"Kills any chance for a search plane," Cork notes, looking at the low, heavy clouds.

"Let's hope it stops soon," Morriseau says. "Otherwise it becomes a hunter's snow."

Cork shakes his head. "Even Henry will be in trouble then."

A hunter's snow. Game's worst enemy. Cork thinks of the number of times a hunter's snow has helped him track and bring down deer.

"It'll make it easier for us to follow these guys," Morriseau says.

"It's already easy," Cork says.

"I'm figuring they were half a day ahead when we started. If we hurry, we might catch them by nightfall."

They follow where the others have gone before them. The snow begins to come down more heavily and stick to the branches of the trees and then begins to cover the ground. It's becoming the hunter's snow they feared. The men they're tracking are far enough ahead that Cork knows it will be some time before their prints become visible in the snow. He has no idea how far ahead of those bastards Rainy and the others might be. He hopes far enough to find shelter and hide before the tracks they might themselves leave in the snow give away their location.

The snowfall intensifies and a wind rises, and it's as if they've stepped into the swirl inside a snow globe. Then the first shot comes, a rifle report like the crack of thunder from somewhere up ahead. Cork and Morriseau, both veterans of law enforcement, drop and take cover.

"Are you hit?" Cork calls. He's rolled behind the cover of a fallen pine.

"Good here," Morriseau says. He's found a gray rock outcrop that gives him good protection.

"Did you see where it came from?" Cork calls.

"Hard to tell in this damn snow," Morriseau says. "But I'd say somewhere above."

Cork crawls to the end of the fallen pine and risks a peek. The swirling snow makes a good blind for whoever has fired on them. The flip side is that it helps to hide Cork and Morriseau as well. He figures whoever the shooter is, he must have spotted their dim images approaching in the snowfall and fired too soon. Not a true hunter. A bit more patience and he might have had a clear shot.

In the wake of the rifle shot, the only sound in the woods is the rush of the wind through the tree branches. Cork and Morriseau remain unmoving, listening for anything that might give them a better idea of the shooter's location. Nothing comes. Cork slides the rifle strap from his shoulder, slowly brings the rifle around, and sights through the scope. Fifty yards ahead is a slope topped by a rock outcropping. Although he can't see the shooter, it seems to him the most logical position. He signals to Morriseau, who is thirty feet to his right, to circle in that direction. Morriseau gives him a thumbs-up and begins maneuvering carefully under the cover of the trees.

Cork stays low. Although the snow is falling heavily and will help to mask him, he moves with extreme caution from one form of cover to the next—fallen log to pine tree, pine tree to spruce, spruce to brush blind—circling gradually and widely.

A rifle shot brings him to a sudden halt. It has come not from ahead, where Cork believes the shooter to be, but from where Morriseau is circling. He wonders if Morriseau has spotted their target or if he's simply trying to draw the shooter's attention. Cold flakes slap Cork's face, melt immediately, and drip into his eyes. With the back of his hand, he wipes away the melt.

Another shot, this one from the outcrop atop the slope. He uses his scope but still can't see any movement there.

He continues to circle until he's fifty yards from the outcrop and slightly behind it. He can see a figure now, dressed in hunter's camo, wedged into a cleft at the top of the outcrop. He can see the rifle snugged against the figure's shoulder. The shooter appears to be intent on aiming. Cork has a clear shot but refrains from taking it. He wants this man alive. He wants answers.

He moves quickly now, but carefully still, until he's twenty yards away and with an easy shot at the figure's back. He slips behind the broad trunk of an ancient cedar, kneels, sights, and calls out, "Drop your rifle!"

The figure doesn't move.

"I said drop it!"

The figure sets the rifle down among the rocks.

"Hands clasped behind your head and stand up."

The man complies. He's powerfully built, with a narrow face and a nose like an ax sunk between his eyes. Early forties, Cork guesses.

"Who are you?"

The man stares, a blank look focused on the swirling snow somewhere beyond Cork.

"I've got him!" Cork shouts.

A few moments later, Morriseau appears. The man doesn't look at either of them. His eyes remain fixed on the distance.

"Three steps away from the rifle," Morriseau says.

The man takes three limping steps forward.

"Who are you?" Cork asks.

He's like a figure cut from ice, unmoving, his cold eyes holding on something far away, something only he can see.

"Where are the others?" Morriseau demands.

Cork can see that the leather of the man's boot is soaked with blood. "There was blood back there on the trail. Yours?" When he gets no reply, he rams the butt of his rifle into the man's stomach. The man doubles over, collapses, struggles to breathe. Cork stands over him. "Whose blood?"

The man slowly gathers himself and says nothing. Cork slams his boot into the man's ribs. The man absorbs the blow, his face clenched in pain, but he holds to silence.

"We're getting nowhere this way," Morriseau says. "Maybe we should torture him a little?"

Cork kneels down and puts his face near the man's ear. "My friend is Ojibwe," he says. "Do you know what that word means? It means 'to pucker,' which is what happens to a man when he's burned alive."

The man replies, finally looking Cork in the eye, "If you want the women alive, you need to move now. Me, I'm going nowhere with this foot."

Cork has seen hard men before and he knows that to break this man would take a good deal of time.

Morriseau understands this, too. "I hate to say it, but he's right. We've got to keep moving or we'll lose them in this snow."

"What do we do with him?" Cork asks.

"I say we tie him to a tree and leave him. We can come back for him after we find Dolores and the others."

"Let's take that knife from his belt, check to see if he has anything else on him, maybe some ID," Cork says.

They frisk him but find nothing that will tell them who the man is.

Morriseau pulls out a pair of flex cuffs from his gear. In response to Cork's look of surprise, he says, "I bring 'em everywhere. You never know."

They take the man's belt, the laces from his boots, seat him on the ground with his back to the trunk of a birch, and use the plastic restraint to secure his hands behind him to the tree.

Cork picks up the rifle the man has dropped. "Savage M10 Stealth. It's fitted with a Leupold VX-2 scope. Expensive."

"We can't leave it," Morriseau says.

"At least not in this condition."

Cork scrapes mud from the snow-wetted ground and stuffs the barrel. Then he takes a rock and smashes the scope. "Should you somehow get free, that piece'll be no good to you now."

Just before they leave, the man says, "Any wolves in these parts?"

"Oh, yeah," Cork replies. "Several packs. Know anything about wolves?"

The man looks up at him. Snow is melting on his face, running like tears down the sides of his nose.

"They're meat eaters. They can smell blood for miles."

"If you're lucky," Morriseau says, "maybe we'll be back before the wolves find you."

They turn and begin again in the direction they were following before the attack. A thin blanket of wet snow covers everything, obscuring any tracks on the ground. But the men have left other signs, crushed vegetation, broken branches. For a while, Cork and Morriseau are able to proceed.

But the snowfall finally grows too heavy and the wind grows too strong and the storm becomes another enemy in their fight to find the ones they love. Because of the thick cloud cover, darkness comes early. As eager as he is in this hunt, Cork knows that if they go on, they risk losing any sense of the trail, and maybe any hope. It's a hard decision, but he knows they have no choice.

"Over there," he says, pointing to an alcove among boulders at the bottom of a rocky slope.

They hunker in the shelter of the boulders, in the lee of the wind. They don't talk. They sit, sunk in their own thoughts.

"The guy we left behind," Morriseau says. "Think he'll be okay in this?"

"He'll suffer but he'll survive," Cork says. "It's those still in front of us I'm worried about."

They both peer into the confusion of swirling snow.

"We've done everything we can for the moment," Cork says, fighting a blanket of discouragement as wet and heavy as anything the storm promises to deliver. "Now, it's up to Henry."

PART EIGHT

RAINY

CHAPTER 16

When the snow finally comes, it falls in large flakes that drift slowly down. Rainy and her companions have walked since before dawn, covered miles of hard ground. Henry's pace has greatly slowed. Maybe it's because he's seen that Dolores's energy is flagging. But Rainy suspects that Henry is nearing the end of his strength, too. She knows that, despite his age, he walks every day, sometimes all day, and it hasn't been uncommon for him to be gone overnight alone on his wanderings. The woods have always given him strength, clarity of vision, a purposeful life. He's an amazing old man, but he's not superhuman. As the snowfall grows heavier, she can see that his step is beginning to falter.

"We have to stop, Uncle Henry," she finally says.

The old man looks at the sky, at the flakes falling like ashes from a great conflagration, covering the ground. He nods, then turns and starts back the way they've just come.

"What are you doing?" Dolores asks, voicing the confusion that Rainy feels, too.

"Patience," he says in a tired voice.

They trail after him a quarter of a mile to a place where, a few minutes earlier, they crossed the mostly dry, rocky bed of a small creek. He turns and begins to follow the creek bed.

"Remember," he tells them over his shoulder. "Do not dislodge the rocks."

They travel the creek bed for a few hundred yards, Henry scanning the trees around them as they go. The snow has begun to come down more fiercely, and a wind has risen, making the flakes a chaotic flurry that engulfs them. Finally, Henry says, "There," and points toward a deadfall, a place where a long-ago storm toppled several trees, creating a jumble of trunks and branches. They leave the creek bed and step among the fallen trunks, snapping off brittle branches that block their way, and at last seat themselves on a bed of soft, rotting leaves at the center of the deadfall. Rainy spreads her blanket over the mesh of branches above them to create a thin roofing against the falling snow, then joins the others beneath.

They are so tired that for a long while none of them speak. Along the way, they have refreshed themselves with the plentiful water the forest has offered, but they have eaten sparingly. What they brought with them the day before may have to last awhile. Rainy parcels out jerky, dried cranberries and nuts, and the last of their biscuits, and they sit in the shelter created by the confusion of fallen trees.

Rainy is thinking of her family. What is Cork doing now? He must be searching for them. She thinks about the worry of Stephen and Jenny and beautiful little Waaboo and Daniel. She fights against the sinking feeling that has come with her fatigue, the oppressing sense that their flight is hopeless. She looks at Dolores and can see the gloom on her face as well. Henry, however, is sitting with his back against one of the fallen tree trunks, his eyes closed, apparently peacefully asleep. Despite the grim circumstances, Rainy finds herself smiling.

Then she brings her attention to bear on Dolores Morriseau,

this woman who walked into her life only the day before and who now has altered everything. Who is she really? What does Rainy actually know about her? Something Henry said has been knocking around in Rainy's thinking as they've walked the long miles. Earlier that day, as they rested, Henry had leveled a penetrating look on Dolores and said, "Like a beautiful face, snow can hide much beneath it." Which seemed like a casual remark, but it has stuck with Rainy.

"Dolores?" she says quietly.

The woman is still chewing on some jerky. She swallows. "Yes?"

"You told us you had no idea why a man might pretend to be your husband, and that you have no idea who these guys are that are tracking us."

"None."

"When you left your home in the Cities, did you tell anyone where you were going?"

"My neighbor when I asked her to collect my mail."

"Did you tell your husband?"

"Lou was gone, off on one of his frequent business trips to Canada. It was something we argued about."

"Why?"

"I insisted on going with him this time. He absolutely refused."

"Did he say why?"

"No, but I have my suspicions." She closes her eyes, shakes her head. "I think he's seeing someone there. Another woman."

"What makes you think that?"

"Lou works out of his office in our home. Sometimes lately I'll walk in when he's on the phone, and he'll tell me to get out. I've heard him say her name before he knows I'm there." She pauses, then says as if she's just tasted something rancid, "Katie."

"Just Katie?"

"Just Katie. If I had a last name, I might have tried to . . . I don't know what."

"Are you sure he really goes to Canada?"

"I'm not sure of anything anymore."

"Did you let him know you were leaving?"

"I left him a long note."

"You couldn't have called him?"

"I tried. He didn't answer his phone. And then I decided I wanted to do this on my own, and I was afraid he might try to talk me out of it. Lou's not like the rest of his family."

"What do you mean?"

"He's not keen on where he comes from."

"Being Anishinaabe, you mean?"

"Yeah. He's three-quarters Ojibwe, but Lou can easily pass for white. He's always concerned about what clients think if they know he's Native. Still a lot of prejudice out there."

"Who are his clients?"

She shrugs. "Rich people mostly. Although he does some work with First Nations people. Like I said, he goes to Canada a lot. I'm not exactly sure what he does for them. He doesn't talk much about that."

"He's in real estate law, right?"

"I think he often acts as a kind of middleman between people who want to buy something and people who have what those people want to buy. It's always been a little fuzzy to me."

"Could it have anything to do with these men who are after us?"

"I don't know. If Lou would just talk to me more, I might have an idea."

Henry says, "Two birds in a nest but you do not sing to each other." His eyes are still closed, and he has spoken so softly that it would be easy to believe he is speaking in his sleep.

"Are you all right, Henry?" Rainy rests her hand on his arm.

He opens his eyes. "My heart is still beating and my mind is still clear. My legs are complaining, but I have learned not to listen to them." He looks at Dolores. "You have said that you love your husband."

"With all my heart."

"Is it his heart you question?"

"He's not like he used to be, and I don't understand why. Is it me or is it him? That's why I came to you. You told me when we first met that if I needed you, you would be there for me. I wasn't sure you'd even remember me."

"I remembered," Henry says gently.

Rainy watches the woman's eyes. They're the green of willow leaves, a startling and beautiful color. They're moist now with what seem like tears of gratitude. But Rainy wonders if they're like the snow, and if so, what do they hide?

The snow continues to come down heavily as an early dark descends. Dolores is sleeping, wrapped in her blanket. Rainy has nodded off, too. She doesn't know how long she's slept when she feels the light touch of Henry's hand on her arm. He holds a finger to his lips and motions her to follow.

They crawl quietly from the shelter of the fallen trees. The snow has finally stopped, and the storm clouds have moved east, leaving behind a twilight sky full of stars. Half an inch of snow has collected on the ground. Henry leads the way across the empty creek bed to a rise on the far side. Rainy can see the indentation of earlier tracks and understands that while she and Dolores have slept, Henry has been out reconnoitering. He kneels behind an upthrust of bare rock that crowns the rise. Rainy kneels beside him. He nods in the direction he wants her to look, and she sees the reason he's brought her there. She estimates the fire to be less than a quarter mile away.

"Who?" she whispers. "Cork, maybe?"

"Only if he is foolish enough to build a fire and give himself away."

"The people who are after us, then? Or even someone else maybe?"

"I would like to know."

"I would, too, Uncle Henry."

His eyes rest on her expectantly and she finally understands. "You want me to check them out?"

"You can run if you have to. Me, they would catch easily."

Rainy considers and finally draws a deep breath. "Maybe I should take the rifle, just in case."

"It will slow you down. It might also make you careless. Better to take with you only caution. And patience."

She stands, leaves the cover of the rocks, and in the blue twilight, begins to make her way toward the distant campfire.

She is a trained public health nurse and a Mide. She has always been focused on healing. She has never been a hunter, and this mission Henry has sent her on, this reconnaissance, feels alien. She thinks of the deer she frightens so often in sudden encounters on her walks near Crow Point, how they are so silent in the forest that she never suspects them, how swift they are when they bolt, how suddenly they vanish. She tries to think of herself like a deer.

She moves from tree to tree, bush to bush, pausing, listening. Before she can see anything around the fire clearly, she hears the low timbre of voices carrying in the cold air. Men's voices, she can tell. She pauses a long time behind a thicket of sumac, listening carefully, trying to hear if one of the voices is familiar. She would know Cork's voice from a thousand miles.

The voices rise suddenly, angry, and she knows that Cork is not among the men. She steals around the sumac, crouches, then darts for the trunk of a big spruce and presses herself against it. She is fifty yards from the fire, but her heart is hammering so fast and hard against her breastbone, it seems like a noisy drum that will give her away. She breathes deeply several times, trying to calm herself.

She can make out some of the words now.

"They're just a couple of women and an old man, for God's sake."

"A man we really know nothing about."

"You told me you could track them."

"And I have. If it hadn't been for Herring and the snow, we'd have caught up with them."

"I'm not paying you for excuses."

The voices stop suddenly. Rainy risks a look around the trunk of the spruce.

Two men sit at the fire. One has his back to her. In the firelight, she can see that the other appears to be Native. He's a stranger, though. Both men wear camo, just like the men who invaded Crow Point. They aren't mere campers. One man has a satellite phone to his ear, listening.

Rainy has the information she's come for. Carefully she back-tracks. Though she would love to run, she tells herself, *Caution. Patience.*

When she mounts the rise where Henry is waiting for her, she sees that he's holding the rifle. "Just in case," he says. "What did you find, Niece?"

"It's them, the ones who came for us on Crow Point. But there are only two of them now. On Crow Point, there were four. Do you think your trap worked?"

"One stick, one man. But what about the other?"

She eyes the deep woods all around them. "Could he be out there somewhere?"

"Maybe he has gone ahead," Henry says. "Maybe he stayed behind. I do not think he would be wandering these woods alone."

"At least they didn't see where we followed the creek," Rainy says.

Henry looks up at the sky, where the stars have emerged like bright little fish rising from a blue-black sea. "They will realize their mistake tomorrow, but we will be long gone." He smiles to himself. "It is time to turn back toward Allouette. Only two men track us now. Our odds are improving."

PART NINE

THE WOLF

CHAPTER 17

The storm begins deceptively, with flakes soft and delicate and dancing as they descend. But soon, the snowfall grows heavier and a stiff wind rises. The soil is quickly covered with a thin coat of white, which eliminates ground tracking for prints. LeLoup's eyes have moved up as he searches for disturbed brush, bent branches, spiderwebs broken in someone's recent passage. The trail grows vague, but not impossible to follow, and LeLoup presses on with Kimball at his back.

To LeLoup, there is something sacred in the fall of snow or of rain. Blessings from the heavens, they sustain life. And if sometimes they create difficulties for humans, that's not the fault of nature. The fault is in the nature of man. Humans, LeLoup believes, are far too focused on doing and not enough on being. Usually when he's in a wilderness like this, his inclination is to stop, sit, meditate, absorb, appreciate. He feels as if the woods speak to him. Those moments are the best in his life.

But this is a different kind of moment, one that requires another part of himself. He's focused on doing. Much to his dismay, he begins to see the snow as an obstacle, an enemy instead of a thing of mystery and beauty. The storm has descended in force and he can barely see the woods around them. Their prey might well be anywhere and, maybe like Herring, just waiting for them to come into rifle range. The wind whips the bushes and brush and he can no longer see signs. He finally delivers the news to Kimball. "We have to stop."

"This storm will make them stop, too. We can still catch up with them."

"We won't."

"Christ, if we stop, we'll lose them."

"We've already lost them."

"You lost their trail?"

"A while back. I've just been moving in the direction they were headed. They could have veered off, taken a turn. In fact, if I were them, that's exactly what I would have done and counted on the snow to hide the fact. They could be anywhere now. Best to stop, wait for the storm to pass, and pick up their trail after. We may have to wait until morning."

"They could be long gone by morning."

"They're tired. I could see that in the signs they were leaving before the storm hit. If they're smart, and believe me they are, they'll hole up somewhere and wait for the storm to pass. Without a moon, it will be too dark for them to see their way, so they won't move until morning, and they won't be able to walk without leaving tracks. I'll find them then."

Even in the cold wind and snow, Kimball's eyes blaze. "I want them today."

"Look around you." LeLoup swings his hand in a wide arc across a landscape where the storm makes everything appear as if seen through a layer of gauze. Tree trunks are vague black stripes against a white wall, and deeper, the woods are nothing but vague suggestions of shape. "They could be anywhere, sighting a rifle on us even now, and we'd never know it until we were hit."

"You think they have a rifle?"

"The gun rack in the old man's cabin was empty."

"A man a hundred years old who probably can't see well enough to shoot anything except his own foot."

"Maybe one of the women with him can shoot. You want to take that chance?"

"Son of a bitch," Kimball whispers and studies the storm. "What about the men behind us?"

"Herring might be able to take care of them. If not, the snow will give them the same problems it's giving us. If they're smart, they'll wait it out somewhere. If they're not, they'll just get themselves lost."

"All right. Let's call it. But just until the storm passes. We may be able to track them again today."

LeLoup thinks not but refrains from saying so. Instead, he says, "Best find a place to hunker down."

They take shelter in the lee of an outcropping flanked by thickets of sumac. LeLoup gathers wood, shakes off the snow, and gets a fire going. It's not an easy process, but he's built fires under worse conditions. He's dressed well enough to endure the cold, and the fire is less for warmth than to help alter the gloom of the man who's hired him. A fire, LeLoup well knows, can work magic on the human spirit, lift up a flagging soul. Kimball is thinking like a man who believes he's already been beaten. LeLoup needs him to think clearly, and a few hours beside a warming fire and out of the bitter wind might be just the ticket. They have not brought food supplies. That was Kimball's call. A quick in-and-out operation on Crow Point. Extract the woman, silence any witnesses, and disappear. Aside from their sat phones and firearms, Kimball believed no supplies were necessary. LeLoup thinks the man must never have been a Boy Scout. "Be Prepared" means nothing to him.

LeLoup, on the other hand, has brought along sustenance in the form of trail mix and jerky, which he keeps in an inside pocket of his camo jacket. He could have offered food to the others but wisely waited, knowing that if another day was required to bring down their prey, it would be best if they had something to keep their energy from failing them in the home stretch. Now he reaches into his pocket, pulls out a packet of trail mix, and hands it across the fire to Kimball.

"Probably hungry," LeLoup says. "I know I am."

Kimball looks at the offering as if it's as unexpected as a moon rock. "Thanks." He tears it open and downs it greedily. Then he eyes LeLoup. "Not eating?"

"Not yet."

"Got any more?"

LeLoup pulls out a strip of jerky and hands it over.

Kimball tears off a bite of the dried meat. "Oh, God, does this taste good," he says while chewing. When he's finished, he lies back against one of the rocks that shelter them. "Yesterday feels like forever ago. I thought we'd have the woman by now and the info and the job would be done."

"What did you know about the old man before we hit his cabin?"

"Nothing really. The Morriseau woman was our objective. Once we had the location from the tracker Fredricks planted, it was a simple extraction. Whoever this Meloux is, I figured we'd just ice him and disappear the body. Somebody must've tipped them off we were coming."

"You said he's a medicine man of some kind. I knew a healer, a Yellowknife Dene. Old man, but probably not as old as this Meloux. I visited him many times, and every time he seemed to know that I was coming. He told me that the woods talked to him. Maybe the woods talked to this old man Meloux."

Kimball shakes his head. "We've got a leak somewhere. Soon as we're out of these woods, I'll figure out who and plug that leak." He closes his eyes. In a few moments, he's breathing regularly, sleeping.

LeLoup is tired, too. Not much sleep the night before, followed by a long day of tracking. He would like to close his eyes and rest. Instead, he sits with the wind howling past their little shelter and the snow gathering deeper on the ground, and he considers the possibility that somewhere out there is a man who may well beat him in the only thing LeLoup has ever been any good at.

When Kimball wakes, he wakes cranky.

"Goddamn it, why didn't you tell me the storm passed?"

"Stopped snowing only half an hour ago."

"Then we should have been off by now."

"It's twilight. Not enough light left to see anything. And it'll be dark soon."

"That old man is probably out there right now making tracks we can follow."

"Out there where?"

"Isn't that what I pay you to know?"

"You pay me to find them. If I'm out of commission, I can't do that."

"Out of commission? They're just a couple of women and an old man, for God's sake."

"A man we really know nothing about."

"You told me you could track them."

Kimball's sat phone vibrates. He answers it and listens. "Roger that. Have you got the chopper ready to go? Good. Let our people know we'll still make the deadline. And keep me posted." He slips his phone into his jacket. "A search plane is scheduled to take off at first light. If our prey gets spotted, we'll know exactly where they are."

"Fredricks, huh?" LeLoup nods toward the sat phone.

"The man's good at his job. Tapped into all their communications. We'll know everything that search plane knows. I've got a chopper lined up to extract us once we have Dolores Morriseau. But the guys who are tracking us are still on our tails. And they found Herring."

"Did he talk?"

"I'm guessing no. He understands what'll happen to him if he does. But these guys behind us worry me."

"No need to panic. That snow has wiped out every trace of a trail. It's already too dark to see anything clearly. They're not stupid. They'll wait until morning to begin tracking again."

Kimball nods with a look of satisfaction on his face and holds up the sat phone. "Once Fredricks gives us the woman's location, we'll complete this mission and get the hell out of here. We can still meet the deadline."

LeLoup makes a sudden grab for the sat phone, snatches it from the man's hand before Kimball can react. He shatters the device against the wall of their shelter. He picks up his Weatherby MeatEater and levels it on Kimball. "Give me Herring's phone."

"What the hell are you doing?"

"Give me Herring's phone or I'll shoot you where you sit."

"Have you gone crazy?"

"Just give me the phone."

Kimball reaches inside his jacket and brings out the sat phone.

"Toss it to me."

When he has the phone, LeLoup destroys it in the same way he did the other. Then he glares at Kimball and says in a voice whose menace is impossible to miss, "I don't need anyone telling me where they are. I'll find them in my own way."

- PART TEN -

STEPHEN

CHAPTER 18

Stephen watches his father and Anton Morriseau cross the meadow on Crow Point under a graying sky. The forecast is for snow later that day. He can sense the change coming, smell the moisture in the air, feel the last energy of a winter that refuses to abandon its hold on the North Country. Everything in him wants to be with these men, wants to be a part of this important hunt, but he has a different job to do, one of no less importance: Find Lou Morriseau and with him maybe the reason behind all that is happening. No small task, he knows. He has an idea where to begin, but first he heads to the office of Sheriff Marsha Dross.

"Nothing more on our fake Lou Morriseau yet," she tells him. "We know the make of his vehicle. Not that many Escalades in Tamarack County."

"If he's still here."

"We've put out an APB to all adjacent counties, Stephen. There are lots of eyes out there right now looking for this guy."

"Mine'll make two more."

"Do you have any idea where you'll look?"

"I'm heading to Leech Lake. I want to talk to Morriseau's family, see if they can give me any kind of lead."

"You better leave soon. Snow's on the way. I talked to the Forest Service about getting one of their search planes in the air, but that weather front's going to keep everything grounded for a while. I'd send in more help for your dad and the others, but the storm would make finding them in those woods almost impossible. Cork has a sat phone, and if he checks in on the hour as promised, we'll know what's going on every step of the way."

Stephen stands, ready to leave. "You'll call me if anything breaks?"

"I will. And you do the same for me."

Jenny has shut Sam's Place and put a sign in the serving window: CLOSED UNTIL FURTHER NOTICE. Stephen checks in with her and Daniel at the house on Gooseberry Lane and explains the situation.

"The snow's going to complicate everything," she says.

"Dad knows what he's doing."

"I know. Doesn't mean I won't worry."

Waaboo has been playing with Lego blocks in the living room. Now he wanders into the kitchen. "Where's Baa-baa?" he says, looking around as if he might be hiding in a corner.

"He's hunting in the woods," Daniel says.

"Bears?"

"He's looking for Grandma."

"He'll find her," Waaboo says as if it's a given, and he heads back to his Legos.

Stephen looks at his sister and at Daniel. "He's right."

The drive to Leech Lake takes three hours. The farther west Stephen goes, the heavier the cover of threatening clouds. By the time he pulls up to the address in the small town of Bena, which Anton Morriseau gave him earlier, snow has begun to fall, clinging to branches and beginning to coat the ground. He understands that by midafternoon the storm will reach Tamarack County. This will make the search for Rainy, Henry, and Dolores Morriseau far more difficult. If there are truly men hunting them, it will also make the search far more dangerous. Once again, he wishes he were with his father.

Anton Morriseau's father answers Stephen's knock. Vernon Morriseau is a man in his sixties, short but broad in the chest, the build of a lumberjack. Stephen called ahead and is expected.

"*Boozhoo,*" he says in greeting. "Thank you for seeing me."

"Happy to talk to you if it'll clear up what's going on with Lou and Dolores. He's here, Minnie," he calls over his shoulder. "Come on in, son."

The house is small and cozy. A stone fireplace dominates the living room, and across the mantel is an array of family photos. On either side are shelves filled with books. Dozens of photographs adorn the walls, mostly of North Woods scenes, enchanting and tastefully framed. A colorful braided rug takes up most of the floor. The house smells of freshly brewed coffee.

Two women stand watching Stephen expectantly. One is roughly the same age as Vernon Morriseau. The other is much younger, about his own age, Stephen guesses.

"My wife, Minnie, and my daughter, Belle. Ladies, this is Stephen O'Connor."

"Can I get you something?" Minnie Morriseau asks. "I've just brewed coffee."

"Yes, thank you. Black."

She disappears into the kitchen.

Belle says, "Anton called us this morning, told us what was going on. It sounds a little crazy. Kidnapping?"

Stephen says, "At the moment, we think it's more of a hunt, and we're hoping that Henry Meloux can keep our people safe until we locate them."

"We understand Rainy Bisonette is with them, too," Vernon says. "We've met her. She's helped Henry Meloux with the ceremonies here. A good woman."

Minnie returns with a mug of coffee, which she hands to Stephen.

After they're all seated, Stephen goes over what he knows of the situation.

"Somebody pretending to be Lou?" Minnie shakes her head. "Why?"

"That's what I'm trying to find out. That and maybe where your son is. When did you last hear from him?"

"We haven't actually seen Lou for a while. Not since Christmas. He called a couple of weeks ago though."

"Any particular reason for his call?"

"He said he was feeling kind of low. Just wanted to hear our voices."

"Which is so not like him," Belle says. "He's always Mister Sunshine, Mister Got the Tiger by the Tail."

"Then Dolores shows up a couple of days ago asking how to find Henry Meloux," Vernon says.

"Did she say why?"

"She said her and Lou were going through a rough patch. She thought maybe Henry could help sort things out."

"And you know Henry because of the ceremonies he's held here?"

"He's done several traditional burial ceremonies for our community. His spirit is remarkable, and I've never met a human being with a bigger heart. If Dolores is looking for counsel or comfort, I can't think of anyone better to turn to."

"Have you tried to contact Lou today?"

"Bunch of times," Vernon says. "Nothing."

"So, no idea if he's come back from this latest trip to Canada?"

"None."

"If he's still in Canada, any idea where he might be? Where he stays?"

"He's mentioned Winnipeg, but nothing specific. Like I said, Lou's not talking to us much these days."

"Look, this is what I'd like to do." Stephen explains that he intends to drive to Edina. He wants to check their son's home, maybe his office, talk to neighbors, business associates, anyone who might be able to give him a lead on their son.

"Any way we can help?" Vernon asks.

"Do you have a key to your son's house or office?"

"He operates out of an office in his home," Vernon says. "We don't have a key. But Belle can get you in. She stays with Lou and Dolores sometimes."

"I just finished my third year of law school down in the Cities," she explains. "Whenever I've needed a little time away from the stress, Lou and Dolores have let me stay with them for a few days. It's helped a lot."

"So you've been around them a good deal lately?"

"I wouldn't say a good deal, but more than anyone else in our family."

"Any insights about the trouble between them?"

"Lou's a good talker except when it comes to anything personal and emotional. Shuts right down. And Dolores has other people she confides in. That's been fine with me. All my attention's been on law school. But I can get you into their house and maybe help you look for whatever you think might be helpful."

"Just give him the codes for the locks," Vernon says.

"I'm going with him," she replies.

"I don't think . . ." Stephen begins.

"This storm is only going to get worse. If we don't want it to cause us problems, we need to get going." Belle stands. And that's that.

CHAPTER 19

The storm sends a dizzying swirl of white across the highway as they make their way south toward the Cities. The snowfall is heavy, and the wipers of Stephen's old Jeep work hard to keep the windshield clear. The radio has indicated that it's coming down in a narrow band, and Stephen's relieved to know that they'll drive out of it eventually.

"Tell me about your brother," he says.

Belle has been sitting quietly, watching the landscape slide past, woods and isolated houses and small communities that seem ghostly behind the gauzy veil of snow, places where the wise have holed up until the storm passes.

"What kind of guy is he?"

"Smart. Funny. Ambitious. A storyteller."

"Traditional storyteller or twister of truth?"

"Both. I could never tell when he was teasing or when he was serious. I guess that's part of what makes him a good salesman."

"I thought he's in real estate."

"He's a real estate attorney. But a lot of dealing with clients is selling yourself. He's the kind of guy you can't help trusting even though your better instincts tell you that you shouldn't."

"You like him."

"He was always a good big brother."

"So, what's happened that's made him distant now?"

"I wish I knew."

"Something to do with his business?"

"Maybe."

"But you have a different idea."

Belle shrugs. "Lou's an attractive guy. Women have always fallen all over him."

"You're thinking it might have something to do with another woman?"

"After three years of law school, I have a legal mind-set. I'm always searching for additional possibilities, other approaches."

"Did Dolores give any indication she was worried about another woman?"

"No, but Dolores has her own faults."

"Such as?"

"She presents herself in a pretty simplistic way, but she's complicated. Her past is an issue."

"What about her past?"

"She was adopted as an infant, never knew anything about her birth parents. But she told me that whenever she did something wrong, her father would complain that it was the Indian in her. Her folks split up and she went with her mother, her adopted mother. I guess their relationship wasn't the greatest. A couple of years ago, just before she died, she let it slip that Dolores's birth mother was Native."

"Anishinaabe?"

"Dolores doesn't know. She's been trying to find out, but nothing so far. There may have been an issue with the legitimacy of the adoption. Not sure exactly what, but it wouldn't be the first time a Native kid ended up in a white family no questions asked."

"I've seen a picture of her. She doesn't look Native."

Belle gives him a long, hard look.

"Sorry. I can't believe I said that."

"I like Dolores, but I can't help thinking that this relentless search of hers for her heritage has grated on Lou, who would like nothing more than to forget his own Native heritage. It's like suddenly they're going in different directions."

"I'm not married, but maybe that's what marriage does to you, sends you in different directions," Stephen says.

"That hasn't been my experience."

"You're married?"

"I mean, looking at my parents," she replies quickly.

They pass a car that's pulled to the side of the road, its flashers blinking. Stephen's about to pull off and offer help when he sees a man on the far side of the vehicle clearly making a bit of yellow snow. He drives on.

"When was the last time you had a good heart-to-heart with your brother?" he asks.

"His birthday last November. He turned thirty."

"He came up to celebrate with you?"

She shakes her head. "We all went down to the Cities. Big to-do at his country club. Lots of his friends, who, in truth, were mostly his business associates. And us. It was a little awkward, honestly. We were the only Native people there. It was clear that most of the guests felt uncomfortable trying to talk to us. The nearest a lot of them had ever been to Native people was watching *Dances with Wolves*. Or panhandlers in the Cities."

"But your brother's Ojibwe."

"Three-quarters, like Anton and me. But in Lou, it's the Irish blood that shows. Anyway, money is the great equalizer, and Lou has plenty of it."

In an hour, they drive out of the storm, leaving the thick band of dark clouds behind. It's late afternoon. The sky is a brilliant blue, and it's as if they've entered a different world where everything is green and broadcasts that it's spring. They pass through Brainerd and Little Falls, and Stephen presses down a bit harder on the accelerator to make up for time lost to the storm.

"You said you've finished law school. So, you're a lawyer?"

"I've got to pass the bar first."

"What will you do then?" Stephen asks. "Join your brother in the real estate business?"

"I'm not like Lou. I plan to return to the rez and work for an organization called Mother Earth Always. I worked with them for a while before I got accepted to law school."

"I know that group. Environmentalists, right?"

"More than that. We focus on issues related to preserving the natural habitat. Not just on the rez but also in a broader way. We work with similar organizations on a number of other reservations. We fight back against encroachment, the continued theft of the land, misrepresentation of all kinds of projects proposed in the name of the greater public good. Could you pull off at the next exit? I need to use a restroom."

Stephen gases up the Jeep and makes a call to the Sheriff's Office in Aurora. Marsha Dross reports that his father and the others are following a clear trail heading into the Boundary Waters.

"At last check-in, they were somewhere your father called the Hungry Hills," Dross tells him.

"I know the place," Stephen says. "Any sign of Rainy and Henry and Dolores?"

"The men he's tracking have pretty much destroyed any sign that might have been there before they passed through, so no word on the others yet. But your dad's pretty confident he'll find them."

"How's the storm up there?"

"Intense but brief. Still, by the time it passes, it'll be too late to get a search plane into the air. If need be, we'll have one up there at first light tomorrow. Where are you?"

"On my way to Lou Morriseau's house in Edina. His sister's with me."

"What are you hoping to find?"

"I don't know. Anything that might help."

"Keep me posted."

When they're on the road again, Belle says, "I have a confession. I've read your sister's books. I understand they're based on real events in her life." She glances at him. "Is that right?"

"Occasionally she sacrifices the truth for suspense, but generally speaking, yes."

"In the stories, there's a brother who has visions and wants to be a Mide. You?"

"A literary version of me."

"Do you really have visions?"

"I have since I was a kid. They come as dreams. They usually require some interpretation."

"Do you interpret them?"

"Sometimes I have help. Henry Meloux is good at that."

"The brother in the stories was shot in the back."

"Two bullets. The doctors were afraid I wouldn't walk again. As you can see, I get around pretty well. Just don't ask me to sprint."

"You come off nicely in the stories."

"It can be a tough image to live up to."

She smiles. "You're doing a pretty good job."

*   *   *

At twilight, they arrive in Edina, a wealthy community on the west side of the Twin Cities. With Belle's help, Stephen locates the home of Lou and Dolores Morriseau. It's a huge house on a street lined with nothing but huge houses. Lou Morriseau's home is two stories with a stucco exterior and an expansive lawn and garden that only a team of landscape workers could maintain. When he pulls into the long, curving driveway in his Jeep, mud-spattered from the back roads up north, Stephen feels a little like a beggar knocking at the palace gate. He gives a low whistle. "Your brother's done pretty well for himself."

"If money's the measure," she says, and Stephen hears the note of censure in her voice.

The house is dark. Stephen follows Belle to the front door. The lock is a dead bolt with a keypad. Belle keys in the code. She opens the door, steps inside, and turns to the alarm keypad next to the entrance. But her finger stops before touching any of the keys.

"It's already disabled," she says, then calls into the dark house, "Lou!"

The house is vast, quiet, creepy. Belle turns on a few lights, then stands looking around the living room, clearly at a loss. "I was hoping he might be here. Just not answering his phone."

"I was hoping the same thing," Stephen says. "Is his car here?"

They check the attached garage, which is empty.

"We should check his bedroom," Belle suggests. "See if he's slept here."

The bed is made, no sign that anyone's been there. They scope out the four additional bedrooms. Stephen finds himself wondering why two people feel the need for so much space. As if reading his mind, Belle says, "Dolores wanted a big family, a slew of kids."

"But?"

"Endometriosis. A year after they were married, she had a hysterectomy."

"They could adopt."

"She was okay with it. Lou not so much. They don't talk about it around me, but I've gathered that it's been an issue."

"Let's check the rooms downstairs," Stephen suggests.

As they descend the stairs, the doorbell rings. When Belle opens the front door, two policemen confront them, glaring at them in the porch light.

"Yes?" she says.

"Identification please," the taller of the two officers demands.

"Why? What's this all about?"

"Identification, ma'am." No *please* this time.

The other cop looks at Stephen. "You, too."

Stephen withdraws his driver's license from his wallet and hands it over. Belle retrieves her purse from the hallway table, pulls out her license, and offers it. The tall cop scrutinizes both licenses, then hands them to the shorter cop, who says, "Wait here. I'll be right back." He heads to the cruiser parked behind Stephen's mud-spattered Jeep.

The tall cop eyes Belle. "Your license says Morriseau. Any relation to Louis Morriseau?"

"I'm his sister."

"Beg your pardon, ma'am, but we've heard a story like that before."

"I don't understand."

"Just be patient. We'll explain."

They stand silent until the second cop returns. "Nothing," he says and hands back the two licenses.

"Okay, how about an explanation now," Belle demands.

"We received a call from neighbors," the tall cop says. "That Jeep in the driveway doesn't exactly blend in out here."

"That's it?" Belle's voice is edged toward outrage. "Our vehicle doesn't fit the neighborhood profile."

"It's not just that, ma'am. We had some trouble here a couple of nights ago."

"What kind of trouble?" Stephen asks.

The shorter cop eyes him. "And who are you exactly?"

"A friend of the family," Belle snaps before Stephen can reply.

"We had a report of prowlers," the tall cop says. "When Officer Riley here responded, he found a man on the back patio attempting to enter the house. He asked for identification and was given a driver's license for Louis Morriseau."

"The ID matched, but there was something about the guy that just struck me wrong," the shorter cop says.

"What did you do?" Belle asks.

"I wasn't able to do anything at that moment."

"Why?" Stephen says.

The tall cop doesn't quite stifle a grin. "Riley got his clock cleaned."

"The hell I did," the shorter cop says. "He sucker-punched me."

"And got away," the tall cop says. "We had several cruisers searching the neighborhood. Didn't find him."

"What did he look like?" Stephen asks.

"About your height, sandy hair, fortyish," short cop says.

"Someone tried to impersonate Lou Morriseau up in Aurora, too," Stephen tells them.

"Aurora? Where's that?"

"Tamarack County," the tall cop says. "Gateway to the Boundary Waters. You never get up north, Riley?" The tall cop returns his attention to Stephen. "What about this impersonator?"

"Our sheriff up there is looking into it. Not sure what's going on yet. You can contact her."

"We've been trying to reach Morriseau but no luck so far. When we got the call tonight, you can understand our concern. Ms. Morriseau, do you know where your brother is?"

"That's what we're here trying to figure out."

"We understand he's married. Any idea where his wife might be?"

Stephen glances at Belle, who says, "She's up north at the moment. She doesn't know where Lou is either."

The tall cop says, "All right, then. If you see him or if he contacts you, let him know we'd like to talk to him. And sorry about the interruption, but I hope you understand. You folks have a good evening."

They watch the cops drive away, then close the door.

"What the hell?" Stephen says.

"God, this just gets worse and worse."

They turn and start toward the living room. And the doorbell rings again.

CHAPTER 20

Stephen opens the door to a woman with a worried face.

"Who . . . ?" the woman begins, then looks past him and says with relief, "Belle!"

"Penny," Belle replies. "Come in, come in."

Stephen stands aside and the woman enters. He scans the yard and the street, sees nothing that causes him concern, and closes the door. The two women have moved to the living room. Stephen joins them.

"Penny, this is Stephen O'Connor. Stephen, this is Penny Fidler."

Penny Fidler is tall and slender. Her hair is long and caramel-colored, her eyes blue and intense. There's something athletic in the way she moves, as if she's preparing to sprint or to wrestle.

"Stephen's helping me look for Lou," Belle explains.

"Lou still hasn't come home?"

"Come home from where?"

"Another one of his damn trips to Canada. It was kind of a last straw for Dolores, and she took off herself. Asked me to collect her mail." She puts a stack of envelopes and catalogs on the coffee table. "She said she was going to track down an Ojibwe man who might be able to help clear her thinking."

"Henry Meloux," Stephen says.

"That sounds right."

"If you don't mind me asking, who are you to Dolores and Lou?" Stephen asks.

"I live across the street. Dolores and I jog together in the mornings."

"I've jogged with them sometimes," Belle says. "Penny barely breaks a sweat."

"We're golf partners, too." She moves to the mantel and lifts a trophy. "We won this together at the country club last year. Lord, can that girl putt."

Stephen can't quite place the woman's accent. "You're not from around here."

"Arkansas," she says. "Moved here when I was in my twenties for a job. Told my grandmother I'd be back in two years. Didn't count on meeting Bob and putting down roots, but that's the way it goes." She sets the trophy back on the mantel. "I didn't mean to sic the cops on you, Belle. I saw the Jeep, and well, after that prowler the other night. You understand."

"Of course," Belle says. "Can you stay for a few minutes?"

"Happy to."

"Coffee?"

"Dolores keeps a bottle of good bourbon in that cabinet over there. I'm sure she wouldn't mind if you poured me a little. I take it neat."

When they've settled and Penny Fidler is sipping her bourbon, Stephen says, "A man showed up in Aurora yesterday pretending to be Lou. He was looking for Dolores."

"Whatever for?"

"We don't know. What we do know is that Dolores was with

Henry Meloux, and some men came for her. It looks like their intentions weren't good. As nearly as we can tell, Dolores and Henry and Stephen's stepmother fled into the woods to get away. The men followed them."

"Oh, my God. Are they okay?"

"People are searching for them right now, but there's a snowstorm that's complicated things," Belle says.

Penny sips her bourbon, shakes her head. "It's something to do with Lou, I swear to God. Dolores told me she was hoping this Meloux might be able to help her figure out what's going on. She's tried to be patient, but lately that man could wear the horns off a goat."

"Why do you say that?" Stephen asks.

"There's nothing but darkness in him lately. Dolores has tried to get him to talk to her, but he won't say boo about it. You ask me, he's the one could use some help from this Meloux."

"You think it has something to do with his trips to Canada?"

"Dolores thinks that for sure," Penny says.

"Lou handles properties in Canada, too," Belle explains. "Our dad is Canadian. Actually, Kekekozibii Anishinaabe out of Manitoba. Lou, Anton, and I were born here, so we have dual citizenship. Lou is licensed to practice in Canada as well as the U.S."

"Is this all about real estate, about business?" Stephen says.

Penny takes another sip of bourbon and makes a disapproving sound in her throat.

"What is it?" Stephen asks.

"I'm not one to speak out of school. But the business he's about could well be monkey business."

"What?" Stephen presses.

"Katie," Penny says, as if the word is obscene.

"Who's Katie?"

"Dolores told me—in strictest confidence," she emphasizes—"that she thought Lou might be having an affair."

"With a woman named Katie?" Belle looks at Stephen. "See? What did I tell you?"

"Is there a last name?" Stephen asks.

"Katie is all Dolores knew. She overheard Lou talking on his cell phone and mentioning her name. When she asked him about it, he clammed up."

"She overheard him talking just the once?"

"A few times, I guess. But when she pressed the issue, he blew up at her. And there's something else. Bob and Lou play a lot of golf together. A couple of weeks ago, when Bob came back from playing, he told me about something strange that happened on the course."

"What was that?" Stephen says.

"Lou was having a great round, then he gets a call on his cell phone. He talks for a while and the name Katie comes up a bunch of times. When he ended the call, he looked like he'd just seen a banshee or something. His face had gone white, his hands shaking. He played one more hole, badly, then begged off. Said he wasn't feeling well. Now you tell me what kind of woman would scare a man to death."

"Let's hold on a minute," Stephen says. "Even if your brother is having an affair, what possible connection could that have with the people who are chasing Rainy and Henry and Dolores? Seems to me, there's got to be more at stake here. The prowler the other night, was he looking for Lou or for Dolores?"

"They were gone. So maybe something the guy thought might be here in the house?" Belle offers.

They're all quiet a moment, then Stephen remembers a detail. "When we got here, the alarm system was already disabled. That prowler, did the cops catch him going in, or did they catch him coming out?"

Penny shrugs. "Don't know."

"The man pretending to be Lou said he found a note Dolores left," Stephen says. "And also a journal she kept. That's what led him to Aurora and Henry Meloux."

"Dolores wrote in her journal every day," Penny says. "If she had some kind of insight while we were jogging or golfing, she'd say, 'I need to put that in my journal.' A little too compulsive that way, you ask me."

"Any idea where she keeps her journal?" Stephen asks.

"She uses one of the spare bedrooms as a kind of office for herself," Belle says. "Whenever I've stayed with them, she's spent a while in there writing before going to bed at night. So maybe the spare bedroom?"

Belle leads the way upstairs. In the bedroom, there's a small writing table by a window, but it's bare except for a clay jar that holds pens and pencils.

"Maybe she hides it," Stephen suggests. "Doesn't want anyone prying."

They search the room, then the master bedroom and the other spare bedrooms, but find nothing.

"The cops showed up before we had a chance to check the rooms downstairs," Stephen says. "Maybe it's somewhere down there."

In a large back room, the room Belle says is Lou's office, the file drawers have been opened and files scattered about the floor. The chair at the computer desk has been shoved away and the drawers there stand open.

Belle takes a deep breath, lets out a sigh. "Pretty clear that guy the other night got inside."

"Could be there's some good news in this," Stephen says.

"Good news?" Belle looks at him as if he's a little nuts. "What good news could there possibly be?"

"From what I'm seeing here, I'm guessing whatever they're after, they think Lou has it. If that's true, maybe they're after Dolores because they think she can lead them to him. Which could mean your brother's hiding out somewhere and is okay."

"Then why doesn't he answer his cell phone?"

"Maybe he's afraid they'll use the signal to track him."

"He could call from a different phone, couldn't he?" Belle's voice carries a sharp edge.

"Honey, relax. Stephen's just trying to look at this in a positive light." Penny glances around and shakes her head. "Look, I should be getting home. But listen, you get any news or you need anything, you give me holler, okay?" She gives Belle a hug. "I'll see myself out."

When she's gone, Belle says, "I haven't eaten since lunch. I'm hungry. How about you?"

The mess in the office cries out to be sorted through, but Stephen knows it'll be a daunting task. "I could eat."

They work together on the meal. Stephen whips up an omelet with mushrooms, ham, and cheese, and Belle makes toast. They eat at the counter in the huge kitchen. "Where'd you learn to cook?" Belle asks.

"We've owned a burger joint forever. I grew up cooking."

"You look like you might have some Native blood in you."

"My great-grandmother Dilsey was pure-blood Iron Lake Ojibwe."

"Mother's side or father's?"

"Dad's family."

"My mother's half Irish," Belle says. "Flaherty. That's where Lou gets his Irish good looks. Like I said, in Anton and me, it's our beautiful Ojibwe genes that show."

"I'm the only sibling in my family whose Ojibwe genes show. Even though she was Irish, my mother was proud of the Native side of my heritage and wanted to be sure I was proud of it, too."

"Was?"

"She died a few years ago."

"I'm sorry."

"She was an attorney. She represented the Iron Lake Ojibwe."

"Good for her," Belle says.

"What made you want to go into law?" Stephen asks. "Following in your brother's footsteps?"

"Lou left the rez and did well on his own, but he hasn't been particularly generous with our people. I wanted to give back in some way. We have more legal fights than you can shake a stick at, so I decided to join the battle."

"Noble," Stephen says.

"Necessary," she responds. "What about you? Going to take over the family burger business?"

"I'm just finishing up my associate degree in criminal justice at our local community college."

"Going to be a cop then?"

"Maybe. Or maybe a lawyer like my mother. And you," he says with a smile. "Not sure yet. I've been accepted at the U of M for the fall. I'll just see how the spirit moves me there."

It's late by the time they've cleaned up. Stephen makes a final call to the Tamarack County Sheriff's Office. His stomach draws taut as Marsha Dross delivers the details of the rifle assault on his father and Anton Morriseau. He's relieved that no one was hurt. Stephen tells her about the prowler but admits that he has nothing concrete to offer on his end. When he hangs up, he reports everything to Belle.

"These people are willing to kill," she says. "Why?"

"Henry Meloux would say that we're seeing the web the spider has woven, but we still have to find the spider. Maybe things will be clearer in the morning. I think we should turn in."

Belle says, "I'll take the room across from Lou and Dolores's bedroom. It's where I usually sleep. You can take any of the others."

"I think I'll just crash on the living room sofa, if that's okay. It's as big as a bed."

"Suit yourself. What do we do tomorrow?"

"I'll think about that. Maybe I'll have an answer in the morning. But before you go upstairs, let's reset the alarm and the door locks with new codes."

"New codes? Why?"

"The alarm wasn't set when we came in. That could mean that the prowler was able to disarm it, which may mean he had the code. He also got into the house in the first place, which may mean he had the code for the door lock as well. If we don't want to be surprised in the night, we should change the codes."

"I don't know how."

"I do." When Belle gives him a questioning look, Stephen replies, "I told you my dad was a cop. He's a PI now. I've learned a few things from him. Come on."

When he's finished keying in the new codes, Stephen wishes her good night, then watches as she heads upstairs. Her hair is long and black, like a river of liquid onyx. What he tries to think about is how sharp her mind is and how good her heart. But he can't help noticing as well how nice she looks as she climbs the stairs.

CHAPTER 21

Stephen stands at the edge of the woods. It's night, the moon is full, and the snow is deep. He's watching the man at the center of the clearing. The man is tense, waiting, listening. He turns in a slow circle as if watching for something and doesn't know from which direction it will come. The man is chanting, quietly but fervently. Stephen can't hear the words, only the desperate tone. Then he hears the air-shattering shriek and understands the reason for the man's vigilance and fear.

The Windigo steps from the forest on the far side of the clearing. It's a huge creature with fiery red eyes, the body of a hairy beast, a heart of ice, and, Stephen knows, an insatiable hunger for human flesh. Its foul odor of rot carries on the wind and assaults Stephen's nostrils. The man in the clearing turns to face the creature. He's still chanting, more desperately than ever. But as the great beast comes to devour him, the man changes, grows, becomes huge and hairy, a twin to the Windigo. They meet at the center of the clearing and the battle begins. But it begins oddly, with the sound of breaking glass.

* * *

Stephen wakes from his dream and is up in an instant, listening. The alarm hasn't gone off, but he's certain that he's heard something. The house is lit with ambient light from the streetlamps. Stephen can make out the living room and dining room, everything cast in gradations of black and gray. He reaches toward a Tiffany lamp on an end table, then draws back his hand. He walks silently to the mantel and lifts Dolores Morriseau's golf trophy. The base is heavy granite. He hefts the trophy, creeps to the hallway, and stands listening again. Everything is quiet, but through the open door of Morriseau's office comes a glow that seems to vary in intensity. Stephen realizes that it's from a flashlight beam searching the room. He returns to the sofa, grabs his cell phone from the coffee table, and calls 911. He disarms the security alarm and cracks open the front door for the police.

Then he returns to the hallway, trophy in hand, and waits.

A minute later, the flashlight beam cuts into the hallway and whoever is behind it exits Morriseau's office. Stephen steps behind the corner of the hallway wall and watches as the beam moves toward him along the carpeting. He grips the trophy tight and readies to swing it if necessary.

"Stephen?" Belle calls from the top of the stairway.

The flashlight beam stops moving, then goes out.

"Stephen, is that you?" The light at the top of the stairs comes on.

The prowler is past him in an instant, running for the front door. Stephen is on his tail. They hit the night outside, the prowler only steps ahead. Stephen drops the trophy and, as the man dashes across the broad front lawn, dives for his legs. The man goes down hard and Stephen is on him. But the man is powerful, and in an instant, he's got Stephen beneath him with his hands around Stephen's neck; the fingers are like a vise, choking. Stephen tries to pry loose the grip, then drives his fists desperately into the man's ribs, but to no avail. The fingers tighten even more.

Suddenly, the man goes limp and slumps to the ground. Belle stands over him, holding the trophy Stephen discarded. "He's out cold, I think."

Stephen rolls away, stands up slowly, breathing hard, feeling at his neck. His heart is kicking in his chest from the flood of adrenaline. On the grass, the prowler lies still, blood along the side of his face glistening in the glare of the streetlamp. Stephen glances at Belle. She's wearing only a T-shirt and underwear. Her feet are bare. Stephen's dressed pretty much the same, in T-shirt and boxer shorts, feet bare. From a distance but drawing nearer comes the sound of a siren.

"Thanks," Stephen says. Then he nods toward her bare legs. "You might want to put on your jeans before the cops arrive."

The prowler has no ID on him. He's conscious but not cogent, and his head wound where Belle smacked him with the trophy worries the Edina police enough to warrant a trip to the ER. In the house, fully dressed now, Belle and Stephen talk with the two officers who responded earlier and a detective named Griggs from the major crimes unit. The shorter cop has identified the prowler as the man he'd encountered a couple nights earlier. "Broken window in your brother's office. He must've entered that way."

"Why didn't the alarm go off?" Belle asks.

"If he'd tried to open the window, it would have," the cop explains. "Your brother's system wasn't installed with the option of a sensor for breaking glass. Either our prowler knew that or he just got lucky."

"Any idea what he was looking for?" Griggs asks.

Stephen lays out what's been going on in Tamarack County. "We believe these people are really interested in Lou Morriseau, and they probably believe his wife knows where he is. That's why they're after her."

"Any idea what's behind this interest in Mr. Morriseau?"

"None at the moment. That's why we're here, just trying to put the pieces together."

"You said someone searched the office earlier. Any idea what they might have been looking for?" Griggs asks. "Why they came back?"

"None," Stephen says.

"All right." Griggs closes his little notebook. "I'm going to contact your Sheriff Dross up in Tamarack County, see what she has to say. I'll be talking with our offender once he's able to make sense. I'd like you both to come down to the department tomorrow for an official statement. In the meantime, I'm going to post a cruiser out front to make sure there's no more trouble tonight. Okay?"

When the police have left, Stephen and Belle sit on the sofa. They're both quiet. Stephen's trying to wrap his thinking around what's happened, but he's getting nowhere.

Belle lays her head back and stares at the ceiling. "He came back for something. Maybe for us."

"Why?"

Belle shrugs. "Because he thought we might know where Lou is?"

Stephen considers this, then offers, "Or maybe he was looking for something he thought might be here now that wasn't here before."

"Like what? Something we brought with us?"

"Maybe. Or . . ." Stephen eyes the stack of mail Penny Fidler delivered. "Maybe something that arrived today." He picks up the mail and sorts through. "Here's one addressed to you. At least I think it is." The handwriting is barely legible. He hands the envelope to Belle.

"No return address," she says. "But the postmark is from Canada."

Belle tears open the envelope and extracts a folded map and a thumb drive. She sets the thumb drive aside and spreads the map on the coffee table.

"Canada," she says. "But what's with all those black lines?"

With a Sharpie, someone has drawn a network of interconnecting, serpentine lines across the entire country.

Stephen shakes head. "No idea."

There's black bleeding through the map, and Stephen turns it over. Scrawled across the reverse side in bold but shaky capital letters is the word *KILLCATIE*. Below it is a number: *5110*.

"Killcatie? What does that mean?" Belle says. "Is it even a word?"

"And what's with the number?"

Stephen takes out his cell phone, Googles *killcatie*, and scrolls through the offerings. "There's a village in Ireland called Killcatherine, but I don't see anything else that looks useful."

Belle says, "Maybe it's supposed to be two words. *Kill* and *Catie*." She looks at Stephen, her eyes wide. "The other woman. Not *Katie* with a *K*. *Catie* with a *C*."

"Kill Catie? That seems kind of drastic." Stephen turns the map over to the side with all the black lines. "What do they mean?"

"Could it be somebody tracking Lou's movements around Canada?" Belle says. "Maybe Dolores hired somebody to follow him?"

"Possible, I suppose. But judging from these lines, he went to some pretty remote areas. You said he does a good deal of work with the First Nations reserves."

"Along with his traveling companion Catie?" Belle frowns. "Maybe we'll know more when we see what's on this thumb drive."

They move to Lou Morriseau's office. The floor beneath one of the two windows is littered with shattered glass. Belle leaves and returns with a blanket, which they pin over the broken window, then she turns on the computer. She keys in a password. "Lou let me use his computer sometimes," she explains. She inserts the thumb drive. "Damn. Pass code protected." She looks at Stephen. "Your dad's a private detective, right? Did he teach you anything about getting around pass codes?"

"He's old school. But it seems to me that since the envelope was addressed to you, it probably came from your brother and there's a reason he sent it to you. Maybe a legal reason?"

"Kill Catie," Belle says. "Maybe things blew up between him and his girlfriend in a big way and he wants me to hire a hit man."

"You've been watching too many movies. Try *Killcatie*."

Belle types in the word. It gets them nowhere. She includes the number 5110. Still nothing. She tries several combinations of the word and number, then pass code possibilities based on her knowledge of her brother. Finally, she sits back and sighs heavily.

"Hold on a sec," Stephen says. He puts his finger below the first 1 in the number 5110 on the map. "Is that a one, or is it a slash?"

"Could be a slash," Belle says. "It's all pretty messy."

"So maybe it's a date. Five ten. May tenth."

"That's only a few days from now."

"Kill Catie on May tenth." Belle looks at Stephen. "That's kind of crazy."

"Whatever it is, we don't have much time. Especially since we've got no idea who she is."

"Maybe it's not Lou who wants her dead," Belle says. "Maybe he's trying to save her from being killed on May tenth."

"Try *Killcatie* and the number with a slash."

She gives this a shot, but like all the other attempts, it gets them nowhere.

"Nothing," Belle says, sounding exhausted, defeated.

The adrenaline that fueled Stephen's attack on the prowler has drained away, and he feels as tired as Belle looks. "I'm not sure I can think straight right now. Maybe if we get some sleep, we'll see everything more clearly in the morning."

At the bottom of the stairs, they stand together and Belle smiles. "You told me you couldn't sprint. You looked pretty fast tonight."

"Sometimes I surprise myself."

"*Migwech.*"

"Thank you for what?"

"Helping."

He returns her smile. "Seems to me we're in this together."

There is a long, awkward moment, in which Stephen feels overwhelmingly drawn to this woman he has known for less than a day, and he wonders, is she waiting for him to kiss her?

"Well," she says lightly. "See you in the morning."

And for the second time that night, Stephen watches her climb the stairs alone.

PART ELEVEN

CORK

CHAPTER 22

In the early morning, Cork hears a plane passing overhead, flying low and slow. He spots it, a de Havilland Beaver from the U.S. Forest Service fitted with pontoons, cruising just high enough to reflect the light of the sun, which is not yet above the horizon. He gets on the sat phone.

"The pilot has the coordinates you gave us last night," Dross says. "He's flying ahead of you. Deputy Foster is with him. Keep me posted on what you're finding, and I'll keep Foster posted."

Then she tells him about her conversations with Stephen and with a detective from the Edina Police Department concerning the events of the night before.

"The guy in custody isn't cooperating. Won't say a word. They don't have an ID on him yet, but they're working on it."

"Does Stephen have any idea what the guy was after?"

"The Morriseaus' mail was being collected by a neighbor. After Dolores left, they got an envelope from Canada addressed to Lou's sister, Belle, containing a map of that country with lots of lines drawn across it, along with a cryptic message: *KILLCATIE.* It looks like one word, but Stephen thinks it's really two words. *Kill* and *Catie*. Below it is a number, five-ten. Stephen believes it's a date. Maybe the date this Catie is supposed to be killed. There was also a thumb drive, but it's pass code protected, so no idea what's on it. Stephen hasn't got any of this figured out yet, but it's the only lead he has at the moment. I've sent two of my men to pick up the guy you cuffed to a tree yesterday. They'll bring him out of the woods and we'll book him. But if you need help, they can always bypass him and come straight to you."

Cork assures her they're fine and they agree to check in at hour intervals unless something comes up that needs immediate attention. He reports what he's learned to Morriseau.

"A map of Canada?" Morriseau says. He's chewing on a Slim Jim and an apple that he packed in. "Lou goes to Canada a lot these days. He's told us it has to do with some land deals up there. But what the hell does 'Kill Catie' mean?"

"Let's hope that Stephen can make some sense of it and soon," Cork says. "In the meantime, we've got a trail to try to pick up."

The early light of the day colors everything blue. They head in the general direction the trail they followed the day before was taking them. The snow is half an inch deep and the only tracks they find have been left by rabbits and red squirrels. Periodically, they hear the plane engine as it flies a grid, but nothing new comes over the sat phone. Although Cork holds to his faith in Henry Meloux, there is a devil in his head telling him that Meloux is more than a hundred years old. No one that old can hold up long under the kind of hardships he and the two women are facing. Rainy is strong, raised in the North Country, and Cork tells himself that even if Henry falters, she can fend for herself. But as they go one mile, then two, then three with no sign of Henry and the others and no sign of the trackers, the voice of doubt in his head begins to drown out his hope.

"We've lost them," Morriseau finally says.

"They could be anywhere now," Cork agrees grimly.

"Do you know this area?" Morriseau asks. "Any idea at all where the old man might be taking them? Or is he just trying his best to stay ahead of these goons?"

Cork pulls out the topographic map he's brought and on which he's been keeping track of their progress. Meloux's been heading relentlessly north. The Boundary Waters is enormous, but Meloux has been traveling through this wilderness his whole life, and Cork doubts that there's a single acre the old man hasn't explored. Cork, however, has only a vague knowledge of the area they're in now. Looking at the map, he has no idea what's in Meloux's head, no idea if the old man has a grand plan or if he and Rainy and Dolores Morriseau are just running for their lives. He recalls Meloux's advice to quiet all the noise in his head so that he can hear nature speaking to him. He tries, closes his eyes, works to calm himself. But the voice of doubt keeps chipping away at his resolve and from the woods he hears only silence.

"Suggestions?" he says.

"If it was me out there, I'd circle east and try to get back to the reservation, to Allouette or to someone there who could help," Morriseau says.

A good possibility, Cork believes. Still, his own inclination is to continue north, and he says so.

"Maybe we should split up," Morriseau suggests.

"We have one sat phone," Cork points out. "How do we communicate?"

"Finding them is the important thing. If they're headed east and I locate them, I can give them some protection. You're going north, deeper into the wilderness. I think you should keep the phone."

"You may stumble onto the trackers before you stumble onto our people. Two men with firearms, the odds'll be against you."

Morriseau says, "I'll take that chance."

They check the map, make educated guesses about the route Meloux might have followed east or north, and Cork reports their decision to Dross.

"Any luck with the search plane?" he asks.

"Nothing so far. But the tree cover's pretty thick. Unless they build a signal fire or find some high, open ground and stay put, they could be hard to spot."

"Keep me posted."

He wishes Morriseau good luck and the two men separate.

As Cork plods north, he studies the relief of the land, trying to get a sense of Meloux's thinking. Was the old man wanting an easy passage and so he kept between ridges? Or did he want to make it more difficult for those tracking him and so took to the rocky higher ground when possible? Cork knows that the white blanket of snow may hide soft, marshy ground. So did Meloux perhaps try to thread his way through a bog before the snow fell, hoping the trackers would find themselves hopelessly mired? *Christ*, he tells himself. *So many possibilities and no signs at all.*

The sun, high above the horizon now, is brilliant in the hard blue of the cloudless sky. The wilderness is a patchwork of stark shadows and pale white. The day is warming quickly, however, and the snow is turning to slush under his feet, already vanishing in the sunniest places. He can't hear the drone of the plane anymore and wonders where it's gone in the search.

Then he comes to the footprints in the snow, two sets of booted feet. The trackers. He's confused, however. The footprints come from the north and head south. They turn east along a creek bed where a thread of snowmelt is running between rocks. He resists the urge to plunge up the creek bed. Instead, he follows the boot prints for another quarter mile until he comes to the char of a fire in the protected lee of an outcropping. The same boot prints continue north from there, with an identical set returning south.

Cork tries to make sense of what he sees. He figures that the men weathered the storm in the protection of the rocks. In the morning, they set out again, headed in the general direction Meloux and the others had followed the day before. But they turned around, came back, and followed the creek bed. Why? What did they find that made them turn back? Or maybe they found nothing and that was the reason. A tracker, when he's lost the trail, returns to where the last sign or most obvious option occurred. The creek bed.

Cork thinks about Meloux. If they'd come to the creek before the snow gave away their tracks, the old man could have chosen to follow it. The creek bed may well have been dry yesterday and would have been a reasonable point to divert from the relentless trek north. If luck was with them—though Cork suspected that with Meloux, nothing was the result of pure luck—the fall of snow would cover any signs they may have accidentally left.

The trackers, Cork understands, have caught on to Meloux's thinking. He turns, double-times back to the creek, and follows the boot prints.

A few hundred yards up the creek bed, he finds tracks that issue from a deadfall of tree limbs. The tracks were made by moccasins. But there's a set of small boot prints among them. *Rainy,* Cork thinks with great relief.

He reports what he's found to Dross, who relays the information to the pilot of the search plane. Cork hurries east along the creek bed, hope once again fueling his pace.

The call from Dross comes before the next hour's check-in.

"Cork, the search plane spotted smoke from a small fire at Fisheye Lake. They flew over the lake. It's too small for a safe landing, but they saw the fire, a smoldering campfire, and something else."

From the tone of her voice, he's not sure he wants to hear the rest. "Go on."

"It appears to be Henry Meloux. He's lying on the ground next to the fire. He didn't move when the plane flew over."

"Did they see anyone else?"

"Meloux appeared to be alone."

"And not moving, you say?"

"That's right."

"Hang on."

Cork unshoulders his pack, pulls out the topo map, and unfolds it. He looks for Fisheye Lake, one of the thousand small bodies of water in that great wilderness and one that he's not familiar with. "Found it," he finally says. "It's about three miles from my location."

"The search plane is running low on fuel. They're returning now. After they've refueled, they'll fly back out. Another thing. If Rainy and Dolores had to leave Meloux, I'm guessing they'll be headed toward the reservation. We've got a slew of volunteers from the rez just itching to join the search. I'm going to send some of them toward Fisheye Lake along with Deputy Azevedo. God willing, they'll get to our people before the trackers do."

Cork takes a deep breath. "I'm on my way."

CHAPTER 23

A bright sun and warm wind have followed the storm. The snow cover has melted rapidly, shrinking to thin, isolated patches beneath the thickest tree cover and in protected hollows. The trail of mixed tracks that Cork had been following has vanished, but the wet ground left in the wake of the snow still offers lots of signs. Plus, Cork knows exactly where he's going.

He's moving fast. Between the warming day and his physical effort, his body's pouring out a river of sweat. He removes his jacket, bundles it, and slips it into his pack. But it's not just the rising temperature or his own exertion that's making him sweat. It's something he remembers from several months earlier, something troubling.

Stephen has had visions since he was a child, usually visions of dire warning. Stephen foresaw his mother's death in a vision. He foresaw the shooting that nearly left him crippled. He foresaw the fall of a plane from the sky that killed a prominent U.S. senator. And several months ago, in a vision, he saw Henry Meloux lying on the ground, dead. When he shared that vision with Meloux, the old man's response had been a simple "I know."

That vision has been heavy on the mind of everyone who cares about the old man. Every life must end, but a world without Henry Meloux is a world Cork doesn't want to begin to imagine. The Mide has been a part of his life and life on the Iron Lake Reservation for as long as even the oldest of the old can remember. Meloux's guidance has helped Cork and so many others untie the difficult, knotted threads of their lives. Imagining the world without Meloux would be like trying to imagine the world without sunshine or the songs of birds.

And here's another worry. If Meloux is alone, where are Rainy and Dolores? If they'd been with Meloux, wouldn't they have done their best to signal the plane? They wouldn't have abandoned the old man, would they? Cork doesn't believe this for a moment. Unless Meloux was beyond helping them and beyond their help as well. As in dead.

The terrain is a rugged sculpting of ridges, marshes, and streams coursing with the runoff from the snowmelt. Bushwhacking his way through the wilderness, Cork progresses much more slowly than he'd anticipated.

At last he mounts what the topo map indicates is the final ridge between him and Fisheye Lake. He pauses, winded. From where he stands, he can see the small oval of water less than a mile away. A thin finger of smoke rises, marking the location of the fire. Cork pulls out his field glasses and tries to get a better look, but the source of the smoke is hidden by tree cover.

As he stands catching his breath, Cork also catches a sudden noise, distant and faint. It's barely a whisper of a sound, but in his current state of deep concern, he worries that it might have been a gunshot. It comes not from the direction of Fisheye Lake but from the south instead. He listens intently, strains to hear more. A minute later, another faint crack, like the breaking of a small twig. Now he's certain. Gunshots. Anton Morriseau is somewhere to the south, but is he near enough that Cork would hear the report of his rifle if he fired or was fired at?

Cork stands atop the ridge, trying to put the pieces together. When the search plane flew over Fisheye Lake, Meloux didn't move. And he was alone. As much as Cork hates to think it, he has to consider the real possibility that the old man is dead and that, to save themselves, Rainy and Dolores have abandoned him. According to the topo map, the rez is less than ten miles south of Fisheye Lake. If the women move quickly, they might be able to make it before dark. They might even run into some of the search party from the rez with Deputy Azevedo. This is the scenario he would love to believe, but the shots are like razor blades that cut into his desperate hope.

He's wasted enough time. He starts down the ridge slope, moving faster than he should, fueled by his growing dread that the worst of his fears is playing out, that those he cares about so deeply are dying. Halfway down the ridge, his right foot slips out from under him on a bedding of leaves still slick from the snowmelt. He falls, tumbling over and over until he slams into the jagged edge of a small rock outcrop. He's hit chest first, a painful blow, and he lies stunned, staring up at a sky broken into blue pieces by the branches of a sapling birch.

For a couple of minutes, he lies still, gathering himself and his wits, then he tries to stand. The pain is sharp enough that he cries out. Carefully, he brings himself to a kneeling position. He sluffs off his pack, unbuttons his flannel shirt, and checks his chest. The impact site is a flaming pink streak just left of his sternum. He presses gingerly there and is rewarded with another lightning bolt of pain. *Broken*, he thinks. *One rib, maybe two.*

He works at standing fully upright. When he's erect, he lifts his pack and sets it on the rock that ended his tumble. He digs into the pocket where he's kept the sat phone, thinking he needs to let

Dross know the situation. What he brings out is a useless piece of electronics cracked and broken in his fall.

He looks around for the rifle he was carrying, but it's nowhere to be seen. He steels himself and begins the slow climb up the slope. The rifle is just below the mess of leaves that was his undoing. He grips it, turns, but before beginning his descent, sits a moment to rest. The water of Fisheye Lake is still visible to him, opalescent amid all the evergreens. It's not so far, but to Cork at that moment it seems as distant as Mars.

PART TWELVE

RAINY

CHAPTER 24

Huddled together inside the deadfall of trees and limbs, exhausted, Rainy and the others have slept the night through. Rainy wakes in the thinnest light of dawn and finds that even Henry has not stirred. She wonders about the day ahead. Can the old man maintain the pace they've kept in order to outrun their pursuers? Will the snow help throw those men off their trail completely? And still at the heart of everything, the questions of who the hell are they and what do they want.

As she lies staring up at the interlacing of branches covered by her blanket, she mulls over more questions. When Dolores arrived on Crow Point in the company of her brother-in-law, Anton, and asked for Henry's help and hers, Rainy could see that Dolores was in pain. She told them she needed to find herself and was looking for their guidance. Before he would probe more deeply the source of her pain, Henry suggested a sweat. He told Dolores that sometimes in a sweat, answers come to important questions. Rainy has seen this happen many times. During the sweat, the woman prayed, and although she'd kept those prayers to herself, Rainy could see from her body language that they were fervent prayers and the answers she was seeking were real and necessary. Now she wonders about all those prayers, and what really the woman was seeking, and if it has anything to do with the questionable situation in which they've found themselves. Is it possible that Dolores knows more than she's let on about these wolves who are after them?

Henry wakes. There are branches that poke into the shelter, and the old man carefully avoids them as he slowly sits up. He sees that Rainy is watching him and signals for her to join him outside the shelter. Rainy crawls out, and Henry follows. When he stands, she can hear the cracking of his old bones. Although the sun won't dawn for some time, Rainy can already feel the difference in the air, the warmth on the breeze.

"This snow's going to melt soon, Henry. All our tracks will disappear."

"The ground will be wet."

She understands what he's saying, that if the men somehow pick up their trail, they will see the soaked earth that holds their prints. No matter how careful they might try to be, they will leave signs.

She studies her great-uncle, a man she's known, respected, learned from, and loved her entire life. She remembers a time when he was all muscle and sinew and walked with his spine erect and his shoulders back. She remembers that when she was a child and Henry would come to visit, the women of the Lac Courte Oreilles Reservation spoke among themselves of how handsome he was and how magnetic and mysterious. There is still something vital about Henry, something age hasn't diminished, and she sees it in him now as his dark eyes scan the silent, snow-covered woods, and for reasons known only to this enigmatic old man, he smiles.

"What is it?" she asks.

"It is a day of reckoning, Niece. Do you not feel it?"

"What I feel now, Uncle Henry, is the need to be moving. We have to be gone in case those men find our tracks."

"And they will," the old man says. His eyes are focused now to the north, where the trackers have spent the night waiting out the storm and resting. "One of them understands the woods. One of them listens."

"And he'd love to hear us standing here talking instead of walking. We need to go."

At Rainy's touch, Dolores wakes from her sleep.

"Where's Henry?"

"Waiting for us."

"I'm hungry," Dolores says, yawning.

"We'll eat in a while. Right now, we need to be moving."

Rainy pulls the blanket from the top of the deadfall and shakes off the snow. She rolls it and ties it to her knapsack. Dolores crawls out and follows, bringing Henry's old Winchester. Rainy shoulders the knapsack, takes the rifle, and with Henry leading the way, they move out while the sun is still below the horizon.

They shadow the creek bed east for an hour until they come to a ridge. Henry turns and follows the ridgeline. The sun is up now, firing the trees atop the ridge, and a soft wind is pushing out of the south, bringing a welcome warmth. Along the ridgetop where the sun hits fully, Rainy can already see patches that are clearing of snow. There is something promising in the warmth, and she wonders if this was the reason for Henry's enigmatic smile.

Two hours after they quit the deadfall, they stop. The women do their morning business behind a thicket of sumac, and when they return, Henry says, "We should eat."

There's very little left of what Rainy quickly threw together before they fled Crow Point: a piece of jerky for each of them, a handful of dried cranberries and nuts. It's not much, but it's something, and with the sun and warmth, a deep sense of hope descends.

"When we're out of here," Rainy says, "the first thing I'm going to do is bake a loaf of wild rice bread, slather half a dozen slices in butter and blueberry jam, and wash it all down with a pot of strong coffee."

"Coffee," Dolores says, closing her eyes. "What I wouldn't give right now to be sitting on my patio with the morning paper and a good latte."

"And your husband?" Rainy asks.

"Lou used to join me. Not so much anymore."

"The other woman?" Rainy says.

"Katie." She says the name with venom.

"What do you know about her?"

"Nothing at all. Except that when I brought her name up, Lou went ballistic. But . . ."

"But what?"

Dolores is quiet a moment, pondering. "When I think about it now, it seemed to me that Lou wasn't so much angry as afraid. During our sweat, Rainy, do you know what I prayed for? That Lou was safe. I wasn't sure why then. But with these wolves on our heels, it's pretty obvious now."

"So this is all about Lou?"

"I don't know. I should have pushed him more, but honestly I was scared I might push him away completely. Everything has seemed so fragile lately."

"Is it possible he's been trying to protect you?"

At that, Dolores's eyes widen. "I never thought of it that way. Lou's been trying to keep me safe?" A hopeful smile plays across her lips.

"We have stopped long enough," Henry says. "We should go."

With her brow furrowed, Dolores stands. She follows Henry, but Rainy can see that her mind is elsewhere.

East they go, toward the risen sun, which warms Rainy's face and continues to lift her spirits. Henry has led them on a serpentine journey, weaving among ridges, hills, and bogs. Rainy can see that her great-uncle has been following deer trails. They're making good time, and he seems not worried about the men behind them being able to follow. She wonders if they'll ever head south, toward the Iron Lake Reservation. By her own calculation, they're maybe eight or ten miles north of Allouette. Even if they had to bushwhack their way through the forest groundcover, they could be there by sundown.

They come to a small lake where the water feeds out over a natural rock dam. Henry carefully crosses the rocks. Rainy follows and can feel the slippery surface of the stones under her boot soles. Dolores comes next. But her foot slips on one of the rocks. She gives a cry and tumbles into the lake. When she attempts to stand, her face contorts, and she lets out a groan.

"My ankle," she says, reaching out for help.

Rainy steps into the water and offers her hand. She lifts Dolores and supports her as they climb onto the shore of the lake. Dolores sits immediately, clutching her ankle with both hands.

"Let me look at it," Rainy says.

Before she came to Crow Point years ago to tend her aging great-uncle and to learn from him the ways of the Midewiwin, she was a trained nurse. She's seen lots of sprains, and this is yet another.

"Not broken," she says. "But it's going to be hard for you to walk."

"And I'm freezing," Dolores says, clutching herself through her wet clothing.

Rainy looks to Henry. Henry looks to the west, from where they have come and where the trackers must still be following. He smiles, as if he's known all along it would come to this.

"We will build a fire," the old man says.

CHAPTER 25

Rainy gathers dead wood and strips away the wet outer bark. Henry cuts a mound of dry shavings, then creates a pile of kindling and builds a small fire. Patiently, he adds larger fuel, and in a short while, a warm blaze has grown.

By the time Dolores strips off her wet clothing, she's shivering. She wraps herself in a blanket. Rainy hangs her things from sticks set in the ground and angled near the flames. She strips sheets of birch bark as dry seating, and they sit around the fire. The whole while, Rainy looks west across the little lake, watching for the trackers. She keeps Henry's old Winchester always within reach.

"I got you into this," Dolores says. "I'm sorry."

Rainy puts a comforting hand on her shoulder. "You had no way of knowing."

"When you asked for my help, you told me you wished to know the truth of who you are," Henry says. "You were sincere in this, I could see. But I could also see that there was more to it. What else?"

The woman stares into the fire, then looks at Rainy and Henry. "I want what you have," she finally says.

"And what is that?" Henry asks.

"I never knew my real mother or my real father. I was adopted at birth. My folks were not a happy couple. I was supposed to make things better between them. In the end, I think I only made things worse. They divorced when I was ten. My mother got custody, but I've always believed I was just one more thing she didn't want my father to have. My father died three years ago. Cirrhosis of the liver. My mother passed away last year. I'd been estranged from them both for a very long time." She pulls the blanket tighter around her, as if, despite the fire, she's still cold. "When I was a child and did something wrong, my father would say it was the Indian in me. I thought it was just his way of saying I was wild. But before she died, my mother told me something about my real mother, that she was hardly more than a child, just fifteen. Mom couldn't remember her name, and she claimed to have lost the adoption papers long ago. But what she did remember was that the girl, as my mother put it, was a little squaw."

"Native," Rainy says.

"I assume my real father must be white. I mean, look at me. I've tried to track down the adoption agency, but I've had no luck. When I met Lou, I felt an immediate connection with him. I chalked it up to Cupid. But when I learned the truth of my real mother, I thought different. I've tried to understand what it means to be Native. I've asked Lou's help, but he's done his best to turn his back on his heritage. So, it's been like trying to get a hold on something that just keeps slipping through my fingers. Then last year, we attended the funeral for Lou's uncle. You did the ceremony, Henry."

"I remember," the old man says.

"Do you remember that we talked?"

"You told me that you wished you had a belief as strong as those at the ceremony."

"And you said it's like a fire you build from a match. You told me I needed to find the match. I came looking for it. I thought maybe you could help."

"That match, Dolores Morriseau, is not mine to give."

She nods. "I know. I just wish . . ."

"What?" Rainy asks.

"I may not have that match, but I wish Lou had it. I would like him to understand how important his family is and his people. He has no idea what it's like to feel as if you have no history, no real identity. To come from nothing."

"You did not come from nothing," Henry says. "You came out of the heart of the Creator. And the match you so desire for your husband, maybe that is you."

Dolores looks at him and shakes her head. "I don't understand."

"There is already a flame inside you, Dolores Morriseau. It is what brought you here among us."

"Only to get you all killed."

The old man smiles. "We are not dead yet."

Then to Rainy's profound surprise, her great-uncle slips off his moccasins, stands, and begins to undress himself.

"Uncle Henry?"

"I will give Dolores Morriseau my dry clothes. We are not so different in build."

"And then what?"

"You must be moving."

"*We* must be moving," Rainy says.

Henry has already shed his jacket and shirt. He is unbuckling his belt and unzippering his pants. "You have a good heart, Niece. But your head is a little slow sometimes."

"You're not staying, Uncle Henry."

He stands in his union suit, holding out the rest of his clothing to Dolores. "Your ankle will slow you down. You will need all the time I can give you."

"I can't," she says.

"You came to me for help. This is the only help I have to offer now."

"Uncle Henry . . ." Rainy begins with an iron tone.

"Do you want to sacrifice everyone, Niece?"

"Of course not. But what are you going to do, Uncle Henry?"

"What I am very good at. I will wait."

"For what? To be killed?" Rainy's anger and fear nearly choke her.

"You speak as if you already know the outcome, Niece. Do you see the future?"

"I know the vision Stephen had. Uncle Henry, please don't do this."

"It is done." He drops his clothing into the lap of Dolores Morriseau.

"I can't," she says.

"Listen to me. Since I first entered this world, what awaits has always been before me. If I turn this way or that, it is still there, waiting, more patient than any human being." He faces Rainy. "If Stephen O'Connor's vision is a true one, then who am I to deny it?"

"Uncle Henry," Rainy begins.

"Go."

It is like the voice of rock, and Rainy knows she is beaten. "Give him your blanket, Dolores, and put on his clothes."

The woman stands, passes her blanket to Henry, and begins to don his clothing. The old man was right. The shirt is a little tight around the chest and the pants snug at the waist, but they fit. His jacket is almost perfect for her, as are his moccasins.

Rainy watches the exchange with a sinking heart. She understands the wisdom of her great-uncle's thinking. Staying puts them all in danger. But she can't bring herself to abandon this old man she loves with her whole heart.

"I'm not going."

"You are," Henry says. This time it's not a quiet suggestion. There's steel in his voice and fire in his dark eyes. "I am at the edge of my time and you know this. Now or a year from now or two, what difference does it make? But you have a lifetime still ahead. Continue your journey and leave me to the path the Creator set before me from the beginning."

"I can't just abandon you."

"You will not leave me. You are here." He touches his chest.

She hugs the old man, feels his bones and the bump of his heart.

He whispers to her, "She is in your hands. Promise me that you will do your best to keep her safe."

"I promise, Uncle Henry."

She steps away and it's Dolores's turn. "*Migwech, Mishomis,*" she says.

"Granddaughter," he replies and allows her to embrace him.

"Here." Rainy holds out the old Winchester. "Take this, Henry."

He shakes his head. "As a young man, I once shot the eye out of a moose at three hundred yards. Now I would be lucky if I did not shoot my foot. Keep the rifle, Niece. And if you need to use it, keep your hands steady. Leave me only my medicine bag and my flint and steel."

Rainy hands these items to Henry. "Let's go," she says. Despite the determination in her voice, there are tears in her eyes.

"Stay south," Henry says. "Always south. You will be home tonight."

Dolores turns and begins hobbling away. Rainy lingers a few moments. The beloved old man nods for her to go. And so she does.

PART THIRTEEN

THE WOLF

CHAPTER 26

LeLoup wakes in the dark, sitting with his back to the rocks. The fire is nothing but embers and ash. He checks his watch. Still a couple of hours before sunrise. He has slept fitfully, but not just because of the cold and his awkward position. He has dreamed again.

For LeLoup, dreams are a dangerous territory. In dreams, the past is not the past. The terrors of his childhood in the residential school still plague him. A lifetime of trespass haunts him. Nameless faces loom before him. The voices of dead men speak.

In dreams, LeLoup sees things he cannot explain.

In the dream that awakened him, he saw a man in the clearing of a forest transform into a huge beast and begin a battle with another beast that was its twin. In this dream, he not only stood watching the battle; he was the transformed man, and he was deep in the fight, claws ripping, teeth gnashing. Even when he wakes, the fury of the dream still unsettles him.

His dreams have sometimes proven to be premonitions. Once, in a dream that came to him while he was working under Kimball as a private military contractor hired by the government to help secure the diamond district of Sierra Leone, he saw a swarm of ants engulf a hyena and devour it, only to be swallowed themselves by another hyena. The next day he was scheduled to be part of a team assigned to help with the search of a village suspected of harboring RUF insurgents. The dream had greatly disturbed him, and he found an excuse to be released from the mission. The team, when it entered the village, was set upon by the villagers en masse and suffered devastating casualties. LeLoup, along with Kimball, was part of the large force sent the following day to secure the area. When they'd finished their mission, not one villager was left alive nor any building left standing.

He makes no excuses for his past. But in his sleep, he has no control over his conscience and his dreams sometimes punish him.

He rises and steps away from the rocks to relieve himself. As he stands pissing onto the snow, he gazes up at the stars. He has read that the Dakota people believe stars reside in the branches of cottonwood trees and when the spirits of the night sky require more, they shake the stars loose with a fierce wind. He has looked at the inside of a cottonwood branch and has seen the star there. The part of him shaped by his urban upbringing in the residential school tells him what nonsense it all is. But there is a deeper part of him that is more than willing to embrace the beauty of the story.

"God damn this night," Kimball says from behind. "Can't sleep. Can't go after them. And since you killed our communications, we've got no idea what's going on out there. We're blind."

When LeLoup has finished his business and turns, he sees the other man adding sticks to the embers and blowing flames to life.

"They're not far from us," LeLoup says. "We'll catch them soon after it's light."

"You said we'd catch them yesterday."

"Fate intervened. And who can control fate?"

"What if something intervenes today?"

"The sky's clear. And can't you feel that south wind? The day's already warming. By midmorning, all this snow will be gone. Nothing to stop us today."

"I'll believe that when we have Dolores Morriseau in hand."

"You can have the woman," LeLoup says. "I want the old man."

"Outfoxed you yesterday. Got under your skin, did he?"

"Let's just say he intrigues me."

Kimball settles back as flames grow in the fire. "Got any of that jerky left?"

"We ate it all last night."

This is a lie, but LeLoup has no intention of further depleting his supply. Despite the reassurances he's given Kimball, he's not certain of the day's outcome. The wily old man they're tracking may have more tricks up his sleeve. The hunt has already gone on far longer than any of them anticipated. It could go on even longer. In a way, LeLoup hopes that it does. He's eager for the challenge.

"Remember the job in Colombia?" Kimball says. "When we took down that operation, you didn't want any of the drugs we found. You could have made a fortune. A lot of the guys did. You were just satisfied that you tracked down those cokeheads. That was your real payoff. It was you against the jungle then. This time around it's you against this wilderness and that goddamned old man."

"You see everything as a fight, Kimball. It's not that way. I'm not fighting this wilderness. And I'm not fighting the old man."

"No? What then?"

"Think of it as a dance, and I'm trying to hear the music."

"You like music, do you? Well here's a little ditty for you. If we lose the Morriseau woman, we could be history, you and me. And I don't just mean we'll never work together again. I mean the people that hired us may decide to cancel our futures, and believe me, nobody will ever find our bodies."

"You always did have a penchant for melodrama, Kimball."

"I'm not the one who smashed our sat phones against the rocks."

"And I'm not the one who neglected the recon that would have told us who we're up against out here."

"Hell, he's not a ghost or a monster."

"I don't know what he is." LeLoup looks at the sky and sees the first faint suggestion of daylight. "But I intend to find out soon."

They've gone less than a mile north when LeLoup stops, turns around, and starts back in the direction from which they've just come.

"What the hell are you doing?" Kimball says.

"We've lost them."

"You said you'd find them."

"I will. But not by going in this direction. They turned off somewhere."

"Where?"

"I have an idea."

"Christ, I should never have trusted you. You and your damn instincts."

"This old man, whoever he is, knows these woods. I've just been following him. It's time I began to anticipate. Come on, double time."

LeLoup breaks into a trot heading south, following the tracks he and Kimball have just made. The sun has risen, and the day is warming rapidly. The snow is becoming slush under their boot soles. They pass the rocks where they spent the night. A quarter mile farther, they come to a stream bed that was dry the day before; now a rivulet of snowmelt is already threading its way among the rocks.

The creek bed runs east and west. LeLoup pauses a moment, considering. "Which way?"

"West," Kimball says. "A few miles west then south and they'll walk right into Aurora."

"A white man's thinking. East and south is the reservation. We go east."

It's a few hundred yards before LeLoup finds the tracks. They lead from a deadfall of trees and branches. He can see the bare area over the top where a blanket had been laid to keep out the snow. A far better place to have weathered the storm than in the lee of some rocks. Did the old man know it was there? Is he just lucky, or is something else at work, something Kimball would call superstitious mumbo jumbo?

"He hears the music," LeLoup says, mostly to himself.

"What?"

"Never mind. We need to keep moving fast."

The tracks, while LeLoup follows them, grow more and more shallow as the snow that holds them melts away. The two men come to a ridge running north and south. What's left of the snow clearly shows that the old man and the woman have turned north.

"Heading into the damn wilderness again," Kimball complains.

LeLoup takes the topo map from a pocket inside his jacket and studies the terrain. "There's a series of three ridges ahead of us. He's gone north to get around this one. But he'll head south along one of the troughs between the ridges. If we cut due east now, over this ridge, we'll intercept them or the trail they've left on the other side. If not there, then on the other side of the next ridge. They'll still have a good ten miles of hard walking before they hit Allouette, the rez town. We'll have them in hand before that."

Kimball eyes the slope of the ridge slick with snow slush. "Looks like a broken ankle just waiting to happen."

"After you," LeLoup says.

CHAPTER 27

LeLoup discovers no trail beyond the next ridge or the next. Although the snow has melted in all but the most protected nooks and crannies, the wet ground is a perfect receptor for footprints, yet LeLoup finds none.

"You're going to tell me the old man just vanished into thin air?" Kimball says.

"He's gone farther east than I anticipated is all. Beyond the final ridge. Must be something there he needs to reach."

LeLoup takes another look at the topo map. Beyond the next ridge is a small lake called Fisheye. A stream also called by that name heads south from there and threads its way to Iron Lake, its mouth less than a mile from the town of Allouette.

"Got him," LeLoup says. "He's taking them south along Fisheye Creek. They'll come out on Iron Lake. It's exactly how I'd go if I were him."

They can hear the engine of the plane approaching and they move into the shadow of a tall spruce. In a minute, a de Havilland Beaver passes overhead.

"Damn it to hell," Kimball screams. "They're going to find these people before we can get to them."

"But they won't be able to extract them," LeLoup tells him. "This Fisheye Lake is too small for a landing, and there's not a big enough body of water between Fisheye and Iron Lake. Even if the plane is able to report their position, there's no way help can reach them before we do."

"I'm sick of your empty assurances."

"We'll never grab them if we stand here arguing." LeLoup starts up the slope of the final ridge.

At the top, he's greeted by a surprising discovery. Less than a mile away lies the lake, an oval that in its opalescence does, in fact, resemble the eye of a fish. A thread of gray smoke rises from the shore. LeLoup watches as the search plane circles, then heads south and out of sight.

Kimball smiles with grim delight. "Just like you said, the plane couldn't land to pick them up. We've got them now. Let's go."

But LeLoup hesitates in his descent of the ridge. "Why did they stop?"

"Who cares? They've stopped. Big mistake."

"This old man doesn't make mistakes."

"You think it's a trap? Like the sharp stick?"

"I don't know. But I don't want to rush into anything. Let's take it slow until we know what's what."

They carefully descend the slope of the ridge, which is slick from the residue of the snowmelt. A hundred yards beyond the base of the ridge, LeLoup finally sees the tracks he's been anticipating, tracks so clear that even a man as blind as Kimball could follow them.

Remembering the empty rifle rack in the old man's cabin, Le-Loup approaches the lake with caution. He and Kimball find cover on the near shoreline to assess the situation. LeLoup takes field glasses from the soft case looped on his belt. He can see the fire, which has dwindled to a thread of gray smoke. He can't see any people, but there appears to be a body lying near the fire. He hands the glasses to Kimball, who spends a minute with the lenses to his eyes.

"Not moving. Dead?" Kimball says. "We've been pushing them hard. Maybe the old man had a heart attack."

"Maybe. It would explain why the others have abandoned him."

But LeLoup hopes that's not the case. He would be disappointed if he didn't get a chance to confront this confounding old man, this worthy adversary.

"On the other hand, maybe a trap," LeLoup says. "As soon as we show ourselves, whoever's holding the rifle shoots us from wherever they're hiding."

"That's assuming they can shoot."

"Considering everything else they've shown us, that's not an unreasonable assumption. There's something odd going on here. I don't like this."

"Okay, this is how we play it," Kimball says. "You go in first, I'll cover you."

LeLoup takes back the field glasses and studies the trees that rise up behind the body lying next to the fire. The woods are a mix of bright sun and hard shadow, with lots of good cover for a shooter. He checks the end of the lake where water spills over a jumble of rocks, feeding the stream that runs to Iron Lake.

"If I go first, I'm not dancing across those rocks," he says. "I'd be a perfect target for about six seconds. I'll circle the lake, come in from the north."

"And waste another fifteen minutes?"

"Fine, then you cross those rocks and I'll cover you."

Kimball weighs his options, finally says, "Go."

In five minutes, LeLoup is kneeling behind a stand of tall ferns, studying the scene around the dying fire. He can see that the body is that of an old man. He moves silently through the undergrowth beneath the tree cover, checking for a shooter who might be hiding there. He finds no one. Finally, he steps from the forest onto the lakeshore and signals all clear to Kimball.

He stands looking down at the old man, who's lying on a blanket, his eyes closed, no sign of breathing. LeLoup is surprised at the intensity of the regret he feels, as if he's suffered a deeply personal loss. He has never seen this old man before, but he's seen all the evidence of the old man's mind and experience at work, and he can't help feeling that something rare has passed away.

"Good," Kimball says, after he's crossed the stones. "Mother nature iced this one for us. And you think he's the one responsible for keeping the Morriseau woman out of our reach?"

"It was him all right."

"God, he's old."

"I would have said beautiful."

"Christ, you're a strange one, LeLoup. Come on, let's get started after the others. They can't be that far ahead."

"*Boozhoo.*"

When the old man speaks, LeLoup actually takes a step back in surprise. Kimball brings up his rifle and prepares to shoot. LeLoup grabs the barrel and shoves it away. "Wait!"

The old man opens his eyes, which are dark and deep and shine in the sunlight as if with a fire of their own. He brings himself into a sitting position on the blanket and returns the wary gazes of the men with a look that LeLoup swears is filled with bemusement.

"You're going to die, old man," he says.

"All men are going to die."

"He means now," Kimball says.

"Why?"

"I don't need a reason beyond all the trouble you've caused me," Kimball replies.

"The others, why did they leave you?" LeLoup asks.

"I told them to leave me."

"Why did you stay?"

The old man looks at him in a way that makes LeLoup feel as if an arrow has pierced his soul. "I stayed for you."

"You don't even know me."

"Better than you think. I know that you listen to the woods and have already learned many lessons. I have suspected all along that the blood of The People runs through your heart. I have seen you coming for me in dreams. And I think that you must dream, too."

"Which way did they go, old man?" Kimball demands.

"I already told you which way they went," LeLoup snaps at him. "South, following Fisheye Creek."

"Then ice this old man and let's go."

LeLoup makes no move. Kimball says, "Christ, then I will." He lifts his rifle again.

LeLoup strikes him, a hard right hook, and Kimball goes down, dropping his rifle.

"What the hell's got into you?" Kimball rises slowly, rubbing his jaw.

"We don't kill the old man."

"Fine. I don't give a shit. It's the Morriseau woman we're after."

"You know where she is. Just follow the creek."

"What about you?"

"I'm staying here."

"Good God, what for?"

It's the old man who answers. "To learn," he says.

Kimball stands, his empty hands clenched into hard, bloodless fists. He glares at LeLoup, his eyes narrowed into dark, angry slits. Finally he says, "You still have your sat phone?"

LeLoup nods.

"I'll need it to get the chopper."

LeLoup reaches to a pocket inside his coat, brings out the device, and tosses it to Kimball.

"I'm going to get the Morriseau woman and call for the chopper to extract us," Kimball says. "Then I'll be waiting for you. You'll have to come out of these woods sometime. When you do, you son of a bitch, I'll find you and shoot you down like the ungrateful dog you are."

"I could kill you here and now," LeLoup reminds him. "It's the Morriseau woman you want. You have no use for the old man."

"No use maybe, but he's caused me a shitstorm of trouble. I want him dead."

"Won't happen. Not today. And every minute you stand here arguing, those women move farther away."

"Damn you!" It's feeble, but with LeLoup's rifle barrel pointed at his chest, it's the best the man can muster. He carefully lifts the fallen rifle from the ground and starts after the women, following Fisheye Creek.

LeLoup watches until he's certain Kimball has gone for good, then faces the figure still sitting peacefully on the blanket. This man called Meloux has already surprised him in many ways, and LeLoup finds himself surprised yet again by his first clear look at what has been his prey for the past two days. Meloux is wearing a light down jacket that looks rather feminine in its design. The collar of the blue work shirt beneath is embroidered with flowers. His jeans are ill-fitting and hang on him loosely. Then there is the old man himself. His face has more lines than sun-cracked mud. His hair is the silky white of milkweed fluff. The skin on the back of his hands is splashed with dark age spots. Still, there is nothing

old about his eyes. They seem ageless in the way they regard Le-
Loup, a look absent of any trace of fear.

"You said I'm here to learn. Learn what?" LeLoup asks.

"What you came to me for."

"I came to kill you."

The old man shakes his head. "That is why the others came."
The man rises slowly, cinches the belt about his waist a little
tighter in order to hold up the ill-fitting jeans. He lifts the beaded
bag that has lain next to him and slips it over his shoulder. He nods
toward the blanket on the ground. "We'll need that."

"Where are we going?" LeLoup asks.

"No questions," Meloux says. "To learn you must listen."

PART FOURTEEN

STEPHEN

CHAPTER 28

Because of the disturbance the night before, Stephen wakes late, but rises to the good smell of fresh-brewed coffee. He finds Belle in the kitchen looking well rested.

"Good morning," she says cheerily. "I thought about waking you, but decided I'd let you sleep a little longer before breakfast. You have time to shower if you'd like."

"Coffee first," Stephen says.

He pours from the pot on the coffeemaker. "Anything I can do to help?"

"Just relax and drink your coffee. Penny Fidler dropped by this morning. She saw all the hullabaloo last night and wanted to check on us, make sure everything's okay. She brought quiche for breakfast. I'll heat it now and cut up a little fruit to go with it."

"A good neighbor," Stephen observes.

"A generous woman, and I'd say Dolores's best friend."

He watches her work, watches her move with grace and assuredness in the bright sunlight that slants through the big kitchen windows.

"What are you smiling at?" she asks.

"Just thinking about your name. Belle means 'beautiful' in French, right?"

"More or less."

"Suits you."

"*Merci.*"

"Tell you what. In exchange for breakfast, I'll fix the window our prowler broke last night."

"I've put a blanket over it for the moment. I'll get someone out to fix it later. We have more important things to worry about. Like where's my brother and what's up with that map and thumb drive."

"We were pretty tired last night. Maybe this morning we'll see something we missed. In the meantime, I'll check in with Sheriff Dross and see what's happening in Aurora."

He makes the call and relays to Belle the essence of what he's learned. "Dad and Anton lost the trail in the snow, but a search plane is in the air now. Dross promises to keep us posted."

"Why don't we eat?" Belle suggests. "Then we can think about where we go from here."

As they finish their breakfast, Belle says, "I'm thinking we should go through the files in Lou's office carefully. Maybe this Catie isn't a lover. Maybe she's involved with Lou in another way, maybe business of some kind."

"The office is a mess. It's going to take forever to get things organized. I'm pretty sure our burglar last night came back because he already went through the files and didn't find what he was looking for."

"He was looking for the map and key, right?"

"I don't know if we can say that for sure, but it's probably a good guess."

"Then maybe there's information in the files he didn't care about but we might. And do you have another suggestion?"

Before Stephen can reply, Belle's cell phone rings. "This is Belle Morriseau." She listens and nods. "You'll keep me informed?" She listens again, then says, "Thanks very much. And if we think of anything, we'll be sure to let you know." She ends the call. "That was Detective Griggs. He says they haven't been able to identify the man who broke in. His fingerprints aren't in the FBI database. And he's not talking. For the moment, they're going to charge him as a John Doe. Griggs would still like us to come in today and give an official statement."

"Maybe we should have told him about the map and thumb drive and 'Kill Catie,'" Stephen says.

Belle shakes her head. "I think we should hold off until we have something more substantial."

Stephen looks toward the back room. "Well, are you ready?"

"Let's get to those files," Belle says.

It's nearly noon when Stephen gets the next call from Sheriff Marsha Dross. Her voice is weighted. "I have some news, Stephen."

"What is it?"

"The search plane has spotted someone."

"That's good news, right?"

"Just one person. They think it's Henry Meloux."

"And?"

"He was lying on the ground at the edge of a lake, Stephen. He didn't move when the search plane flew over, didn't try to signal at all."

There's silence on her end, and although Stephen doesn't want to say the words that are screaming in his head, he can't stop them. "He's dead?"

"I can't say that for sure, but it's certainly not looking good. Your dad's on his way there now. We should be getting an update from him soon. Stephen, I'm sorry. I know what Henry means to you."

Although he's numb, he replies, "Thank you."

"A search party from the reservation is also headed to that lake. One way or the other, we'll have some answers soon," Dross promises.

When the call is ended, he sits and stares at the papers in the open file folder on the desk in Lou Morriseau's office. It feels as if his heart has been sucked out of his chest and with it has gone his very soul.

"What is it, Stephen?" Belle asks. She's sitting on the other side of the desk, files stacked before her.

Lifting his eyes is like lifting heavy weights. He feels as if he's trying to breathe underwater. Words are trapped in his throat. "Henry Meloux," he finally says. "They spotted him."

"That's good, right?"

"They think he's dead."

"Oh, Stephen, I'm sorry." Belle abandons her chair, comes around the desk quickly, and wraps her arms around him.

He feels her heart beating against him, and it helps his own heart return. "They're not certain," he says. "But . . ."

Belle draws back and looks deep into his eyes. "Yes?"

"I told you that sometimes I see things," Stephen says.

"I remember."

"Months ago, I saw Henry. I saw him dead."

Belle says nothing, but her expression is soft, her face filled with a look of compassion.

"I told him my vision, and he said, 'I know.' As if he'd seen it, too."

"But they're not sure," Belle reminds him.

"I know what I saw. And Henry saw it, too. He's dead, Belle."

"What about the others?" she asks in a gentle voice.

Stephen shakes his head. "Nothing. They didn't spot anyone except Henry." Stephen feels the slow crawl of a tear down his cheek, a thread of ice that chills him to the marrow. He wipes it away brusquely with the back of his hand. "I don't know who these guys are or what they want, but I swear on Henry's soul we're going to get them. I swear I'm going to make them pay."

CHAPTER 29

It's taken hours to organize and go through the files that were left scattered on the floor of Lou Morriseau's office. Stephen's eyes have gone blurry, Belle is sitting slumped in her chair. The room is quiet and has the somber feel of a funeral visitation.

"Nothing," Belle finally says.

Stephen arches his back and feels the cracking of his spine. "All I can guess is that whatever's going on, it doesn't have a thing to do with your brother's business dealings. It must be something personal. The envelope was addressed to you, Belle. Any idea why? You're about to become a lawyer, so maybe something legal?"

"Kill Catie? It doesn't take a lawyer to know that's definitely against the law," Belle replies.

"You said you've done work with Mother Earth Always, right?"

"Yes."

"And you said that even though Lou has pretty much turned his back on his Native heritage, he sometimes has dealings with First Nations folks. Is it possible whatever's going on has some-

thing to do with those dealings, something that might be important for Mother Earth Always to know about?"

Belle ponders that possibility for a few moments. "Maybe."

"Let's look at that map again." Stephen clears the folder files
from Morriseau's desk and lays out the map with all the interconnecting lines. "Belle, can you pull up a map of Canada on Lou's
computer?"

A minute later, she has it on the screen. They stare at it for a
while, then Belle says, "If you're right and it's about First Nations
business, let's take a look at the reserves."

She maneuvers the mouse and taps some keys, revealing a different map of Canada, one with shaded areas here and there across
the broad stretch of the country.

Stephen sees it immediately. "The lines on our map. So many
of them connect to First Nations reserves."

"What are they?" Belle says.

"I don't know. Roads? Rivers? Maybe communication lines of
some kind? Broadband connections maybe?"

"Could they be cultural connections?" Belle offers. "Clan connections?"

"Or pipelines? We're getting a lot of our oil from Canada these
days."

Belle shakes her head. "Too many and they don't go anywhere
near the tar sands."

Stephen's cell phone rings. It's Sheriff Dross.

"Some troubling news, Stephen," she says without preamble.
"We've lost communication with your dad. He hasn't checked
in for several hours and we can't raise him on the sat phone. He
should have reached Fisheye Lake, but we can't be certain if he did
or what he found. And there's more, something we don't know
how to interpret."

She hesitates and Stephen prepares himself for more bad news.

"The search plane has flown over the area several times since refueling. They can't see Henry Meloux's body."

An ember of hope begins to glow in Stephen's heart. "Maybe he wasn't dead."

"His body could have been moved, Stephen. Buried or thrown in the lake to hide it. We won't know anything for sure until the search party gets there. They're bushwhacking their way through but still a couple of hours from the lake."

"Any sign of Rainy and the others?"

"None."

"And the men tracking them?"

"Nothing. It's dense forest. Hard to spot anything. How are you progressing down there? Anything helpful?"

Stephen explains what they've just discovered, but that they still don't understand the connection.

"What about the thumb drive?"

"We haven't cracked the pass code, so no. But we'll keep working, and when we come up with something, we'll let you know," Stephen promises.

When he's ended the call, he reports the gist of his conversation to Belle.

"They think Henry might still be alive?"

"Marsha wasn't willing to go that far."

"What about your vision?"

"Henry has often said that a vision may not be the thing itself, only the reflection of the thing. What it means is that sometimes the vision doesn't show you something concrete. It shows you a representation that requires interpreting. So, Henry dead might not be Henry dead."

Belle takes Stephen's hand and squeezes it warmly. "Let's hold to that hope."

"I think I need a break," Stephen says. "My brain is fried."

"It's hours past lunch," Belle says. "Let's take a break and grab a bite."

She puts together two plates—peanut butter and jelly sandwiches with some chips—which she takes to the living room, where Stephen has spread out the map of Canada on the coffee table. They're quiet as they eat, and although he feels as if his brain is turning to mush, he can't help continuing to study the spiderweb of lines, trying to decipher their meaning.

"Maybe this map and the map of the reserves have absolutely nothing to do with each other," he says. "As far as you know, your brother has no interest in Native affairs."

"Maybe that's changed. We haven't seen him much in the last few months."

"I don't even know what he looks like."

She stands up and goes to a framed photograph sitting on a shelf near the mantel. She brings it back and sets it on the coffee table where Stephen can see it.

"Is that you?" Stephen says.

"When I graduated from law school. Lou was ecstatic for me."

"And that's Lou?"

"Yeah."

Stephen studies the man in the photograph, and slowly something emerges from deep in his recollection. "Oh, my God."

"What is it?"

"I've seen him before."

"Where?"

Stephen looks at her, wondering if she will believe him. "In a dream," he says.

"You saw Lou in a dream? Do you mean a vision?" Belle doesn't sound disbelieving, for which Stephen is grateful.

"That's how my visions come to me, in dreams."

"When did you see him?"

"Last night."

Stephen tells her about the dream of the man in the clearing and the two battling Windigos.

"And you're sure the man was Lou?"

"I'm sure."

"Maybe you saw him in another photograph while we were searching the house and he became part of your dream."

"It's possible. But the dream still means something."

"You saw Lou become a Windigo." She sits, puts the photograph on the coffee table, and studies it. "If Lou is one of the Windigos, who is the other?"

"Catie, maybe?" Stephen offers.

"Catie," Belle says, standing and walking away from the desk. "I don't even know who she is, and I hate her with a passion."

"Unless your brother's trying to save her," Stephen says. "Maybe she's, I don't know, some kind of pawn in whatever's going on."

"And what the hell could that be?"

Stephen stares at the map again. "Real estate, maybe? That's what your brother deals in. A lot of the lines connect with First Nations reserves, so maybe it has something to do with buying or selling Native holdings."

"He's worked with land transfers on reserves in Canada before. On reservations here in the States, too. The issues can be complex, and it's one of his areas of expertise. But what would the lines have to do with reserve landholdings?"

"Could they be right of ways?" Stephen offers.

"Right of ways?" Belle considers the map. "Maybe, but like you've said, not for oil pipelines. So what then?"

The doorbell rings and almost immediately rings again, as if the visitor is impatient. Belle rises to answer, and the doorbell rings a third time. Stephen doesn't like the aggressiveness of their caller, and he gets up, too.

Belle opens the door with Stephen beside her. Two men stand in the shade of the porch. They're dressed in dark gray suits. Their faces have a dour, gray aspect as well. One appears to be in his early fifties, thinning hair. The other is a good deal younger. Both stand as rigid as fence posts. The older man lifts an ID holder for them to see.

"I'm Officer Peterson and this is Officer Orlock," he says. "We're from the Canadian Intelligence and Security Service. We're looking for Louis Morriseau."

CHAPTER 30

"What's this all about?" Belle asks the two officers.

"As I just said, we're looking for Louis Morriseau," Peterson, the older officer, replies.

"He's not here."

"And you are?"

"The woman who's asking what this is all about."

Peterson turns his gray eyes on Stephen. "And you, sir?"

"A friend," Stephen says.

"Of Mr. Morriseau?"

"Of the woman who's asking what this is all about."

Orlock, the younger officer, glances back, checking the street and the neighborhood. "May we come in?"

"Not until I know what you want," Belle replies.

"You already know," Peterson says. "If you allow us in, we'll explain why."

"Could we see those IDs again," Stephen says. "We've had some trouble with people misrepresenting themselves lately."

When he and Belle are satisfied, they allow the men inside. As they enter the living room, Stephen realizes that the map is still open on the coffee table. He moves ahead of the others, snatches it up, and folds it. But when he turns back, it's clear that Peterson and Orlock have seen. They eye him and the map like vultures. He slips the folded map into the back pocket of his jeans.

Light from the late afternoon sun streams through the tall windows that overlook the back patio and gardens. The two men sit in chairs facing the sofa. Where the sunlight strikes the right sides of their faces, their skin is gold. The left side of each man's face floats in shadow. Belle and Stephen settle onto the sofa. Belle explains who she is.

"And Dolores Morriseau? Where is she?" Peterson asks.

"Not here," Belle replies and leaves it at that.

"Ms. Morriseau, are you aware that your brother has made a significant number of trips into Canada in the past six months?"

"I am."

"Do you know why?"

"Real estate deals, I imagine. That's what he does. Negotiates land transfers."

"Has he talked to you at all about these trips?"

"Lou keeps his business to himself."

"You're Ojibwe, is that correct?"

"Anishinaabe."

"How do you feel about oil pipelines?"

"I believe they're a dangerous mistake."

"Yet you haven't been a part of any protests."

When they first arrived, they appeared not to know who Belle is, yet they know this about her already. Stephen wonders why they lied and what else they might know.

"I'm a lawyer," Belle replies. "Well, almost. I protest through legal channels."

"Just tell her, Peterson," Orlock, the younger officer, says.

"We believe there's a group of First Nations activists planning a series of attacks on oil pipelines in Canada."

"And you believe Lou is involved? I can assure you he's not," Belle says.

"We believe that, too. But we also believe your brother may have stumbled onto some of the details of their plan, information vital to preventing these attacks."

"How exactly did Lou get this information?" Belle asks.

"For some time, your brother has been working with a First Nations reserve to reacquire land given over to the provincial government as part of an agreement in the mid-1950s. The deal was rather unscrupulous, involving a good deal of bribery on both sides of the table. We believe that in digging through the documents involved in that transaction and in the current negotiations, your brother stumbled onto something that clued him in to the plotting of these activists. We believe he may be in grave danger. He was recently in Winnipeg, but he's not there anymore, and we've been unable to locate him. We were hoping that your brother might have returned home. We need to talk to him."

"Did you check with the border authorities?" Belle asks. "If he'd crossed back into the United States, there should have been a record of it."

"We're aware that your brother hasn't always crossed the border at legal checkpoints, but we're not sure why. As I said, we don't believe he's one of the activists, but we do believe he's in danger. Because we can't locate him, we believe he's aware of the danger and may have gone into hiding."

"How do you know he has this information?" Stephen asks.

"It's our business to know this kind of thing."

"If you already know so much, why do you need to talk to my brother?"

"A few important questions remain unanswered. In return, we'd like to offer him protection."

They all sit for a few moments, staring at one another in silence. Then Stephen says, "May tenth."

It's clear that he's startled both men.

"Is that the date these attacks are supposed to take place?" When Stephen gets no reply, he says, "What about Catie?"

They've been pleasant, but their demeanor suddenly changes. "What do you know about Catie?" Peterson demands.

"Someone wants her dead."

The younger officer says, "Her?"

"Shut up, Orlock," Peterson snaps. He leans forward, his eyes narrowed to slits of gray menace. "Tell me about Catie."

"You first," Stephen replies.

"That's not how this goes."

"Maybe not in Canada," Stephen says, "but things are different here."

"That map you grabbed as we came in. I'd like to see it."

"It's nothing," Stephen says.

"Then show it to me."

"I don't think so."

Peterson sits back, scrutinizes Stephen, then Belle. "We'll just see about that. Let's go, Orlock."

The two men head to the front door with Stephen and Belle following. After they step outside, Peterson turns. "Things here are not so different as you might imagine, son. We'll be back."

Stephen and Belle watch the men get into their black sedan and drive away in the long, orange slant of the late afternoon sunlight. They close and lock the door.

"What do you think?" Stephen says.

"Their IDs seemed legitimate. First Nations activists have disrupted train lines and sabotaged mining and logging operations in the past. But I think they were selling snake oil."

Stephen returns to the living room and stands at the large picture window that looks out on the broad front lawn and the street beyond. Belle stands beside him.

"I think they're right about one thing," Stephen says. "Your brother's gone into hiding. The question is where."

"I think they were right about something else, too," Belle says. "Things might not be so different here. He said he'd be back, and I get the distinct feeling powerful forces are at work. No telling who or what he might bring with him."

"I don't know what else we're going to accomplish here. Maybe it's time we left."

"Back to my parents' house in Bena? Will it be any safer?"

"Call your folks. Check it out. I'm going to get the thumb drive."

When he returns from Lou Morriseau's office, Belle is still on her cell phone. She glances at Stephen, a troubled look on her face. "Okay, if they come back, you'll let me know, right?" She listens. "We'll be careful. You, too. Love you."

"If who comes back?" Stephen asks when she's ended the call.

"They got a visit a little while ago, two men who claimed to be from Border Patrol asking about Lou. They believe he has important information about smuggling."

"Smuggling what?"

"Guns, explosives."

"That's ridiculous, right?" But Stephen can tell she's holding something back. "What is it?"

"Lou and Anton, in their much younger days, used to take things across the border illegally. Nothing major. Alcohol and weed, just for their friends on the rez. They knew a lot of unpatrolled routes into and out of Canada. They were just teenagers and it was mostly for kicks. When Dad got wind of it, he laid into them, and they stopped. But guns? Explosives? That's ridiculous."

Stephen unfolds the map and lays it again on the coffee table. "These black lines, could they be smuggling routes?"

"That makes about as much sense as a plot to blow up pipelines. And if he's smuggling, why don't any of those lines cross into the States?"

"You can see where they would." Stephen points to several of the lines that hit the international border in the midsection of the country and stop there.

Belle studies the map, then shakes her head vigorously. "I still don't believe it. Not for an instant. Not Lou."

Beyond the broad front window, Stephen spots a black sedan pull into the circular front drive and park behind his Jeep. It's followed by another black sedan and another. Half a dozen men in dark suits exit the vehicles, Peterson and Orlock among them.

"Out the back way," Stephen says, snatching up the map.

"Wait. Shouldn't we see who they are?"

"Run first. Ask questions later."

He sprints toward the doors that open onto the rear patio, Belle on his heels. They leave the house and make for the back privacy fence. It's eight feet high, a tough scramble, but fueled by adrenaline, they pull themselves up and over and land in the backyard of the house there.

"What now?" Belle says, breathing hard.

"We need a car."

"Penny," Belle says. "She'll help us. Come on."

They cross the yard and reach the next street. Belle leads Stephen on a circuitous route that brings them eventually to the door of Penny Fidler's back patio. She knocks, and few moments later, Penny slides the door open.

"Damn, girl, what's up? Looks like a convention of the men in black at your brother's place."

"It's bad, Penny. You've got to trust me. I need to borrow your car."

"Okay," the woman says without hesitation.

"Can you drive around to the next street?" Stephen asks. "If they see us, we're sunk."

"Whatever will help. Wait on the corner."

In five minutes, they rendezvous and Penny drops the keys to her BMW into Belle's hand. "I don't know what this is all about."

"I'll explain things when I can, Penny. Just know this is for Dolores and Lou."

Penny gives her a hug. "Godspeed to you both."

They get in, Belle in the driver's seat, and head away, leaving Penny Fidler on the sidewalk, shaking her head as she watches them go.

- PART FIFTEEN -

RAINY

CHAPTER 31

They have left Henry, left him to the hunters. Rainy understands the necessity of what Henry has asked, and she appreciates her great-uncle's sacrifice, but she's not sure that she'll be able to live with herself. Already guilt and grief have created a black hole in her spirit that sucks her down into a darkness more profound than any of the fears she's felt during their flight. But Henry has tasked her with getting Dolores to safety, and this is what drives her now. This final promise.

The way is difficult. There's no deer trail to follow, and the women bushwhack along the creek. Dolores is struggling but bravely so. She limps and with each breath puffs out a little grunt of pain. There's no hope of hiding their trail, and Rainy doesn't even try. What she hopes is that somehow Henry can delay the men. He was certain they would follow, certain there is one among them who understands the wilderness as he does, but she has no idea how far behind them the trackers might be.

After an hour, Dolores begs to stop and rest. They sit on a pine felled in some past storm. The day has warmed and Rainy is sweating. She removes her jacket, bundles it, and shoves it in the knapsack.

"Is that creek water safe to drink?" Dolores asks. "My throat is parched."

For two days, they have been drinking water supplied by the wilderness. Each time, Dolores has asked this same question. Rainy gives her the same answer she's given before. "Probably, but there's always the risk of giardia." Which is a parasite that can cause all kinds of stomach distress.

Dolores hobbles to the creek, kneels, and drinks, but Rainy stays where she is, her eyes on the woods in the direction they've come from. Behind her, she hears Dolores say, "I'm sorry."

"Don't keep saying that. This isn't your fault."

"If I hadn't come, you wouldn't be in this mess."

"But you might. And didn't you come for our help?"

Dolores returns and sits beside her on the felled pine. "Lou's family has talked about the visions that sometimes come to people during ceremonies or in sweats. Since Lou stopped talking to me, I've been desperate. In the sweat, I prayed for a vision, something to tell me how to help him, how to help us." She gives Rainy a troubled look. "I didn't get a vision. Instead, I got a pack of wolves wanting to rip us apart. Did I offend the spirits?"

"This has nothing to do with your prayers in the sweat, Dolores. In a sweat, if you're sincere in your prayer, there's no offending of spirits."

"It's Lou these men are after. Maybe he's hiding from them, and they think I know where he is."

"Is it personal or business?" Rainy asks.

"I've been hoping it might be both. Maybe he's not having an affair with this Katie. Maybe he's somehow in business with her, and she's got them both in deep trouble."

"You said your husband deals in real estate and that he's been going to Canada a lot lately. Could it be related?"

"I suppose. Lou sometimes acts as a middleman in land negotiations with reserves in Manitoba. That's where his father's family is from. He has lots of clan connections, but I think he hasn't always been on their side." She breathes deeply, a little sadly. "He's made a lot of money from his Canadian business associations. Maybe it's begun to bother him. Some of the darkness that's crept over him, maybe it's the result of guilt." She looks to Rainy as if for confirmation.

"You believe he might have been helping steal land from his people? It wouldn't be the first time that's happened," Rainy says, with a note of bitterness. "But how is this Katie involved?"

"That's what I'd like to know."

"I'm going to find you a walking stick, and we're going to get out of these woods. Then Cork can help us with figuring out Katie." She smiles. "He really is a good PI."

They walk another mile and come to a place where the creek threads through marshland a couple of hundred yards across whose shoreline is populated by tamaracks. Rainy looks back at the trail they've left and thinks about the sharpened stake Henry planted in the trail along the bog the day before. She knows there are only two men tracking them now. Because of the slow pace Dolores's injured ankle forces them to keep, Rainy is certain the men will overtake them long before they can reach the reservation. She makes a decision.

"You go that way. I'll meet you at the other end of the marsh, where the creek flows free again."

"Why split up?" Dolores asks, her concern clear.

"To confuse them and separate them," Rainy answers. "Like we did before."

"What difference does it make if we separate them? It's not going to slow them down much."

But simply slowing them down isn't what Rainy's thinking of now. "Just do it," she says, a little harshly.

Dolores shrugs and turns away to circle the marsh.

As she moves ahead, Rainy looks for the advantage she prays she can find. She wants a high, protected place. Nothing presents itself until she reaches the far end of the marsh, where Dolores is waiting. That's when Rainy spots what she's been looking for. The creek exits the marsh and runs again in a clear stream. A hundred yards south, the water makes a curve around a rocky knoll. The two women continue along the creek, but as soon as they've passed the knoll, Rainy stops.

"You go on. Stay with the creek and it will take you to safety."

"You're not coming with me?" Dolores says.

"I'll join you in a bit."

"I can't just leave you."

"I'll join you later, Dolores, I promise. You need to keep moving as quickly as possible."

"I'm not leaving you."

"Henry sacrificed himself for you. I won't have that be a sacrifice made in vain. Go. Now."

Dolores stands firm. "We've come this far together. We're finishing this together. However it goes." She eyes the Winchester in Rainy's hands. "A last stand, is that it? Are you any good with the rifle?"

"Yes," Rainy says.

"Then what needs to be done we do together."

They stand a long time facing each other, until at last Rainy gives a nod.

CHAPTER 32

Rainy has been in tight spots before. When she was young, she married a man who turned out to be connected to a drug cartel, and it nearly got her and her two children killed. But as a result, she learned how to shoot firearms with pinpoint accuracy. As she waits for the trackers to come, she tells herself this is nothing new. She can do this thing.

She is atop the knoll, which is capped by greenstone, a ubiquitous rock in the Boundary Waters. She has settled herself behind the greenstone with the barrel of the Winchester resting on the rock. Dolores is below, standing in plain sight of the marsh. It was her idea, using herself as bait. "If they're focused on me, they won't see you," she insisted. "Make sure you don't miss," she added.

As the waiting goes on, Rainy yields to her fear that neither she nor Dolores will walk out of these woods, and her thinking turns to Cork and their life together. She's been happy in their marriage, happier than she can ever remember. He's a good man, a gentle man, a flawed man for sure, but his heart is noble. He's never been one to speak his emotions in fancy phrases, but she feels his love like a shower of rose petals. And oh, does she love him in return. She closes her eyes and imagines them old together, walking hand in hand toward some final sunset.

Then she snaps herself out of her maudlin imagining, opens her eyes, and comes back to the reality of the moment. Which presents her with a conundrum. Cork is *ogichidaa*, a warrior, and she is not. She is Mide, a healer. She nurtures life. Yet here she sits with a rifle in her hands, prepared to kill.

What does the Creator expect of me?

It's a question she wishes she hadn't asked herself because it weakens her resolve. And in the next moment, she spies a man moving double time along the edge of the marsh, head down, reading the trail she's left. She recognizes him, one of the two men at the campfire the night before. She looks to the east, expecting to see the second man coming, following the trail Dolores left, but no one is there. She returns her attention to the lone man.

He lifts his head from the trail signs and hesitates a moment. He's seen Dolores. And Dolores has seen him. She turns with her walking stick in her hand and starts to hobble off. The man breaks into a lope.

He's sixty yards away when Rainy breathes in, breathes out, leads him with her aim, and slowly squeezes the Winchester's trigger. The rifle bucks against her shoulder and in almost the same instant the man goes down. Rainy watches him scramble behind the protection of a tamarack, a narrow trunk that barely conceals him. She sights again on the edge of his shoulder, which is still visible. She should pull off another round, ensure that he's dead or so severely wounded that he's no longer a threat. But she can't quite bring herself to squeeze the trigger a second time. She glances east again, just to be certain that the second man isn't coming to his aid. In the moment she averts her eyes, the downed man dashes from the tamarack into the protection of a fallen pine.

Dolores has made her way behind the cover of the knoll, and she stares expectantly up at Rainy, waiting to know the outcome.

Now it becomes a waiting game. Rainy feels a sliver of relief in her thinking that she hasn't actually killed the man. The weight of murder isn't on her heart.

She begins to ponder the fact that the man is alone. What about his partner? Henry, she thinks, with a twisting of her gut. The other predator is dealing with Henry. But maybe it's not too late, she hopes desperately.

It's been a while and the man hasn't shown any movement. She begins to suspect that her shot might have been a mortal wounding after all. If that's true, then she needs to go back now and see about Henry. She lifts her rifle, rises just a bit to turn and descend the backside of the knoll.

The greenstone explodes. Rainy feels a piercing pain in her left upper arm. She drops low and continues down the slope. She checks her arm, sees blood on the sleeve of her shirt. When she pulls the sleeve back, she can see that it's a superficial wound, a slicing probably caused by a piece of the exploding greenstone.

Her instincts tell her to grab Dolores and make a run for it. But her hope for Henry has set a hook in all her thinking.

"Go on," she tells Dolores. "Stay with the creek like I told you. You'll reach Iron Lake and safety."

"What about you?"

"I'll make sure this guy won't follow you, then I'm going back for Henry."

"I can't—"

"You can. You have to. You'll slow me up too much if you go back with me. I need to get to Henry fast. Please, Dolores, just do this."

On the woman's face, Rainy can see pain. Not from the swollen ankle, she understands. Dolores hugs her, then turns and hobbles south.

Rainy crosses the creek and slips into the trees on the other side. She carefully makes her way in a wide arc that eventually brings her to a place fifty yards west of the fallen pine where the downed man took shelter. She can see him, prone behind the trunk, still alive and moving. He's gripping his right thigh and his fingers are a bloody mess. She could easily put another round into him, but at this point she knows it would be cold-blooded murder, and she's not sure she could live with that.

It's clear he's not going to be chasing Dolores, and Rainy decides that she's finished with him. It's time to see about Henry.

Despite the urgency she feels, she moves stealthily through the pines. She does her best to stay in sight of the trail she and Dolores took earlier, just in case the second man has finished his business with Henry and is now on their trail. But the landscape is rugged and sometimes she can't see the other side of the creek, and she knows she might miss the last tracker. And so, as she makes her way, she prays: *Creator, be kind.*

She returns to the lake in a little over an hour. She crosses the stones where the creek runs and finds the cold ash and char of the fire Henry built. Her great-uncle is nowhere to be seen. She calls out his name and receives no answer. She's on the verge of collapse, physically and spiritually, and all she can think of is Henry dead, his body thrown in the lake or tossed into the woods like the carcass of a worthless animal.

Her strength finally gives out, and she collapses beside the ashes.

The sun is in the western sky, and she feels as if a warm hand is on her face. She closes her eyes, thinking that she's ready to give in to the terrible finality she has imagined, give in to grief. Except she finds that she cannot. There is still some iron in her spirit that will not yield. Not yet. She opens her eyes, stands, and studies the area around the fire. Things are missing. The blanket and Dolores's clothing, which she left with Henry. Also, the old man's medicine bag. What could those monsters of men want with any of these things?

No, she decides with a burst of resolve. Henry is not dead. It is Henry who has taken the blanket and the medicine bag. And if this is true, then he must be alive and has left a trail.

She begins carefully to read the signs on the lakeshore and finally finds the faint impression of a moccasin alongside another big boot print. The toes of the prints point north, deeper into the great wilderness. Henry, she thinks, has fled, but he's being pursued by the last of the hunters.

Once again, she's filled with a desperate purpose, and without hesitation, she follows where the signs lead.

PART SIXTEEN

CORK

CHAPTER 33

When he finally reaches Fisheye Lake, Cork finds that the fire is nothing but ash and warm char. He also finds that Meloux has vanished. He tries to read the confusion of signs, prints everywhere. Some of what he sees makes sense, and some makes no sense at all.

He finds tracks heading south toward the rez—one set of moccasins and the boot prints he knows belong to Rainy. Mixed with them are the larger boot prints of the trackers. But only one of the trackers. He searches for the boot prints of the second tracker and for the set of moccasin prints Henry would have left. It takes him precious time, but at last, in the soft bed of needles at the edge of the pines, he finds what he's looking for: one print from the old man's moccasin and near it the print of a big boot. The toes of both prints are oriented to the north, deeper into the great wilderness. He speculates that Henry split from the women in an attempt to lure the trackers away and one of them followed him. It would be just like Meloux to make that sacrifice.

Cork curses himself for his fall, for the painful ribs and the broken sat phone. He should have been more careful. He should have been here sooner. He should have . . . so many things. He braces himself for the only choice he believes he has, which is to follow the tracks south, the direction Rainy and the Morriseau woman have taken. It's a decision that he knows may eat at him forever.

He turns from the ash and the char and the prints that head north into the wilderness, abandoning Meloux to his fate.

Cork plods south toward the Iron Lake Reservation, easily following the trail that the women, and also the single tracker who's after them, have left. His damaged ribs feel as if a pitchfork is stabbing at his insides. He pushes himself to move on, pushes himself to put behind him the guilt he feels for abandoning Meloux. Twice, he's heard the search plane pass overhead, but he's been under a canopy of evergreens both times with no opportunity to signal. And what would he signal except that he's alive? He has no real additional information to offer, nothing to show for his time in the wilderness but broken ribs and a broken sat phone.

The two shots he heard continue to echo in his head. He thinks about the rifle that the man they handcuffed to the tree was using, a Savage M10 Stealth fitted with a Leupold VX-2 scope. If the final tracker is similarly armed, he could easily have brought down a couple of targets at a long distance. Cork doesn't want to think about who those targets might have been.

He's gone two miles following the trail the others have broken along Fisheye Creek when he comes to the edge of a marshy area through which the creek flows. The tracks in the soft earth divide, one set heading east around the marsh and two heading west. The tracks to the east have been made by feet wearing moccasins. The tracks to the west are boot tracks. Rainy and the man who's hunting Dolores Morriseau.

He increases his pace, ignoring the pain from his angry ribs, making his way through a stand of tamaracks, following the tracks.

Until he comes to the blood. A lot of it. Splashed across a large colony of ostrich ferns, red drops hanging from the leaves like ripe berries. He can see the crushed ferns where someone must have fallen, but looking desperately around him in every direction, he can't locate the body. He moves ahead. There's a trail of blood among the boot prints, Rainy's and the last tracker's. Cork can't tell whose blood it is, and he won't let himself think about that. He comes to the place where the creek flows out of the marsh in a single thread. Moccasin prints mingle with boot prints and blood and head south along the creek. He sheds his pack, lays his rifle down, and kneels next to a tamarack to study the prints more carefully.

The bark of the tamarack explodes next to his head. Cork drops, grabs his rifle, and crawls behind the protection of the tree's trunk. The shot came from somewhere to the south, near enough that the rifle report and the bullet striking the tree were simultaneous. The narrow tamarack provides minimal protection, and Cork eyes the thick, rotting trunk of a fallen red pine a dozen yards to his right. He rises, makes a dash for the downed tree, and dives for cover just as the rifle cracks again. He lies in the lee of the trunk, struggling to breathe, his chest hurting so much that he thinks his broken rib must have punctured a lung.

The pine trunk is a good thirty feet long. Cork crawls to the far end, where roots stick out like a clawed hand. He peers through the roots. A hundred yards ahead is a rocky knoll. He can't see the shooter, but it offers the most likely cover and vantage. He brings his rifle to his shoulder and sights, waiting. A minute passes, then two.

Patience, he tells himself.

He spots the shooter's head easing around one of the rocks. He aims carefully and pulls off a round. The bullet strikes the rock and the shooter's head jerks back. Immediately, Cork rises, runs to his right, and hides himself behind a blind of thimbleberry bushes. He continues circling, tree by tree, while the shooter's rifle is silent. It takes him nearly fifteen minutes to come at the knoll from behind.

He can see the shooter now. The man is sitting with his back to the rock, head down, chin resting on his chest. The rifle is lying on the ground next to him. Cork approaches with his own rifle raised, ready to squeeze off a round if necessary. But it isn't. The man slowly lifts his head. His face is a bloody mess and a dark soaking of blood stains the entire pant leg over his right thigh.

"I made it through Afghanistan, Africa, and South America without so much as a scratch," the man says when Cork is a few feet away. "These woods are cursed."

"What's with the leg?"

"She shot me. From right here where I sit. I walked into her sights. Hell, I figured they'd just run." He shakes his head. "Logistical miscalculation. She got off a good shot, I admit. But then, she didn't have a bullet in her. At least not at that moment."

"What do you mean?"

A grin stretches his thin, pale lips. "Before they disappeared, I got off a round."

"You hit one of them?"

"Friend, I never miss."

"You missed me."

"Bleeding to death makes a difference." He nods toward the makeshift bandaging of thigh. "I'd have put a bullet in you eventually, except that shot of yours sent a rock sliver above my eye. Can't see a thing out of it now."

"Which one of the women did you hit?" Cork's afraid of the answer but desperate to know.

The man doesn't reply, but the grin grows a little broader.

"Get up."

The man shakes his head. "I'm done walking, probably for good."

"Get up."

"Or what? You'll shoot me?" He opens his arms as if inviting it.

Cork swings the rifle butt, catches him on the side of the head. "I said get up."

The man spits blood but doesn't move. "Going to beat me to death, is it? Go ahead. This is as good a place to die as any, I suppose."

"Where's Meloux?"

"The old man? My colleague is taking care of that bastard. As soon as he's finished, he'll come for you. Maybe he's already on his way."

They stare at each other. The grin fades as the man gives in to pain, and the muscles of his face contract in a display of silent agony, scarring him with deep creases. "My guess is that whichever of those bitches I hit, she's bleeding out," he says through gritted teeth. "If she's important to you, you might want to get to her before she's dead."

Everything in Cork pushes him toward pulling the trigger and killing this man. It's what he would do for a wounded beast. Instead, he takes the man's rifle.

"Wolves can smell prey from miles away," he says. "The scent of your blood will promise them an easy meal. Maybe you'll be lucky and die before they get to you."

A few hundred yards after he leaves the stranger, Cork hides the man's rifle in a sea of ferns. With his ribs damaged and strength fading, the weight of the weapon in addition to his own rifle is too great to carry. He plans to retrieve it as soon as he's able, or to send someone for it later. At the moment, his focus is on finding Rainy and Dolores Morriseau, settling the troubling question of which of them the stranger has wounded. The two women have made no attempt to hide their tracks, but there's something that deeply troubles Cork. After a while, he can see only one set of tracks, these left by moccasins. Rainy's boot prints have vanished, which increases his worry to fever pitch.

He's walked a little over half a mile when he hears what sounds like the blades of a helicopter cutting across the sky behind him. He wonders if Marsha Dross has tapped additional resources for the rescue of those still lost in the woods. If so, the chopper is flying in the wrong direction. It's heading where he's been, not where he's going. Dolores Morriseau and Rainy are in front of him. It may be only a coincidence and have nothing to do with the official search, but Cork doesn't believe in coincidence. He can't quite put it all together, and he continues south where, God willing, he'll find Rainy.

The day has grown warm, a dramatic contrast to twenty-four hours earlier, when the snowstorm swept through. Everything the storm dropped has melted away and the ground is drying rapidly under the afternoon sun. He's going so much more slowly than he would like, and his weakness drives home to him the erosion of age.

He's well into his fifties. Meloux sometimes calls him a young whippersnapper, but the Mide is a dinosaur himself, albeit a dinosaur who managed to outwit and outrun the trackers for a good long while before they caught up to him. And maybe even then he was able to delay them in order to give the women a reasonable chance of reaching the rez. But at what cost? Cork thinks of Stephen's vision of the old man lying dead, and another weight, one of overwhelming grief, settles on his shoulders.

He's plodding now, doing his best just to go on. He's stumbling through the profound shade cover under a stand of red pines when the next shot comes. The bullet bites into the bedding of pine needles that covers the ground two feet in front of him. He spins into the protection of a pine trunk, bringing his rifle to the ready.

"Police! Drop your weapon!"

He recognizes the voice of Deputy George Azevedo.

"It's me, Cork O'Connor!" he shouts.

"Throw down your rifle and show yourself with your hands raised!"

Cork does as he's been ordered and steps from behind the tree with his arms lifted high. He's still in the deep shade of the pines.

"Walk ahead until I say stop!"

He takes three steps to a place where the sun cuts through the canopy overhead and he enters a bright patch of sunlight, where he can be clearly seen.

"Stop!"

Azevedo finally shows himself, as do the other searchers, most of them familiar faces from the Iron Lake Reservation. Cork sees that Anton Morriseau has intercepted them and Dolores Morriseau is with them as well. But not Rainy. Cork's almost afraid to ask, but the words cannot be stopped.

"Where's Rainy? Why isn't she with you?"

PART SEVENTEEN

THE WOLF

CHAPTER 34

North they travel, deeper into the wilderness. The old man has already walked steadily for two days, and the pace he keeps is slow but sure. LeLoup understands that Meloux knows exactly where he's going. In Afghanistan, Africa, South America, LeLoup has followed the orders of many different men, men who flailed about in their directions and their resolve. Always, there were questions in his mind about the orders they delivered. But not with this man. There's a yielding in LeLoup that he's never felt before. It's as if he's been moving toward this old man and this moment forever.

They walk for hours, and although LeLoup knows the old man could easily hide their trail, it's clear he doesn't care now if they're being followed. The sun has dropped low in the western sky and the shadows in the woods are slanted long when, at last, they come to a flat tabletop of rock whose far edge plunges fifty feet into the water of a lake that reflects the green pines rising like walls around it and the pale blue of the sky above. The air feels especially fresh here, redolent with the scent of evergreen. LeLoup can smell the clean water, the cool mineral of the rock.

The old man finally speaks. "*Mino-bimaadiziwin.*"

"What does that mean?"

"'The way of the good life.' The answer to the question that brought you to me."

"What question?"

"We must build a fire," the old man says.

The warm day and the sun have dried the wood they gather. LeLoup goes about the business of the fire, which is second nature to him. Always prepared, he has brought a little watertight container of kitchen matches, but when he brings out the matches, the old man shakes his head and offers LeLoup flint and steel instead. LeLoup smiles, accepting the challenge.

He finds dried brown lichen on a nearby rock outcrop and uses it as tinder. The fire is soon blazing. The old man lays out his blanket near the flames. LeLoup sits on the other side of the fire. He waits for the old man to speak, to teach, but as the light slowly fades, the old man sits gazing at the lake.

For more than an hour, they sit this way in silence. LeLoup feeds the fire. The old man seems lost in a trance. Finally LeLoup's stomach grumbles, a noise so loud in the stillness of the place that it seems to him like thunder. He takes what's left of the jerky he's brought and holds out the other half to Meloux. The old man eyes the offering, turns from the lake, and accepts the food. But when LeLoup prepares to eat the jerky he's left for himself, the old man says, "No. You will fast."

LeLoup hands over the last of his food.

"Your name," the old man says.

"LeLoup."

"The wolf," the old man says, translating into English the meaning of this French name. "A noble animal, brother to the Anishinaabeg. And your clan. Let me guess. Ma'iingan," the old man says, using the Ojibwe word for "wolf."

"The clan I chose for myself," LeLoup says. "I never knew my people. I don't know my real clan."

"And LeLoup?"

"I have no birth certificate. I was named by the white people in the orphanage where I was raised. I hated the name they gave me. When I left the orphanage, I chose a new one for myself."

"LeLoup is a good name. But I find it strange that you would be in the company of such lesser beasts. Those other men, I believe they did not understand you."

"I've been in the company of men like them most of my life. Whether they understand me has never been important."

"I think that is not true," the old man says. "It is easy to see that your spirit is a lonely one."

"I know you from dreams. Not you exactly. I don't know how to explain it. But the moment I saw you today, I knew you."

"It is a great web that the Creator spins, and within it, we are all connected. Dreams are sometimes the threads of that connection. In dreams, Ma'iingan, I have seen you, too."

In the same way LeLoup has been awaiting this old man, the old man has been waiting for him. This new knowledge fills LeLoup with a warmth he's never known before. Tears flood his eyes and stream down his cheeks. He has never wept in front of another man, never shown any weakness. But now he lets the tears flow freely.

"You told me I've come to learn something. What is that?"

"I will do my best to help you find the answer for yourself. We must crack you open first. Fasting is the beginning. And tears are good, too."

LeLoup stands, overwhelmed by an urge to embrace the old man.

"Move and I'll shoot you."

The voice at his back is sharp with outrage and cold with purpose. LeLoup freezes.

"Hands behind your head and turn this way, slowly."

He does as he's been instructed and finds a woman standing at the edge of the rock tabletop, a rifle snugged against her shoulder, the barrel leveled on his chest.

Behind him, he hears the old man laugh. "It is good that you have come, Niece. We can use your help."

CHAPTER 35

"Who are you?" the woman demands.

"Who are you?" LeLoup replies.

"Are you okay, Uncle Henry?"

"I am fine. There is no need for the rifle."

She doesn't appear to believe him, and her eyes are nothing but darkness as she regards LeLoup. "I shot your friend and I'll shoot you, too, if you move a muscle."

LeLoup is truly amazed. "You shot Kimball?"

"Whatever his name was, he won't be tracking anyone for a while."

"Dolores Morriseau, is she safe?" the old man asks.

"She should be nearing the reservation by now," the woman says.

"Lower your rifle. This man has come for our help."

"Help?" Her face is a mask of disbelief. "They've been doing their best to kill us, Uncle Henry."

"Has this man harmed us?" the old man asks.

"That was certainly his intent. Wasn't it?" she demands of LeLoup.

"We were after the Morriseau woman. You were just in the way."

"Niece, I will not tell you again," the old man says, this time in a voice of steel. "Lower your rifle. This man is no threat."

LeLoup nods. "It's true. I won't harm you. And the man you shot wasn't my friend."

"Who was he?"

"If you stop pointing that rifle barrel, I'll explain."

He can tell it remains a struggle, but at last, she eases the rifle stock from her shoulder and lowers the weapon. It's still in her hands, and LeLoup knows that if he made a move toward her, he'd be dead in an instant. He respects her for this.

"Sit," she says.

LeLoup eases himself down into the place he sat before. The woman walks to the other side of the fire and sits beside the old man. She continues to eye LeLoup with deep suspicion. "Explain," she says.

"It's what I do," LeLoup replies. "Or did."

"Killing?" the woman says coldly.

"Sometimes, that's been a part of it."

"Women and old men?"

"Mostly soldiers, militants, drug runners. But sometimes . . ." He can't look into her accusing eyes, because she's right. In war, sometimes the innocent die, and he can't say for sure that he was never a part of that.

"You're a soldier?"

"Was. A paid security consultant now."

"A mercenary," she says as if spitting phlegm. "Who hired you and what do they want with Dolores?"

"Kimball, the man you shot, hired me. I have no idea who he was working for. They want the woman because they think she can tell them where her husband is."

"What do they want with him?"

"I don't know. But it's important enough they're willing to kill to get to him."

"Does it have to do with Katie?"

"Who's Katie?"

She studies him intently, and he understands that she's trying to read him. He's done the same when interrogating a prisoner.

"It is the truth, Niece," the old man says.

"And you have no idea where her husband is?"

"I did, but I don't know now. A week ago, I tracked him to a remote cabin in Manitoba, north of Winnipeg. We were supposed to surprise him there, but something went wrong. He got away. The Morriseau woman was the best lead Kimball had left."

"We need to get you back to Aurora. You have to tell our sheriff what you know about all this."

"No," LeLoup says.

"No?" The woman's hands tighten around her rifle.

The old man intervenes. "Not until he has what he came for, Niece."

"Which is what?"

"The answer to a question his heart has been asking forever. You and I, we will help him find that answer."

"We don't have time, Uncle Henry."

"Look at him, Niece. Do you believe he will leave without it?"

The woman's eyes, dark and hard, drill LeLoup. Smoke from the fire rises up between them, and it's as if they look at each other through a curtain. Then something in her eyes changes, softens, yields.

"*Mino-bimaadiziwin*," she says.

The old man nods. "Yes."

*   *   *

They have blackened him with char from the fire. The old man has taken leaves and root from his medicine bag and a small copper cup. In the cup, the woman has fetched water from the lake below, which she's mixed with the leaves and root and has boiled. She's given LeLoup the hot mixture to drink. It's a bitter brew, and it settles uncomfortably in his stomach. As night descends, LeLoup lies back on the blanket they have spread for him near the fire and stares up at the stars. The heavens have always been a constant in his life, a truer guide than any compass. He listens to the old man and the woman sing prayers in a language that he does not understand but that speaks to him in a mysterious way. His vision becomes unfocused. The stars blur into lines like the silver threads of a web. A great warm hand surrounds and cradles him. And LeLoup leaves the world.

He wakes standing in a forest beneath a huge, brilliant full moon. The floor of the forest is splattered with shadow and silver. His knife is in his hand. He has no idea how he came to be in this place, no memory of what preceded. As he stands wondering, a dark shape approaches, moving low and steadily among the shadows. When it finally enters the moonlight, LeLoup sees that it is a wolf. They stare at each other without fear. The wolf turns and trots away. LeLoup follows.

The wolf guides him to the edge of a clearing lit by glaring moonlight. The eyes of the wolf, amber in the glow, look back at LeLoup. He understands and steps forward into the clearing. When he glances back, the wolf is gone.

LeLoup stands waiting, something he's good at. He feels as if his whole life has been a great waiting. Waiting for the appearance of someone who could tell him who he is and where he came from. Waiting to see clearly the path he was meant to walk. Waiting for the warm affection of another human heart. Waiting to know the reason he has always felt like a soul alone in the universe.

But this night, his waiting is brief, because soon a beast steps from the dark on the far side of the clearing and enters the silver glare of the moon. It is a huge creature, manlike in its stature but covered in fur and surrounded by the stench of rotted meat. Its eyes glow like the coals of a fire. It bares its long, yellow fangs, and the moment before it springs toward him, it calls him by his name: "Prophet."

They collide in the center of the clearing. The beast is twice his size and far more powerful than anything LeLoup could have imagined. It lifts and hurls him to the ground. Its clawed hands grab at him, but he rolls from its reach and leaps to his feet. Although the beast is powerful, its great size makes it slow. When it lunges, LeLoup spins easily away. As he slips under the grasp of the beast, he slides the blade of his knife across its belly. The howl of pain that follows is deafening.

LeLoup dances away and crouches. The beast turns and comes at him. Once again, LeLoup evades the attack and manages another slash across its broad, hairy belly. But this time the creature is quicker in its recovery, and before LeLoup is clear, he's once more in the grip of a clawed hand. This time the great beast sinks its teeth into his shoulder. LeLoup screams, pulls free, and with a summoning of all his strength, drives the blade of his knife into the creature's throat. He's bathed in the blood that spews forth. The creature stumbles back, grabbing at its neck. It totters. The fire in its eyes dies. The beast falls and lies unmoving at LeLoup's feet.

LeLoup lifts his face to the full moon and gives out the triumphant howl of a wolf.

*   *   *

He wakes. There is no moon above him, only a black sea filled with stars. He lies among the grasses and wildflowers of a small clearing. The night is quiet. The screams of the beast and his own screams are nothing but a memory. The knife is still in the grip of his right hand, but it is bloodless. With his left hand, he carefully checks himself where the beast's teeth sank deep into his skin. Nothing, no rending of the flesh, not even any pain. His body is the same, but inside him, something has changed. The profound sense of waiting, which has been his constant companion and his tormentor all his life, has vanished.

LeLoup knows his true name: Prophet. It is a relief but still a mystery to him. He rises from the ground. Far away through the trees, he can see the flicker of a campfire. He heads toward the flames, walking like a man reborn.

PART EIGHTEEN

RAINY

CHAPTER 36

Rainy sits by the fire watching LeLoup sleep. She's torn. For days, the man has been her relentless hunter. One of his companions tried to kill her, and she was driven to an act that runs contrary to all her sensibility as a healer, both nurse and Mide. What she has seen in LeLoup is a spirit that is like the sharp edge of a bloodied knife, a spirit that delivers death. But Henry has told her that there is another spirit in him, a deeper, truer spirit, that LeLoup is a man who has always been at war with himself, a man searching for peace.

She and Henry have finished singing their prayers, and she is tired and silent.

"You do not speak, Niece. But I can read your mind."

"What am I thinking, Uncle Henry?"

"That you have chosen to help the enemy."

"I get the feeling he's a man not just used to killing but comfortable with killing. I would be lying if I said he doesn't scare me."

"But you are a woman comfortable with being scared."

"I don't know about that, Uncle Henry."

"A healer's heart is always afraid. It is a great responsibility when a human being puts a life into your hands or asks for the healing of a broken spirit."

"Are you afraid?"

"I always feel as if I am walking a spider's thread."

"What holds you up?"

"A belief in what keeps that thread strong."

"It's never broken?"

"I have failed, of course, fallen. That is what it is to be human. To do your best and still fall. But the thread itself has never failed, only my own belief in it."

LeLoup stirs, leaps suddenly up as if exploding from the ground. He stares at Rainy and Henry like a man possessed. "I will find you! I will kill you!"

"We are not your enemies," Henry says.

But LeLoup seems not to hear. He reaches to the sheath on his belt and snatches a long-bladed knife. He thrusts it forward, the steel a burning reflection of the fire. "I will kill you!"

Adrenaline shoots through Rainy and she grabs for the rifle lying next to her. But Henry says, "Niece," and holds up a hand. She hesitates, her fingers inches from her weapon.

LeLoup spins away and faces the dark wilderness. Then he runs, disappearing into the night.

Rainy's body is shaking. She stares where LeLoup has gone, expecting any moment for him to burst again into the firelight and attack. But minutes pass and he doesn't return.

"Uncle Henry?" she asks.

"He has been called to battle."

"Should we go after him?"

"The battle is his. We have done what we can for the moment. Now there is only the waiting."

*   *   *

An hour passes, then two. Rainy feeds the fire and watches the darkness among the trees. The night is still. The smoke rises straight as a tree trunk toward the heavens. Henry sits nodding, at the edge of sleep. She can't imagine what keeps him upright. He has already endured far more than she thought possible for any human being of his great age. But then, he has always been a man full of surprises.

She's startled when LeLoup steps into the firelight. He has washed the char from his face, and although he looks exhausted, there is a sense of new life about him. Meloux rouses and they watch the man approach. He's the same man who ran into the forest, and yet he is not. Rainy senses a dramatic change, sees a different look in his eyes, in his whole aspect. He sits with them at the fire, in silence for a long while.

"I know my true name," he finally tells them. "But I don't know what it means."

"What name?" Henry asks.

"Prophet."

Rainy leans toward him. "How do you know?"

"It called me by that name."

"It?" Rainy asks.

"The beast."

"Ah," Henry says, as if he understands, then nods. "Prophet."

"I'm no prophet."

"On the path behind you, no," Henry tells him. "Your life now is about the path ahead."

"I don't understand. But one thing I do know. I have to set things right. There's still killing ahead."

"The nature of a wolf," Henry says.

LeLoup lifts his rifle and stands before Henry. "Your people will come looking for me. They can't find me until I do what I have to."

Henry nods.

LeLoup gazes deeply into the eyes of the ancient Mide. "It's just as you said. I feel as if I've been walking toward you my whole life. Thank you."

"*Kitchi-Ottiziwin*," Rainy says to him.

"What does that mean?"

"It's an Ojibwe word. It means 'to live and express yourself kindly and fully from the heart.'"

"There are things I have to do first, then I'll try," he promises. He strides away from the fire. Rainy watches him until he's been eaten by the night. When she looks back at Henry, the old man has laid himself down on his blanket as if preparing to sleep.

"Do you understand where he's going, Uncle Henry?"

"It is not important for me to understand. The wolf has found his name and his true spirit and that will guide his feet."

The nature of a wolf, Henry said. Rainy wonders what LeLoup is hunting now that requires killing before he can set himself on the way to *Kitchi-Ottiziwin.* And she wonders as well why Henry, whose life is about healing, has seemed to sanction it.

She doesn't ponder this long before she hears a crunching in the underbrush beyond the firelight, the approach of footsteps. Henry hears it, too, and sits up.

"The wolf?" she asks.

Henry shakes his head.

Rainy lifts her rifle and calls out, "Who's there?"

A moment passes, then a reply comes, "Are you okay, Rainy?"

She knows that voice intimately and her heart nearly bursts with joy.

- PART NINETEEN -

CORK

CHAPTER 37

Dolores Morriseau is safely on her way out of the wilderness, accompanied by several of the searchers. Cork and Anton Morriseau have headed back toward Fisheye Lake. Deputy Azevedo and the rest of the search party are with them.

They reach the place where Cork abandoned the wounded man. He's gone. They spend precious time looking for the trail he should have left. Finally, Azevedo finds a good deal of crushed vegetation in a flat, open area on the other side of the creek.

"I heard a chopper," Cork tells him. Then says, "We've wasted enough time here. We need to be moving."

At Fisheye Lake, it's Anton Morriseau who finds Rainy's small boot print among vegetation a bit north of the cold ash of the fire someone built on the lakeshore. There are two other prints, as well—belonging to Meloux and the last of the hunters. At first the trail is easy for Cork and the others with him. The signs are surprisingly clear, as if hiding is no longer an issue. But what's even more important to Cork is that they find no blood, not a drop. He holds to the hope that the man Rainy wounded was mistaken or lying when he swore he'd put a bullet in her. *No blood,* he thinks to himself over and over while he and Anton Morriseau and the other searchers struggle to find the trail north of Fisheye Lake. *No blood* has become his mantra.

As daylight fails, the signs begin to disappear into the shadow of night. Cork has brought out his flashlight, as have the others. Long, bright fingers poke at the ground and into the underbrush. He wishes he'd brought a light with the option of a red beam, which would allow him to see more easily any prints that have been left. At first, the beams are concentrated on the ground, searching for prints, but as the night deepens, they swing more wildly in a desperate attempt to find signs in the underbrush.

Cork tells himself that Rainy is whole and healthy and her aim is sure. She can take care of herself. But in the back of his mind is a frightened voice reminding him that only a few years ago, despite a flood of prayers, he lost his first wife, his beloved Jo, to violence.

Finally, Deputy George Azevedo says the obvious. "We've lost the trail. It's no use going on tonight. We'll just get more lost."

"You're thinking we stop here for the night?" Cork says. They're at the edge of a lake that on the topo map is called Minnow. Like its name, it's small, and now reflects a blue-black sky filling with stars.

"The search plane will be out first thing in the morning," Azevedo assures him. "And daylight will help us pick up the trail again."

Cork shakes his head. "I'm not waiting another night to find Rainy and Henry."

"I understand how you feel," Azevedo says. "But this is my call."

"Fine," Cork tells him. "You stop here. I'm going on."

"That's a foolish move and you know it," Azevedo says. "There's no way you can track them now, not in this dark."

"I've got to try, George."

"Let me check in with the sheriff first," Azevedo insists. "Maybe there's some helpful news."

Azevedo makes the call and explains the situation. He hands the sat phone to Cork.

"I understand that you're desperate to find them," Dross tells him. "But going on alone is stupid and dangerous and you know it."

"Henry tells me that if I listen, the woods will speak to me. I'm ready to listen."

"Stay with Azevedo, Cork. I don't want you walking blindly into some disaster because of some nonsense Henry told you."

"I'm going," Cork says.

"Tell her I'm going, too," Morriseau says.

Cork delivers the message. When she replies, "Give the phone to Azevedo," Cork can hear the splinters of iron in her voice.

Azevedo listens, signs off, and says, "Go on if you think you have to. I have a responsibility for the safety of the others. We'll pick up the trail tomorrow and follow it. I hope we don't lose you, too." He gives Cork a sat phone. "Stay in touch."

They are only fifteen miles from the reservation, only fifteen miles from the safety of Allouette, but they might as well be on the other side of the earth, Cork thinks as he makes his way through the dark. With every breath, his damaged ribs torture him. Morriseau walks beside him. They move slowly, searching the ground for prints, the underbrush for branches broken in the passage of others before them, the woods for any small sign of Rainy and Henry and the damn tracker. Cork's head is telling him this is stupid and dangerous, just as Dross and Azevedo said. But he's trying not to listen to his head. He's trying to shut out all the voices there. He wants desperately to listen to the woods, to hear the spirits that

Henry has promised will speak to him. He believes in Henry, and despite the voice of doubt that tries to capture his attention, he believes in the spirits.

When he was ten years old, Cork went into the Boundary Waters with his father and his father's good friend Sam Winter Moon. They were gone ten days. It wasn't his first trip into the wilderness, but it was the longest up till then. The more time passed, the less he felt connected to all that he'd left behind. It was as if the woods had always been his home. Cork's father had brought a topo map of the area, but Sam Winter Moon never once referred to it.

"How do you know where we're going?" Cork had asked him one night as they sat around the campfire.

"The woods tell me," Sam had replied.

"They talk to you?"

"Sure. They talk to you, too. You're just not listening."

"I don't get it," Cork said.

"Everything here is alive with spirit," Sam told him. "If you're able to quiet all the noise inside your head, what you hear is a chorus of voices."

"You mean like birds and stuff."

"Birds have a voice. But so do the pine trees and the tamaracks and the moccasin flowers."

Cork looked to his father for confirmation. "I'm an Irish kid from Chicago, Son. I know concrete and alleyways. Don't ask me about the woods."

Cork had done his best to listen. He believed in the spirits and believed what Sam told him, but although he tried to listen, in the end he seemed deaf, which was a great disappointment.

Now he's trying desperately to blot out all the noise of his thinking, to create a silence he hopes might be filled with the voice of the wilderness guiding him.

But it's Morriseau's voice that intrudes. "I've heard you wore a badge once. True?"

"I was sheriff for a while a few years back. Deputy before that. Chicago cop before that."

"Why'd you quit, you don't mind me asking?"

"Too hard on my family. I prefer the quiet of making burgers for a living. Why are you a tribal cop, you don't mind my asking? Doesn't matter that you're Ojibwe, that badge still puts you at odds with lots of your own people."

"I think of it as doing my best to make sure justice has a fair shot in my community."

"Doesn't make you popular, I'd guess."

"Among a certain element. I know the Iron Lake Reservation doesn't have a tribal police force. Maybe it's time that it did. Could use a man with Ojibwe blood in him and a good deal of law enforcement experience."

"You jockeying for the job?" Cork asks.

"I was thinking of you."

"Like I said, I prefer flipping burgers." Cork stops dead in his tracks, turns off his flashlight, and whispers, "Kill your light."

In the utter dark that follows, Cork confirms what he thought he'd seen. Among the trees far ahead, a campfire flickers.

"You go right, I'll go left," Cork whispers.

"In this dark, it's gonna be impossible to approach quietly. I think we should wait for daylight, make our move then."

"Who knows what might happen to Rainy and Henry in the meantime."

"It might not be them. It could just be innocent campers."

"Then be careful with that rifle of yours."

"You're sure you want to do it this way?"

"I'm sure."

"All right."

Morriseau splits away, and Cork can hear the scrape of brush against his clothing as he goes. The man's right. Surprise is going to be impossible. But waiting until morning is out of the question. Cork creeps to the left and begins his own approach to the campfire.

When he's still thirty yards away, a familiar voice calls out, "Who's there?"

Dear God, it's Rainy. Cork's heart leaps and he wants to shout for joy. Instead, he calls back, "Are you okay, Rainy?"

"I am."

"And Henry?"

"He's here, too. We're both fine."

"There's been a man tracking you."

"We know."

"Where is he?"

"Come to the fire and we'll explain."

Despite her assurances, Cork moves cautiously. At last, he steps into the firelight. Henry Meloux sits on the far side, his old face illuminated by the flames. Rainy is standing, and as soon as she sees Cork, she runs and throws her arms around him. He's carrying his rifle and pack, and the embrace is awkward. His ribs still hurt like crazy, but the feel of Rainy in his arms is like holding on to heaven.

"I've been tracking you for days," he says, his cheek against her hair. "I thought . . . I was afraid . . ."

"It's all right. I'm fine."

Cork puts her at arm's length, sees the blood that has soaked her sleeve. "He wasn't lying. He shot you."

"A rock sliver nicked me, that's all," she assures him. "Is he . . . ?"

"You didn't kill him," he tells her. "Just a bad leg wound."

"Thank God for that. He's in custody?"

Cork shakes his head. "I should have killed him, but I didn't. When I came back with Azevedo and the others, he was gone."

"With that bullet through his leg, he couldn't have gone far."

"I heard a chopper. I don't know how he managed it, but he may have gotten himself airlifted out. We would have searched for him, but we came for you instead. Anton!" he calls into the trees. "It's okay. They're safe."

Morriseau slides from the dark. His eyes take in the whole of the scene. "Where's the tracker?"

"Sit by the fire," Henry says. "We need to explain a few things."

CHAPTER 38

"Do not worry about the wolf," Henry says after Cork and Morriseau have seated themselves. "He is no threat to us now."

"What did you do to him?" Cork asks.

"Not a thing," Henry answers.

"Then where is he, *Mishomis*?" Morriseau asks, calling the old man "Grandfather" in the way of respect.

"Anton Morriseau." Henry smiles. "It is good to see you again. Your family is well?"

"Not really. We're worried about my brother, Lou. We haven't heard from him for a while."

Henry nods. "Cause for worry, a silent brother, a silent son. I do not have any news to share with you."

"What about the tracker?" Cork says.

"First, tell me about Dolores Morriseau. Is she safe?" Henry asks.

Cork explains that some of the search party have taken her back to safety. He tells again in more detail of returning to the knoll where he'd found the man Rainy shot, but the man was no longer there. Finally, he gets to Azevedo and the decision to halt the search for the night.

"But you kept coming in the dark," Henry says. "How did you find us?"

"Dumb luck," Cork says.

"Or maybe you listened to the spirits." Then Henry smiles. "But sometimes dumb luck helps."

"About the last tracker," Cork says.

Henry's eyes settle on the flames of the campfire. "We can say nothing about the wolf."

"You called him that before. Why?" Cork asks.

"His name is LeLoup," Rainy explains.

"It is the name he has chosen," Henry says. "He believes he is one of The People. He has embraced the Wolf Clan."

"He's Shinnob?" Morriseau says. "What the hell was he doing with those other cutthroats?"

"It was part of his journey, the road the Creator set before him."

"I know the road law enforcement will set before him," Cork says.

"And that is why we will tell you nothing more about him."

"He was here." Cork looks beyond the edge of the hard, flat rock above the lake. "But he's gone somewhere." He drills Rainy with a look of steel. "Where?"

"Cork, you have to understand I have an obligation. We have an obligation," she says, nodding toward the old Mide. "LeLoup has asked for our help."

"Yeah, right after he tried to kill you."

"He did not threaten us," Henry says. "In fact, he saved my life. The man my niece shot wanted to shoot me. The wolf stopped him."

"So, you just let him go?" Cork is unable to hide his anger. He casts an accusing look at Rainy.

"We didn't just let him go," Rainy replies calmly. "We did what we could for him first."

"And what was that?"

"We helped him see his true spirit," Henry says. "And that is all we will tell you."

"What if he doubles back and runs into Azevedo and the others who are out here trying to help find you?" Cork is still feeling the heat of anger. "What if he kills some of them or is killed himself? How will you have helped then?"

"He won't," Rainy says.

"And you know this how?"

"He's a different man now."

"He's a killer, believe me."

"Why are you so certain?" Rainy asks this gently, but her tone is like a needle pricking at Cork.

"Christ, Rainy, that man led those goons right to you. You're lucky they didn't murder all of you."

"I don't know about the other men, Cork. But I do know about this one. He's no threat to us or to Azevedo and the others. I give you my word."

Which is the death blow to all of Cork's arguments. He knows Rainy, trusts Rainy. He understands that there is nothing for him but to accept her promise. He looks at the black lake below, a mirror of the stars. "So, he's out there somewhere alone, our wolf."

Henry gives his head a slow shake. "Not alone, Corcoran O'Connor."

Cork gives him a questioning look.

"Because he listens," the old Mide answers.

*   *   *

Cork has called Dross on the sat phone Azevedo handed him. He's given her his location and Dross has promised a floatplane will be dispatched first thing in the morning to pick them up.

Now he and Rainy share a blanket on a soft bed of pine needles Rainy has gathered. Before they lay down for the night, she brewed a tea to help ease the pain of his ribs. "Not broken," she told him with the certainty of her training as a nurse. "Just bruised, I think. Give it a week or two and you'll feel like your old self. I'm surprised you were able to bushwhack your way here. It must have been excruciating."

"I was afraid for you."

"I know." She rolls to him and kisses his cheek. "*Ogichidaa.*"

"If it hadn't been for Henry, you'd all be dead."

"If it hadn't been for Uncle Henry, none of us would have been out here in the first place."

"What do you mean?"

"He told me the men didn't come because of Dolores. They came because of him. Their spirits, their fates, were somehow tied to his."

"It seems true for the wolf, anyway."

"Those long walks he's been taking in the forest, those nights he hasn't returned, he told me he's been looking back, and what he sees is a path often splashed with blood."

"I look at my past and I see the same thing."

"You're *ogichidaa,* a warrior. Uncle Henry is a healer."

"And a person can't be both?"

"Of course. But that doesn't mean it's easy, especially when the two spirits are at odds."

"And Henry is at odds with himself?" Cork gives a little laugh.

"If there's anybody who's been certain of what the Creator meant him to do, it's Henry."

"He's standing at a threshold, Cork. He's hesitating between two worlds."

"This one and the next? Stephen's vision?"

"I think so."

"Rainy, that old man just walked through the wilderness for more than two days straight. I know people half his age who couldn't do that. When Marsha told me the search plane had seen Henry's body lying beside Fisheye Lake, I figured that was Stephen's vision. The whole of it."

Rainy says, "I'm not sure Uncle Henry interprets it the same way."

"All right, I understand your concern for your uncle, but my concern is for you. Are you okay? Really?"

"I'm okay. Really."

"If those bastards had harmed you . . ."

"They didn't. I'm here, with you, in one piece. You got hurt far worse than I did." She touches his injured ribs and he winces. "I'll make it all better. Soon. I promise." She kisses him again but not on the cheek this time, and not so gently.

- PART TWENTY -

STEPHEN

CHAPTER 39

Night has settled, moonless, and the landscape Stephen and Belle pass through on their drive north is a curtain of dark jeweled with the solitary yard lights from isolated farmhouses. They've both been quiet a long time. A lot to process.

Finally, Stephen says, "Her."

Belle is behind the wheel. After a few moments pass, as if bringing herself out of her own deep thoughts, she replies, "What?"

"I keep coming back to Catie and what that guy Orlock said back at your brother's house. When I told him that we thought someone wanted her dead, he said, 'Her?' It was a question. Like he was surprised by the gender."

"Catie's a man?"

"Or maybe not a person at all."

"What then?"

"Let me take a look at the map again." He clicks on the overhead light and unfolds the map of Canada.

"This spiderweb of lines," he says. "I suppose they could be oil pipelines. So what those guys said about a May tenth attack could be true. Think about all the uproar over production and transport here to the States. Keystone, Enbridge. Oil production is killing the environment in Canada. It's not hard to believe that some big protest action might happen."

"I'm just pointing out once again that none of the lines go near the tar sands."

"Okay, natural gas maybe. Or what if it's routes for transporting something really lethal. Like spent nuclear fuel. Or maybe uranium ore. Doesn't Canada have huge reserves of that?"

"Maybe. I don't know."

Stephen turns the map over and stares at the bold, black scrawl on the other side. "Kill Catie," he says out loud. He ponders a moment, then says, "All caps."

"What?" Belle glances at him.

"It's written in all caps."

"So?"

"Maybe it's an acronym."

"For what?"

"Let's see."

Stephen pulls out his cell phone and searches for *killcatie*.

"Well?" Belle asks after a minute.

"Hits for *KillKatie* with a *K*, but nothing with a *C*."

"Try just *Catie*."

Stephen keys in that search term. "Here we go. Something in Canada."

"What?"

Stephen reads from his phone screen, "'CATIE, Canada's source for HIV and hepatitis C information.' Never mind." He goes back to the search page. "Centro Agronómico Tropical de Investigación y Enseñanza," he reads haltingly. "Something to do with agriculture in Central America, so probably not what we're looking for." He scrolls for a while, then shakes his head. "There are like twenty-one million results, seriously."

He turns off the overhead light, and once again, they find themselves in darkness.

"Smuggling," Belle says. "Could that really be what the lines are about?"

"He's your brother. What do you think?"

She shakes her head. "Doesn't make sense."

"Border Patrol, Canadian Security and Intelligence, and who- ever all those men in black were at your brother's house. May tenth. That's just a few days away, Belle. Something big is going down, and your brother's at the heart of it."

"We have to find Lou," Belle says. "That's all there is to it."

"Okay. He went to Canada, we know that. Did he come back?"

"If he did, it wasn't to his house."

"Or your parents' house. So where else? Does he have friends? Someone who could hide him?"

"Probably, but I don't know who."

"Okay, if he didn't come back, where could he be in Canada?"

Stephen gets a call while Belle is thinking. It's Dross. "We have Dolores Morriseau. She's safe."

"Thank God. What about Rainy and Henry?"

"They got separated, but your dad's found them. They're both safe. We'll be flying them out in the morning."

"And the guys hunting them?"

"We have one in custody, but he's not talking. The others are still out there. We'll keep looking. How about you? Anything to report."

He fills her in on the events at Lou Morriseau's home. "We're on our way back to Bena, to Belle's parents' place. If we come up with anything, we'll let you know."

After he's ended the call, he gives Belle the hopeful news.

"But we still have to find Lou," she says.

"Okay, like I said, if he's in Canada, do you have any idea where he could be hiding?"

Belle glances at him, and in the faint glow from the dashboard, he sees her smile. "As a matter of fact, I do."

They're driving along the western shore of Lake Mille Lacs, one of the largest lakes in the state. On a windy, moonlit night, the water would be a reflection of shattered moonbeams, a scatter of glittering diamonds on an ebony blanket. But there is no moon, and beside them is only a vast, black emptiness, which Stephen stares at as Belle explains.

"Those two guys from Canadian Intelligence and whatever said Lou was in Winnipeg recently. I told you my father is from Canada. He comes from the Shoal Lake Forty Reserve, about a hundred miles east of Winnipeg. We still have a house there. We used to go a lot when I was a kid but not so much anymore. Or at least I don't. Law school and all. But my folks and Anton still go. And if Lou was looking for a place to hide . . . well, it's worth checking out, don't you think?"

Stephen looks away from the emptiness beside them, studies Belle's silhouette in the glow of the dashboard, sees her turn her hopeful face toward his. He feels a sudden ache, a nameless longing. Some of it is physical—Belle is attractive. Some of it is admiration—Belle is smart and committed to good causes. But it seems to come from a deeper place, an emptiness inside him waiting to be filled.

"I think . . ." But he swallows what he really wants to say and instead says, "Sure."

It's nearing midnight when they arrive in Bena. Belle has called ahead, and Vernon and Minnie Morriseau are up and waiting for them. Minnie has made tea, and they sit around the kitchen table, trying to make sense of things.

"Lou's always been a big player," Vernon says. "But this time, it looks like he's in over his head."

"Guns, ammunition, explosives. I don't believe it for a moment," Minnie says. "That's not Lou. He's done so well in his real estate dealings, why would he become involved in smuggling?"

"They didn't say he's involved in the actual smuggling," Vernon clarifies. "Only that they believe he has important information."

"Did they mention May tenth?" Stephen asks.

Vernon shakes his head. "Why?"

"The guys who claimed to be from Canadian Intelligence and Security told us they believed activists are planning some kind of major disruption of oil pipelines. We think that might be the day."

"Did they tell you how they know about Lou's involvement?" Vernon asks.

"They said they couldn't divulge that."

"So, they could have been lying," Minnie says.

"A lot of that going around," Stephen says.

"Lying about his involvement or the smuggling or what?" Vernon asks.

Before anyone can reply, the doorbell rings. Vernon glances at the clock on the kitchen wall. "Awful late for a visit."

They stand together and walk to the living room. Minnie goes to a front window, parts the curtains a crack. "Too dark. I can't see who it is. Turn on the porch light, Vernon." When he does, Minnie says, "It's a young woman."

"Anyone with her?" Stephen asks.

"Alone, as nearly as I can tell."

The doorbell rings again. Vernon opens the door to their visitor. "Yes?"

She's still outside and Stephen can't see her, but he hears her reply. "I'm looking for Lou Morriseau. I'm a friend."

"He's not here."

"Do you know where he might be?"

"Would you like to come in?"

"Thank you."

She appears to be in her late twenties or early thirties. She's Native. Her eyes are brown, her hair dark as a raven's wing, the ridges of her cheekbones high and proud. She wears jeans and a jean jacket with a pattern of colorful feathers stitched across the front. She scans the gathering.

"My name's Tanya. Tanya Baptiste. Like I said, I'm a friend of Lou." Her eyes settle on Belle. "You must be Belle. He's told me a lot about you."

"What do you want with my son?" Minnie asks.

"I need to talk to him," Tanya says. "It's important."

"Talk to him about what?" Vernon says.

She hesitates as if struggling with an important decision. Finally, she says, "Catie."

CHAPTER 40

After a long moment of silence, Stephen says, "Do you have some identification?"

From a small, beaded purse that hangs over her shoulder, the visitor takes out a wallet. From the wallet she pulls a driver's license. It confirms that her name is Tanya Marie Baptiste. She's twenty-nine years old and lives in Winnipeg. She's an organ donor.

"You're First Nation," Vernon says.

"Beaver Lake Cree."

"How do you know my brother?" Belle asks.

"He came to us with important information."

"Us?"

"The group I work with. A loose connection of like-minded people. All First Nation."

"Got a name for these like-minded people?" Stephen asks.

"Earth Children United."

"Never heard of you."

"Not surprising. We try to stay below the radar. The government is always prying at the edges of indigenous organizations. They see insurrection everywhere."

"But this isn't about insurrection?" Belle asks.

Tanya shakes her head. "It's about a grand scheme that will wreak havoc on the environment of Canada."

"What kind of scheme?"

"To tap the largest reservoir of natural gas in North America and ruin the Arctic in the process."

"Whoa," Stephen says.

"I think we need to sit down," Minnie suggests.

They move back into the kitchen, where the map with black lines is still open on the table. Tanya eyes it and says with a deep of sadness, "That map was drawn by a dead man." She sees the looks of horror on their faces and quickly adds, "Not Lou."

"Sit," Vernon says. It's more an order than an invitation, and Tanya takes a seat.

The others return to their chairs.

"Tell us about Catie," Belle says.

"And the dead man," Vernon adds.

Tanya studies the map. "Do you know anything about Catie?"

"We had a break-in last night," Belle says. "And today we had a visit from a couple of men claiming to be from Canadian Intelligence and Security. When we mentioned Catie, their eyes lit up."

"And two men from Border Patrol paid us a visit this afternoon," Minnie says. "But they claimed it was about smuggling."

"A lot of fingers in this pie," Tanya says. "And a lot of subterfuge."

"Who is Catie?" Belle asks.

"She doesn't exist," Tanya replies.

"Hard to believe." Stephen turns the map over, showing her the scrawled *KILLCATIE*.

"What I mean is that's not her real name. We thought she was one of us, but we know now she was an operative for the other side.

Monte, the man who wrote that, meant it for Lou. Probably as both information and a warning."

"You say you're working with my son," Vernon says. It's clear he's not convinced.

"For a few months now."

"Doing what exactly?"

"Trying to stop this ecological disaster."

"Explain," Vernon says.

Tanya takes a deep breath before diving in. "It's an agreement between governments, yours and ours, and some of the largest oil companies in North America. The vast gas reserves in the Canadian Arctic have been known about for years, but the issue of drilling has been surrounded by all kinds of controversy. We know now that deals have been struck behind closed doors involving lots of money under the table. Legislation has already been passed clearing the way for drilling, transport, and processing."

"That kind of legislation over an issue as sensitive as this, wouldn't it have become public quickly?" Belle says.

"The way has been cleared quietly with riders on a hundred different bills passed by our Parliament and your Congress. It's been a slow, carefully planned, insidious process to devastate the Arctic wilderness."

Stephen looks at her skeptically. "And you know all this how?"

"Because of Lou. He can prove it. That's why it's important that I find him."

"When did you last hear from him?" Vernon asks.

"A week ago. A meeting had been set up at a cabin north of Winnipeg. Lou was going to give us documents exposing this scheme and all those involved."

"Did Lou say what the documents were?" Belle asks.

"Memos of some kind. What we know is that he first stumbled

onto something suspect while he was working with the Lac La Ronge Reserve."

"Helping them get back land lost in a shady deal in the fifties," Stephen says.

"How did you know?"

"The two guys who paid us a visit today. Maybe they really were from Intelligence and Security."

"Or they were just doling out enough information to make it appear so," Belle says.

"Anyway," Tanya goes on, "what your brother initially found was a more recent easement agreement across the southern section of the reserve, signed ten years ago."

"Agreement with whom?"

"Same people who stole the land in the fifties. The provincial government. This easement was described as a right-of-way for a road and adjunct construction. Although it wasn't clearly stated in the agreement, the understanding was that the adjunct construction was to be an extensive system of power lines to bring electricity to isolated communities. Which apparently got your brother interested because there were already lines serving all the communities on the reserve. He began checking and discovered similar agreements with a number of other reserves. It was done quietly, and just like earlier land thefts, with a lot of money passing under the table."

Belle puts a finger on the map. "So, this is the blueprint for the pipeline network?"

"Roughly. Monte forced it out of one of the people on the other side of this issue."

"Forced?" Belle asks.

"This business is deadly serious. Monte was one of the casualties."

"He's the dead man you mentioned? How did he die?"

"That meeting north of Winnipeg? Catie set it up. But like I said, she turned out to be working for the other side. When Monte got to the meeting site, Catie was already there. But he smelled something funny about the situation. He called Lou and warned him off. Then he ran, but not before some goons put a couple of bullets in him. He lived long enough to let us know the true nature of Catie."

"And to send me this map," Belle says.

"Apparently."

"Why me? Why not Lou?"

"Maybe he was afraid they'd get to Lou, too, and he wanted to be sure the map reached someone who would do the right thing with it. Lou is always talking about you, Belle, how proud he is that you're going to be a lawyer and defend indigenous rights. Did Monte send anything else with the map?"

Belle glances at Stephen, then says, "Just the map with that cryptic message and the date May tenth. What's so important about May tenth?"

"I don't think it's a date. Maybe something about longitude or latitude. I say that because of another important piece of the puzzle that we hoped Lou could provide."

"Which is?" Stephen asks.

"The route for the primary pipeline from the Arctic to the processing facility, which we believe will be built somewhere in Alberta or Saskatchewan, central to all the pipelines you see here. Lou indicated to us that it was among the memos and other documents he had and was going to hand over to us."

"Can't you just go public with what you do know?" Stephen says.

"And sound like crazy conspiracy theorists? The public is already primed to dismiss cries of injustice coming from indigenous people. In order to get anyone who counts to listen to us, we need those documents. Ever since that botched meeting, we've been trying to reach Lou on his cell phone, but he doesn't answer. After Catie, he probably doesn't know who to trust."

"It's clear these people are still worried about my brother," Belle says. "So, they haven't got their hands on Lou or the documents."

Tanya looks uncomfortable and says, "It was a long drive here. Mind if I use your bathroom?"

"Down the hallway," Minnie replies. "Second door on your right."

When Tanya has gone, Stephen says quietly, "Why didn't you tell her about the thumb drive, Belle?"

"How can we be sure anything she's saying is true? For all we know, she could be lying to us. She could be Catie."

"She's given us a pretty good idea of what's going on," Minnie says.

"But without the documents to prove it, Mom, all we have is a map full of lines."

"What do you want to do?" Vernon says.

"Take the direct approach," Belle replies.

When Tanya returns, Belle says, "You claim to be working with my brother. Can you prove it?"

Tanya picks up her beaded leather bag and pulls out the wallet that held her driver's license. This time she extracts a photograph. It's a picture of her and Lou standing in front of a statue of Mahatma Gandhi.

"I've seen that statue in Winnipeg," Belle says.

"Read the back."

Belle turns it over. Written in script are the words *Together toward peace.*

"Do you recognize your brother's handwriting?"

Belle passes the photograph around. Minnie nods and says, "Lou always writes with a flourish."

"Kind of convenient," Stephen says. "Having that photo so handy."

"I thought I might need to prove myself. Seemed the easiest way." Tanya slips the photo back into her wallet, which she returns to her beaded bag. "Any other test you want me to pass? Look, we're worried about Lou's safety and why he's gone silent."

"Like you said, maybe he just doesn't know who to trust," Vernon offers.

"He trusts you, doesn't he? But has he called?"

"If these people know who he is and have the kind of reach you seem to believe they have, maybe he's afraid they'll track his calls," Stephen offers.

Tanya slumps a little in her chair. "I should probably get back to Winnipeg. We don't have much time to stop this meeting. If it goes forward, trying anything after that will be like standing in front of a speeding freight train. So much pristine land will be ruined forever."

"It's late and a long drive," Minnie points out. "Would you like to stay here for the night, get an early start tomorrow? We have a spare bedroom. That is, if Stephen doesn't mind sleeping on the couch."

"I don't want to impose."

"I insist," Minnie says. "Maybe things will look brighter in the morning."

Minnie prepares the spare bedroom, the one she says Lou and Anton shared growing up. They bid Tanya good night, and before they all turn in, they discuss the plan for the next day.

"Anton'll be flown out of the woods with the others tomorrow," Vernon says. "He'll want to go with us to Shoal Lake, I'm sure."

"If I know my dad, he'll want to be in on this, too," Stephen says.

"So the question," Vernon says, "is should we take Tanya?"

Belle considers and gives a nod. "If Lou's there, he'll confirm her story or brand her as another liar. If she is who she says she is, she can get the information Lou has to the right people. It's clear that time is of the essence."

Vernon looks to Stephen. "You've got a vote in this."

"Belle's right. She should go with us."

"Okay then," Vernon says. "Let's all get some sleep."

Stephen has agreed to take the living room sofa. Belle brings him a blanket and lingers while her parents head to their room.

"Thank you," she says.

"What for?"

"None of this is really your problem, but here you are."

"Wouldn't miss it for the world," he says.

"Seriously, I'm grateful. We're all grateful."

She's near enough to him that when he looks into the dark wells of her eyes, he sees his own reflection. "You're welcome."

She leans to him, her breath warm against his cheek, and plants a kiss there. "Good night."

Not long after, Stephen drifts into sleep with the feel of that gentle kiss still lingering.

PART TWENTY-ONE

CORK

CHAPTER 41

It's already daylight when Cork wakes. He rolls to his side and a fist of pain punches his ribs. He sucks in a loud breath and groans.

"Finally awake," Rainy says.

She's sitting at the fire with Meloux. Cork rises slowly, feeling like a man decades older than he is. He glances around and asks, "Where's Morriseau?"

"Trying to catch us some breakfast," Rainy says and nods toward the lake.

"Do we know what lake this is?"

Meloux says, "I have always called it Bizaanide'e."

"A place to make peace with your heart," Rainy translates. "On your map, it's called Cloud Lake."

Cork rises and comes to sit by the fire, grunting in pain as he does so.

"It'll be good to get your ribs looked at," Rainy says.

"You told me they weren't broken."

"Only a guess. An X-ray would confirm it. And you need to rest."

Cork shakes his head. "Still a lot of work to be done."

"There are others who can do it," Rainy reminds him.

"I want a piece of whoever's behind all this."

Meloux laughs.

"What's so funny?" Cork asks.

"Blind fox," the old man says, shaking his head.

"Yeah? What am I not seeing, Henry?"

"It is right in front of your eyes. What you have asked for has already been given."

Cork looks at Rainy and his irritation at the old Mide dissolves. Meloux's right. For more than two days, Cork's most fervent prayer was for the safe return of Rainy. His prayer has been answered. Still, the idea of stepping back from tracking down whoever is responsible for this whole mess doesn't sit easily with him.

Anton Morriseau appears, stepping from the woods onto the flat rock above the lake. "Anyone hungry?" He holds up two large-mouth bass.

Meloux smiles. "In my years, this lake has given me fish many times."

Of course, Cork thinks. Meloux has spent a lifetime in this wilderness. He wonders if there is a hill or a hollow the old man doesn't know.

Rainy cooks the fish over the flames and they eat. They are just finishing when Cork hears the distant hum of the search plane engine.

"Let's get down to the lake," he says, rising.

Rainy and Morriseau stand, too, but Meloux doesn't move.

"Uncle Henry?" Rainy says.

"You go," Meloux tells her. "I will walk back on my own and I will take my time."

"That's a long walk, Henry," Cork cautions, then hears the

stupidity of his words. This old man has just spent days on foot in these woods. What's another long walk to him? "All right. Can we leave you anything?"

"The pack. It contains my knife and hatchet and flint and steel. And I have this." The old Mide lifts his medicine bag. "That is all I need."

Rainy bends and kisses her great-uncle's cheek. "For everything, Uncle Henry, *chi migwech*."

Rainy and Anton Morriseau start away, but Cork holds back. "Thank you for keeping her safe, Henry."

"Not me," the old man says and smiles again. "The Creator must have plans for her."

Deputy Dave Foster is in the search plane with the Forest Service pilot. He updates them on all that the Sheriff's Department knows at the moment. The most important piece of information is that Stephen and Lou Morriseau's sister, Belle, are in Bena. They have an idea where Lou Morriseau might be. When he tells them, Anton Morriseau nods.

"Should have thought of that earlier," he says, as if kicking himself mentally.

"We had a lot of other things to think about," Cork reminds him.

Foster looks toward Rainy. "The sheriff's pissed at you and Meloux for letting LeLoup slip away."

"Exactly what crime has he committed?" Rainy asks.

"I don't know. Collusion, maybe. Conspiracy to commit murder. Something. One of those guys shot at you, after all."

"LeLoup wasn't a part of that," Rainy says.

"That's not how the sheriff sees it. Just warning you. She'll be waiting at the dock when we land on Iron Lake."

And she is. As the de Havilland Beaver noses up to the marina, she exits her cruiser and walks to meet them, scowling.

With Rainy's help, Cork steps from the plane, moving stiffly because of his bruised ribs. "Morning, Marsha."

"Good to see you alive, Cork," she says perfunctorily, then eyes Rainy. "What could you possibly have been thinking, you and Henry?"

"LeLoup, you mean?"

"That's exactly what I mean."

"I'm not law enforcement, Marsha. I have a different duty."

"What duty could possibly drive you to set free the man who tracked you down?"

"That's all he did was track us down. He didn't threaten us in any way."

"Tracking you down certainly put you in harm's way." She nods toward Rainy's bloodied shirtsleeve. "You need to have that looked at."

"He kept Henry from being shot," Rainy says.

"Where is Henry?" Dross looks past them into the plane cockpit. Deputy Foster, who was the first out of the plane, is bent over, securing a line from the Beaver to a cleat. She gives him a hard look. "Dave?"

Foster straightens up and says, "He didn't come."

"What? You just left him out there?"

"Not his fault, Marsha," Cork says. "Henry's choice. Let's just leave it at that."

"Come on then," Dross says. "You both need medical attention, and I'll give you an update on the way. Dave, give Mr. Morriseau a ride back to his vehicle, then report to my office."

"Thanks, Anton," Cork says.

The two men shake hands and Morriseau replies, "Any time."

In the cruiser, Dross questions Rainy about LeLoup. Did he tell her anything that would shed light on why the men were after Dolores Morriseau?

"I didn't ask him about that," Rainy tells her. "I had other business with him."

Dross shakes her head. "Could've used a little help with all this."

"What about the man I left tied to the tree?" Cork asks.

"We still haven't identified him and he's not saying a word."

"And the guy Rainy shot?"

"Still missing somewhere out there in the Boundary Waters. Azevedo and the search party spent some time this morning trying to track him down but with no luck. We did locate the Escalade our bogus Lou Morriseau drove to Sam's Place. Abandoned on a logging road off Highway Two. Stolen."

"What about the impostor?"

"Nothing yet. On the plus side, though, Stephen and Morriseau's sister think they've got a lead."

"What is it?"

"A map of some kind, maybe gas lines in Canada. They're not a hundred percent sure. But more important, they think they might know where Lou Morriseau is hiding. They'll check it out today."

"Foster told us," Cork says. "I've got to get to Bena. I'm going with them."

"Not until a doctor examines you and those ribs."

"My ribs are fine."

"How do you know?"

"Rainy told me."

"I didn't tell you that. I just said probably not broken. You need an X-ray at the very least," Rainy insists.

"Take me home, Marsha," Cork says in a cold voice.

"Hospital," Dross says in a voice just as cold.

"Hospital," Rainy says more gently but just as firmly.

Cork looks out the window at the streets of Aurora rolling past. He admits to himself it feels good to be home and to have Rainy safely beside him. But all his training and experience demand that he leave again. Still, arguing with Rainy and Dross won't get him anywhere.

"Hospital," he says. "Make it snappy."

CHAPTER 42

Jenny, Daniel, and little Waaboo greet them at the door as if they've been gone for years. Waaboo wraps his arms around Cork's hips and cries, "Baa-baa!" Then he gives Rainy a big hug as well.

"Marsha's been keeping us in the loop," Jenny tells them. "God, it's good to see you both. But, Dad, you look like hell."

"You need to rest," Rainy tells Cork evenly.

"I'll rest when we have the people behind this whole mess in custody. I'm going upstairs to pack a few things, then I'm taking off to Bena."

"I'll go with you," Daniel says.

Cork shakes his head. "Once again, you need to stay here, make sure everything's quiet on the home front. The man Rainy shot is still out there somewhere. If he makes it out of the Boundary Waters, he could be looking for a little payback. And at least one other accomplice might still be in the area. I want you here."

There's a knock at the front door. Jenny goes to answer and returns with Anton Morriseau. "I just saw Dolores," he reports. "She's doing fine. Your sheriff insists on keeping her awhile, just to be sure she's safe until things have settled down. I'm heading back to Bena."

"Mind if I ride along?" Cork asks.

"Thought you might say that. But what about those ribs of yours?"

"Only bruised. I've got some pain pills."

"Cork—" Rainy begins.

"I'm going and that's that. Give me five minutes to throw some things together, Anton."

He heads up the stairs. Rainy follows him to their bedroom. While she stands watching silently, he grabs a few clean clothes and throws them into an overnight bag.

"Mind getting my toothbrush?" he asks as he digs out a clean pair of hiking boots from the closet.

She returns with the toothbrush, his razor, and a comb. She places them on top of the clothing in the overnight bag. She also drops in his passport and Stephen's. "You'll need these at the border." She takes his face in her hands and stares deep into his eyes. "This is one of the reasons I love you. And also one of the things I hate. You be careful, do you hear me?"

"I promise I'll come back with only bruised ribs. And maybe I'll have Lou Morriseau with me in the bargain."

She kisses him gently, then steps back and lets him go.

"Your wife is a special woman," Morriseau says. They're in Morriseau's truck, a red F-150 a decade old but kept in good shape. They're moving along a section of highway blasted through sheer rock topped with pines. "One of the Midewiwin and a pretty fine shot to boot."

"You married?" Cork asks.

"Been close a couple of times but dodged the bullet. You wore a badge once, so you know how hard it can be on a cop's family. Just seemed to me a better idea to keep myself single." His eyes hold on the road ahead as he asks the next question. "You lost your first wife, right? To some bad players?"

"That's right."

"Hard," Morriseau says. Then he says nothing more most of the way to Bena. Which is fine with Cork because the medication he's taken not only helps with the pain but also makes him drowsy, and he sleeps.

He wakes two hours later, when Anton Morriseau pulls up in front of a house in Bena. The sun has passed its zenith, and when Cork gets out, he feels the warmth on his face in a refreshing way. His ribs still hurt, but the sunshine and the prospect of finding Lou Morriseau brighten his spirits.

The front door opens even before they've reached the porch. A man about Cork's age steps out, followed by a woman who appears to be Rainy's age. Vernon and Minnie Morriseau, Cork guesses. Behind them come Stephen and two young women. The porch becomes a scene of greetings and introductions and then they all enter the house.

Cork can smell freshly brewed coffee and he accepts the offer of a mug from Minnie Morriseau. They sit in the living room, a place that feels comfortable and homey, and Cork relaxes for the first time in days.

"Okay, tell me what you found in Edina. What's this lead?" Cork says to Stephen.

Stephen and the Morriseaus' daughter, Belle, relate the narrative of their time at Lou's house. Cork sips the good, strong coffee Minnie has brought him and listens without interrupting. When they spread the map on the table, Tanya Baptiste explains what's going on north of the border.

"You told us there's an issue about time," Stephen says.

"We know a meeting is going to take place in a few days and the final agreements that will solidly lock in the pipeline network will be signed there. After that, it may be impossible to stop this train wreck of a plan. If we can get word out about the meeting location, we might be able to get media and outraged people there to disrupt things."

"Vox populi," Belle says. "The voice of the people."

"It can make all the difference," Tanya says. "So we have to get to your brother soon. But you still haven't said where he is."

"A place that might be safe. You'll see soon enough," Vernon says.

"He should have just come here," Minnie says. "We're his family. If he's in trouble he should have come to us."

"He's probably trying to keep all of us out of this, Mom," Belle says. "Just trying to keep us safe."

"We're five hours away," Anton Morriseau reminds them. "We should be going."

Cork says, "I'll call Dross, keep her up to date."

"Maybe that's not a good idea, Dad," Stephen says. "I've been thinking. The people behind all this are powerful. It wouldn't surprise me if they're monitoring all our communications."

Silently Cork chides himself. He should have thought of this, too. "Right," he says. "No particulars in our phone communications. I'll just let Dross know we're on our way. Nothing about where, okay?"

"Best take my truck," Anton Morriseau says. "I've got a crew cab."

"I've got my car," Tanya says.

"You'll come with us," Belle tells her. "Your car will be fine here. You can come back for it after our business is finished."

They've decided that Vernon Morriseau will stay back with Minnie, just in case someone of a threatening nature shows up.

The goodbyes are brief, but Minnie manages to pack some cold fried chicken and biscuits for them before they go. They pile into Anton Morriseau's truck and head out of Bena, north toward Canada.

They've been on the road for an hour when Cork gets a call from Rainy. "Watch your back, Cork. They're coming for you."

PART TWENTY-TWO

THE WOLF

CHAPTER 43

It's barely light enough to see, but in the dim blue-gray illumination before dawn he lopes among the trees and underbrush, a steady pace that LeLoup knows he can sustain for hours.

The night before, after he left the two Mides, he'd made his way around the lake, which Meloux had called Bizaanide'e. A place to make peace with the heart. He'd settled himself on the lakeshore, where he could still see the flicker of the campfire atop the distant cliff. It appeared to be no larger than a match flame, but he found it comforting.

Prophet. He'd rolled the word over and over in his mind with no idea why this name had been given to him. The change in him had come so suddenly that he was still reeling a little, stunned. *Prophet.* What did that mean? It sounded like something out of the Old Testament, a dusty relic of the past. Yet there was a familiar sense to it, as if it had always been his shadow but had finally overtaken him.

Kitchi-Ottiziwin. He'd pondered this final word the woman had offered him. To live and express yourself kindly and fully from the heart. *Is this the path before me?* he wondered. It seemed an impossible thing to ask, especially considering all that he'd been a part of in the past. He'd remembered a line from a poem he read in school long ago that for some reason had stayed with him. *Two roads diverged in a yellow wood.*

Sitting in the dark, under a heaven full of stars, and with a little flame flickering in the distance, he'd felt as if he was at a place where two roads diverge. As the night crawled toward morning, he had considered long and hard the choice before him.

Now, as he runs in the growing light of a new day, he understands that outside this wilderness, a great darkness still looms, and that time is of the essence. He has always had an acute sense of direction, of geography, which has served him well in so many of the foreign locales in which he's fought battles that were never his own. He needs no map to guide him as he heads toward Iron Lake.

It's been more than twenty-four hours since he's eaten, but he's gone longer without food before. He's been trained as a soldier, a hunter, a warrior, trained to focus on the dictates of the mission over the dictates of his body. He pauses only to relieve himself and to drink occasionally from the clear water of a stream. In this way, as the sun nears its zenith, he breaks from the woods and stands in the meadow on Crow Point.

It's been only three days since he and the others Kimball had hired first approached the cabin of the Mide, but to LeLoup it feels so much longer, feels as if he's circled the world and returned to this place a different man. He pauses at the edge of the trees, scanning the scene to ensure that he's alone. No smoke from the cabin stovepipes, a good sign. He's about to move forward when he stops and, much to his own surprise, sees the meadow in a different way. The wild grasses are calf high and sway gently in the light, warm breeze. The veins of bloodroot flowers are deep red and the columbine blooms hang down like red bells. The small yellow eyes at the centers of pasqueflowers look on him with kindness. The blue of the sky seems to him a great hand poised in benediction. He stares at the scene and believes he has never felt a place that offers such peace. There is something sacred here, and he regrets that he and the others violated it with their weapons and their violent intentions.

Although he knows he should be moving quickly, he walks instead, breathing in the cleansing scent of evergreen and the good smell of warm, moist earth. He would love to lie down in this meadow and close his eyes and be like the plants, soaking up life from the very ground beneath him. He finally speaks aloud, "Prophet." And in this place, it feels right.

He moves toward the ATV, which, on his earlier visit to Crow Point, he'd observed sitting next to the second cabin. He finds the key still in the ignition and smiles at this simple, rural display of trust. He starts the engine and shatters the beauty of the quiet, the beauty of the moment.

It's time once more to be the wolf. But he promises himself as he heads away, *This will be the last.*

He abandons the ATV a block from the North Star Inn, a nondescript motel at the edge of Aurora. He's wearing camo and carrying his Weatherby MeatEater in the open, but in a town that caters to hunters, this isn't an unusual sight. There's only one vehicle currently parked in front of a room, and LeLoup recognizes the black SUV. He spends several minutes scoping out the area. No housekeeping staff making rounds. Through the window of the office, he can see the young desk clerk, whose eyes are riveted to a videogame on a television screen. LeLoup approaches the door of room number 17. He knocks lightly once, pauses, knocks twice, pauses, then one more rap. He sees the curtain pulled aside just a hair. A moment later, the door opens.

"Kimball's gonna eat you alive," Fredricks says to him. "Get inside."

LeLoup enters and sees that Fredricks is alone. "Where's Kimball?"

"Him and McHugh went to get some intel."

"Where?"

"House of one of the women you guys were chasing out in the wilds. Her and her husband were airlifted out this morning, guy name of O'Connor. He's the one who left Mike Herring cuffed to a tree out there for the wolves to feed on."

"Where's Herring now?" LeLoup asks.

"Locked up in the county jail."

"Has he said anything?"

"Our intel says no. And if he wants to live to a ripe old age, that's the way it'll stay."

"They haven't ID'd him?"

"Not yet. Probably won't if Kimball's done his job well. Course Kimball's had his own problems to worry about."

"Oh?"

"The woman he went after winged him. A bullet through his leg. A chopper brought him out of the woods, the one that was supposed to extract all of you and the Morriseau woman."

"This woman he's gone after now, what's the intel she might have?"

"Kimball got word that her kid might know where Morriseau's hiding, probably somewhere in Canada. The kid's in a burg called Bena. Probably going to head across the border today to find Morriseau. Kimball and McHugh are going to sweat the woman, see if they can get an exact location."

"Do you have an address for her?"

Fredricks gives it to him and says, "Gooseberry Lane. Can you believe that? Sounds like something out of a fucking fairy tale."

Fredricks doesn't see the blow coming. With the butt of his rifle, LeLoup knocks him out cold. He searches the man's pockets and takes the keys for the SUV parked out front. With bedsheets, he ties Fredricks's hands and feet, then he leaves the motel.

- PART TWENTY-THREE -

RAINY

CHAPTER 44

The cut on her arm from the rock chip took eight stitches to close, but in the woods Rainy had already used an ancient healing technique to treat the wound: spiderwebbing. The doctor who'd stitched her up, a young guy new to the North Country, had been skeptical at first, but when he examined the cut and found no evidence of infection, he admitted to being impressed.

Still, Rainy's arm is sore and her whole body aches. The first thing she does after Cork and Anton Morriseau leave is take a long, hot soak in the tub. She lies back in the soothing water, closes her eyes, and offers a prayer of thanks to the Creator for her safe return from the wilderness, and for Cork's. Then she offers a prayer for her great-uncle, who is still out there somewhere. And finally, she prays for the safety of those trying to unravel the mystery at the heart of all this violence.

When she's finished her bath and dressed, she goes downstairs, where things seem unusually quiet. She finds her nephew Daniel alone in the kitchen.

"Where are Jenny and Waaboo?"

"Gone to do some work at Sam's Place so they can open up as soon as Cork and Stephen are back. Hungry, Aunt Rainy?"

"I could eat a moose."

"I'll fix us some lunch. Ham and cheese sandwiches okay?"

"Sounds heavenly."

"Something to drink?"

"I'll put on some hot water for tea, thanks."

As Daniel goes about preparing the meal, Rainy watches him and finally says, "What's troubling you?"

Daniel laughs. "It's that obvious?"

"You usually hum while you work."

"Preoccupied."

"You want to be with Cork and Anton."

"I feel useless here."

"That sandwich you're making is much appreciated."

"You know what I mean."

"You and Cork, cut from the same cloth."

The kettle begins to whistle and Rainy makes herself chamomile tea. Daniel brings the sandwiches to the table and sits with his aunt.

"What's wrong now?" she says when he doesn't eat.

"You let him go."

"LeLoup." She shrugs. "I didn't see him as a danger."

"What do you really know about him? He could be a killer."

"Cork has killed. But I know his heart is a good one."

"The man who tracked you down, who led those others to you, you think he has a good heart?" It's not just skepticism she hears in his voice; it's censure as well.

"He's been a spirit divided. I believe he has a better sense now of the journey the Creator has laid out for him. The road ahead will be a different one."

"And if you're wrong?"

"Then Henry's wrong, too. Do you believe we both could be that wrong?"

But it's clear to Rainy that Daniel, like Cork and Marsha Dross, is bridling against the decision she and Henry made. The truth is that in the safety of the house on Gooseberry Lane, she's beginning to have her own doubts about much of what occurred in the wilderness. Was the man who now thinks of himself as Prophet thinking clearly? And Prophet? What does that mean? Even Henry couldn't say. Maybe Prophet of death?

"One of Henry's basic teachings is that we need to listen more to our hearts and not so much to our heads. I did what my heart told me was the right thing," Rainy says.

"I hope you don't regret it. I hope none of us do."

Daniel's cell phone rings. It's Jenny, asking him to come to Sam's Place and take Waaboo to play in the park while she finishes up.

"You'll be all right?" he asks Rainy.

"I handled myself in the woods. I'm pretty sure I can handle things here."

"I didn't mean . . ."

"Go. I'll clean up here."

She takes her time straightening the kitchen, then drifts into the living room. She wants to call Cork. He should be in Bena by now. Stephen should be telling him about the lead he believes he's found. Whatever that lead, Rainy hopes this will all be over soon and both O'Connors back safely in Aurora. She sits in an easy chair, closes her eyes, begins another prayer to the Creator. Then she hears the squeak of the hinges on the door to the back porch off the kitchen. *Jenny*, she thinks, *or Daniel and Waaboo*. She's sitting with her back to the kitchen. She turns and waits for them to appear. She's not at all prepared for the two men who step through the kitchen doorway with guns in their hands. One is a stranger. The other she's seen before. He glares at her and says, "Thought you killed me, eh?"

CHAPTER 45

"What do you want?" Rainy says from the easy chair where she sits.

"Information," replies the man she shot in the wilderness. He limps toward her. One of his pant legs bulges with what Rainy assumes is thick bandaging. She's not sure how badly she wounded him, but she can see from the strain on his face that walking is torture.

"What kind of information?" she asks.

"LeLoup. Where is he?"

"I don't know. He left us in the Boundary Waters."

The man sits on the sofa and seems relieved to be off his bad leg. His cohort has moved to the window, watching the street.

"We already know that. Where did he go?"

"I told you, I don't know. He just left."

"Did he give you any indication of his intentions?"

"He said he had to set things right."

"Funny, that's what I'm all about, too." He leans toward her, the handgun resting on his knee. The barrel is fitted with a silencer. "Your husband's on his way to meet with your son in a place called Bena. They've found a lead of some kind. Do you know what that is?"

"I don't."

"See my friend over there?" He nods toward the man at the window. The gun he's holding is also fitted with a silencer. "McHugh's an expert." He waits, as if expecting her to ask what kind of expert. When she refuses to reply, he says, "At extracting information."

"I can't tell you what I don't know."

"Maybe you know more than you think you do. When did you last talk to your husband?"

"Not since he left."

"What did he tell you before he left?"

"Just that Stephen and Belle Morriseau had returned to Bena with a lead of some kind. Stephen didn't say what that lead was."

"Did they mention Catie?"

"They didn't mention anyone by that name."

He studies her. "Your husband and son are going to Canada. They think they might know where Lou Morriseau is hiding. Do you know where?"

"You're wasting your time. I don't know anything."

"Leo," the man says to McHugh.

McHugh turns from the window, grinning as if with the expectation of something quite pleasurable for him. He's taken only a single step toward her when he freezes and looks beyond Rainy, his eyes wide with surprise. The wounded man on the sofa is also looking beyond her, clearly stunned. At her back, she hears a voice she recognizes.

"Play this cool and maybe you'll get out alive."

She turns and sees Prophet standing in the kitchen doorway

with the butt of his scoped rifle snugged against his shoulder, the barrel leveled at Leo McHugh.

"LeLoup." McHugh's grin gradually returns. "Glad you could join the party."

"What you're going to do is this," Prophet says. "You're going to lower your weapon to the floor and step away from it."

"Or?"

"I'll shoot you where you stand. You, too, Kimball."

"Put down your gun, McHugh," the man on the sofa says, and he slowly lowers his handgun with its silencer to the floor.

McHugh also complies, but he's still grinning.

"Get up slowly, Kimball," Prophet says.

The man on the sofa rises. "Now what?"

"We're going to leave this lady in peace. Come this way. We'll exit through the back door. Don't want to scare the neighbors."

Rainy watches as the two men approach Prophet, who steps away from the kitchen door to let them pass. "*Migwech,*" she says before he follows them. She hears the door to the back porch open, then she hears the pop of a small firearm, followed by the more powerful crack of a rifle. She leaps from her easy chair and rushes to the kitchen doorway.

The man called McHugh lies on the porch floor, clutching his chest. Prophet stands over him. Kimball is nowhere to be seen.

"What happened?" Rainy says.

"McHugh had another gun hidden. Kimball ran."

Rainy's instincts as a healer kick in and she goes quickly to the wounded man. "He's losing blood. I need to call nine-one-one."

She hurries to the phone hanging on the kitchen wall, punches in the three numbers.

"What did Kimball say to you?" Prophet asks.

"He wanted to know where you went and if I knew anything about where Lou Morriseau might be hiding."

The 911 dispatcher answers and Rainy tells her about the man who's been shot. She gives her address and is told help is on the way and to stay on the line. But she hangs up. She grabs a kitchen towel and returns to the wounded man, who's gone slack, with his eyes closed. She tears open his shirt. His chest is a gush of blood, which she attempts to stanch, pressing the folded kitchen towel hard against the wound.

"What did you say to him?" LeLoup asks.

"That I couldn't tell him what I didn't know."

"I'm sure he thought you were lying. Your husband's gone to a town called Bena, and from there he'll probably head to Canada to find Lou Morriseau. Do you know where?"

She looks up from the wounded man. Her hands are covered in his blood. "How do you know this?"

"Doesn't matter. Do you know where he's going in Canada?"

"I don't."

"You should let him know he'll be tracked."

"Tracked? How?"

"I can't say for sure. But I know these people. Kimball won't stop until he gets what he wants."

From a distance comes the sound of sirens.

LeLoup hands her a card with a cell phone number written on it. "If you find out where he's going, call me."

"What do I tell the sheriff?"

"Whatever you want, just give me a head start."

"Where are you going?"

"If everyone's headed to Canada, guess I am, too. I'll do my best to stop Kimball." He turns to leave.

"Prophet," she says, using the name given him in his vision.

He pauses.

"Think about the road you're on. Is it the one meant for you?"

"Two roads diverged in a yellow wood," he says. Then he vanishes out the back porch door.

When the EMTs arrive, Rainy finally steps away from the bleeding man, returns to the kitchen phone, and dials Cork's cell number. When he answers, she says, "Watch your back, Cork. They're coming for you."

"Did he say anything?" Dross asks.

They're sitting at the kitchen table. The wounded man was long ago rushed to the emergency room of the Aurora community hospital. Rainy has called Jenny, told her what's happened, and asked her to make sure she and Daniel keep Waaboo away from the house, away from the scene of the shooting, away from the blood still staining the floorboards of the back porch.

"He quoted a line from Frost. 'Two roads diverged in a yellow wood,'" Rainy replies.

"What did he mean?"

"He had a choice to make and he made it."

"I don't understand."

"I'm not sure I do either."

"Did you see where he went, what he might be driving?"

Rainy shakes her head.

"Did he give you any idea what this is all about?"

"He didn't."

Dross gives a low growl of frustration, then her cell phone rings. She answers and listens. "I'll be right there." After she ends the call, she says, "Anonymous tip. Our fake Lou Morriseau is waiting for us at the North Star Inn, room seventeen."

"You better hurry."

"According to our anonymous tipster, he's not going any-where." Dross rises from the kitchen chair.

"LeLoup?" Rainy says. "The anonymous tipster?"

"Probably. I wish to God I knew which side he's on."

"Two roads diverged," Rainy says.

"The hell with Frost." Dross walks out, says something to her people in the living room, and Rainy hears her leave, slamming the front door as she goes.

- PART TWENTY-FOUR -

CORK

CHAPTER 46

Considering all the powerful forces that appear to be involved, they decide it's best to fly under the radar, so they don't cross into Canada at a checkpoint. They take a winding back road, two vaguely visible ruts through deep woods. "When I wasn't much more than a teenager, I knew every back route. I used them to bring petty stuff across the border. Cigarettes, booze, a little weed for my friends," Anton Morriseau explains. "Back then, I thought it was a kick."

"Pretty serious if you'd been caught," Cork says. "Stain on your record like that and you'd never have been a cop."

Morriseau shakes his head. "The things you do when you're young and stupid."

"But handy now," Stephen points out.

"Keeps us hidden from any eyes that might be watching for us," Morriseau agrees.

They move slowly along this back route. At last, they emerge on a highway and continue north. After an hour, they make a pit stop at a convenience store. Cork and Tanya Baptiste use the restrooms while Stephen and Belle grab some bottled water. For another hour, they follow the highway that winds through flat forest land until they reach the Trans-Canada Highway. From there, they head east fifteen miles, and finally south again on a narrow track of serpentine dirt.

"I've seen snakes crawl straighter than the route here," Stephen says at one point.

"Shoal Lake Forty is on a man-made island, pretty remote," Morriseau tells them. "We've been campaigning for years to get a real road built to the reserve. We call it Freedom Road. Until this year, the only way to reach the island was an old ferry that runs out of Kejick, other side of the lake. They finally deigned to build us a bridge, but until they construct a real road instead of this wagon track, it's kind of a bridge to nowhere."

"Our people didn't always live on an island," Belle says. "A hundred years ago, typhoid fever was rampant in Winnipeg, and the city was desperate for a source of clean drinking water. They looked to Shoal Lake, where our ancestors lived. The study the government made indicated that, in their words, 'only a few Indians' lived there."

"So no problem confiscating our land," Morriseau says. "Old story, right?"

"They relocated our people to the end of a peninsula," Belle continues. "Then they dug a diversion canal across the neck, creating an island and cutting us off from the mainland. For a hundred years, the only way to get into or out of the reserve has been by boat when Shoal Lake was open or, in winter, a dangerous walk across frozen water."

"A lot of our people have died making that crossing," Morriseau says. "We've had a ferry operating for the last forty years, but she's an old tub of a thing now, barely seaworthy."

"To make matters worse," Belle says, "the government built a dike to make sure the drinking water to Winnipeg remained clean, diverting the Falcon River toward the island. The water of that river is fouled with tannin. It's become so bad that for the past twenty years the reserve's been under a boil water advisory and our drinking water has been hauled from the mainland in bottles. We've been fighting the provincial and federal governments for years to construct a decent road, which would allow us to build a water treatment plant."

"Have you had a hand in that fight?" Stephen asks.

She shakes her head. "There are good people here carrying on that battle, and there are still lots of indigenous battles to be fought south of the border."

After a gut-rattling journey of several miles, they come to a bridge that spans a narrow stretch of water, but Morriseau stops before crossing. He parks, gets out, and the others follow.

They stand on the bridge, peering over the railing. Dusk has come, the clouds in the east blooming with magenta, the water is like a mirror reflecting their images and above them the darkening sky.

"This is the diversion canal. What you see on the other side is the man-made island," Morriseau tells them.

"Is that where we're headed?" Tanya asks. "Lou's over there?"

"One of the possibilities," Morriseau says. "We have a house on the island, but there's also an old cabin on Fox Creek belongs to my family. We've used it mostly for hunting." He nods toward the south. "We'll check the house first."

They return to the truck and continue across the bridge. A few miles on the other side, they turn north along a rutted dirt road between stands of maple and pine and arrive at a two-story house set on the lakeshore. The structure is old, but well maintained. In the twilight, beneath the canopy formed by two large maple trees and with the calm lake at its back, it seems a welcoming place.

"We used to spend the whole summer here," Belle says. "With

our grandparents before they passed. We don't get here as often as I'd like. Busy lives."

"Busy lives," Anton Morriseau echoes sadly.

"Doesn't look like anybody's been here for a while," Cork says.

"Let's check inside." Morriseau bends and reaches beneath the front steps. When he straightens, there's a key in his hand. He unlocks the front door. Inside, the place is cold and feels empty. They check the rooms and find that nothing appears to have been disturbed.

"Nobody's been here since we closed up last fall," Belle says.

"So much for this possibility," Morriseau says. "Let's keep our fingers crossed for Fox Creek."

"Fox," Cork says with a nod toward Stephen.

"What is it?" Belle asks.

"When I was a kid, Henry Meloux gave me the spirit name Makadewagosh," Stephen replies.

"Black fox," Morriseau translates.

"It's a sign," Belle says with a hopeful smile.

They exit, and Morriseau locks the house behind them. As they head toward the truck, a mud-spattered pickup drives up the dirt road and parks, blocking their exit. A man steps out, Native, big, stern-looking, wearing a bead-studded jean jacket. He eyes them all dourly for a moment, then breaks into a wide smile.

"Anton, Belle. Haven't seen you in a month of Sundays."

"Edgar," Morriseau says. "*Boozhoo.*" He introduces the man to others as Edgar Green. "Our nearest neighbor. Half a mile down the shoreline."

"Saw your truck. Wondered what's up," Green says. "Come to open up for the season?"

"We're looking for Lou. Have you seen him?"

"Haven't. Told those other folks the same thing."

"Other folks?"

"Week ago. Some men came asking about your brother."

"What did they want?"

"Just Lou."

"What did you tell them?"

"The truth. Haven't seen him in months."

"Did you tell them about the cabin?"

"They didn't ask. Wouldn't have told them if they did. Main-landers. Government people." He spit on the ground. "Freedom Road, eh? It'll be good for us, but it'll also make it easier for outsiders to come calling." He glances to the south. "Heard Buck Redsky's seen a light where Fox Creek feeds into Anger Bay. Could be Lou at your old cabin. But if it was, he's kept to himself. Never was as neighborly as you and Belle and your folks."

"Thanks, Edgar."

"Vernon and Minnie?"

Belle says, "They're good."

"Sticking around for a while?"

"We'll see once we find Lou," Morriseau says.

"If we find Lou," Belle adds.

"I'll pass the word." Green nods to them, returns to his pickup, and drives away.

"Government people," Belle says. She looks to Stephen. "From Intelligence and Security Services?"

"The guys we talked to didn't mention coming here."

"An oversight?" Belle says. "Or obfuscation?"

"Or just a lot of fingers in this pie," Stephen says. "What do you think, Tanya?"

The woman is gazing south. Somewhere in that direction sits the cabin on Fox Creek. She doesn't seem to have heard Stephen's question, so he repeats it.

"Oh," she says, bringing her attention back to the moment. "Could be any one of a dozen agencies. A project of this scope crosses a lot of departmental boundaries, provincial and federal."

"In which case, lots of people must know about the project, so it can't be that secret," Stephen points out.

"You know how a government works. Each little part knows only what it's supposed to know and not an iota more. The people they've sent after Lou probably don't know anything except that he's a threat of some kind to those in powerful places. So, what next?"

"We'll check the cabin."

"How do we get there?"

"The other side of the bridge there's a cutoff south. We passed it, but it's easy to miss because it's not much more than a couple tire depressions leading into the woods. Nothing down the trail but the cabin, about two miles in. Sits in a grove of birches on Fox Creek."

"It's getting dark," Tanya says, looking at the sky, where the first stars are showing in the east.

"We better hurry," Morriseau says.

They pile into his truck, return to the main road, and back the way they came. But a couple of hundred yards before they reach the bridge over the diversion canal, Morriseau brakes to a stop. "What the hell?"

Two black SUVs parked nose to nose form a roadblock on the far side of the bridge. Several men stand beside them shouldering rifles.

"What do we do?" Belle asks.

Tanya opens her door and gets quickly out. "Go back to the house. Give me half an hour. I'll have the bridge cleared."

"How the hell are you going to do that?" Morriseau says.

She reaches into the beaded bag she's brought and pulls out a pistol. "Draw them away. You need to stay out of sight until I do. We have to make sure they don't find Lou."

"These people play for keeps," Cork says.

"And you think I don't?" Tanya replies. "Mother Earth is more important than the fate of any one person. I promise you I'll get that bridge cleared."

Cork says, "Way too dangerous. There's got to be another way."

"We don't have time to argue about this," Tanya says. "Go. Now." She steps back from the truck, clearly determined.

"So be it," Anton Morriseau says. Then he adds, "Good luck, *nishiime*," using the Ojibwe word for "little sister." He makes a U-turn and heads away.

Cork looks back. He watches as Tanya stands facing the blockade. "Brave girl, but I don't like her odds. Or ours."

"At the very least, she might buy us time to come up with a backup plan," Stephen says.

"One way or another, we have to get to Fox Creek." Belle glances at her brother. "What about a boat, Anton?"

CHAPTER 47

Morriseau doesn't turn on to the dirt lane that leads to the welcoming little house under the maples. He drives another quarter mile and turns down another similar dirt lane.

"We're going to Edgar and Lacey's," he explains. "We'll borrow Edgar's boat to get to Anger Bay."

Morriseau parks beside the mud-spattered pickup in front of a one-story frame house with a broad view of the lake at its back. Edgar Green pushes open the screen door of the porch and steps out.

A woman follows him, wearing a colorful knit sweater, wiping her hands on a dish towel, and smiling. "Edgar told me you were on the island."

"*Boozhoo*, Lacey." Belle gives the woman a warm hug.

"You look like a man in need, Anton," Green says. Morriseau explains the situation, and Green nods. "Take the boat. Then I think I'll get a few of our guys together and we'll just go see about that blockade."

"Don't start any trouble for yourselves," Belle says.

"Been fighting government people our whole lives here. How's this any different?" Green says.

"Cork," Morriseau says and motions him to follow.

Morriseau unlocks a long storage box in the bed of his truck, lifts out a rifle in a camo cover, and hands it to Cork. Cork unzips the cover and pulls out a Winchester Model 94. "Figure you know your way around one of those," Morriseau says. He takes out a second rifle for himself, a Winchester identical to the one Cork holds. He grabs a box of cartridges, and the two men rejoin the others.

They hurry to a tiny dock on the lakeshore where an old aluminum Lund is moored. The boat's fitted with a Mercury outboard engine that appears to be of the same ancient vintage.

"Not much of a looker," Green admits. "But she runs good. And I just filled her with gas this morning."

"*Migwech*, Edgar," Morriseau says and shakes the man's hand.

"Getting dark. You should go before you get lost," Lacey says.

One at a time, they get into the little craft. Morriseau takes the stern and grabs the tiller. Green unties the mooring rope and gives the bow a shove. Morriseau starts the engine, and they motor away onto a lake where the water is as dark as the evening sky.

"Anger Bay," Cork says. "Quite a name."

"On maps, you'll find it identified as Enger Bay," Morriseau says. "Officially it was named after my mother's great-uncle, an elder in our community whose white name was Enger. His Ojibwe name was Animikiikaa."

"Thunder," Stephen says.

"Had himself a temper. When Winnipeg stole our water, he wanted to go to war, and when our people didn't, he stormed off and spent his remaining years in isolation in a cabin he built where Fox Creek empties into the lake, refused to have anything to do with the rest of us. White mapmakers dubbed the big inlet Enger after that bitter old man, but we've always called it Anger Bay." Morriseau's quiet for a few moments, then says, "I don't know. Maybe that old man was right. Maybe we should've fought."

"We're fighting now," Belle says. "The arc of the moral universe is long, but it bends toward justice."

"Hold on to that thought," Anton Morriseau says.

The sky is already freckling with stars when Morriseau points to a light among the trees whose tops are silhouetted black against the last dim illumination of the day. "That light's coming from the cabin on Fox Creek."

"Lou's got to be there," Belle says triumphantly.

Morriseau nudges the bow onto a pebbled beach. He kills the engine and they disembark and head toward the cabin. It's a tiny affair, nestled in a stand of birches, the kind of hunting cabin Cork has seen a hundred times in the deep woods of Tamarack County. There are thin curtains over all the windows except for one that looks onto the lake, where a light shines through. Cork and Morriseau grab their rifles from the boat, and they circle to the front of the cabin, where a dusty Jeep Cherokee sits parked.

"That's Lou's," Belle says. "He's definitely here."

Morriseau heads to the front door. He holds his rifle at the ready and nods to Cork. The door isn't locked and Cork swings it open.

The interior of the cabin is rustic. A potbellied stove with a cooktop occupies the center. Near it is a table, old and scarred, with a chair on either side and a kerosene lantern burning on the tabletop. Next to the lantern lies an old leather satchel. In one corner, there's a sink, where water is supplied by a pump-handle spigot. The sink is filled with opened tin cans and food wrappings. Against the back wall stands a set of bunk beds. The lower bunk is currently occupied by a man staring at them with glazed eyes.

"Lou!" Belle says and rushes to him.

Lou Morriseau mumbles, "Belle?"

"We were afraid we'd never find you." Belle hugs him, then pulls back. "My God, you're burning up with fever."

"My leg," Lou says, barely able to get the words out.

Belle pulls back the thin blanket covering him. His pant leg is cut away, showing a thigh bound up with bloody wrapping that looks as if it's been torn from a sheet. Belle delicately removes the blood-soaked binding and reveals a mess of crusted, ugly-looking skin with a bullet hole just off center. It reminds Cork of the wound Rainy delivered to the man in the Boundary Waters.

"What happened?" Belle asks.

"Catie," Lou replies. "Water. Please." His tongue is thick, and when he speaks, the words are barely discernible.

Anton goes to the sink and eyes all the opened tins and discarded wrappings. "Is this what you've been living on?"

"Haven't eaten . . . couple of days."

Anton pumps water into a tin cup and brings it back. "Can you sit up?"

"I'll try."

"Here." Belle helps ease her brother into a sitting position. He closes his eyes a moment, as if gathering what little strength he has, then sips some water from the cup Belle holds.

"Who shot you?" Anton asks.

"People behind Catie. Somebody tipped them off."

"We know about Catie," Belle says. "She's an operative for the other side. Tanya Baptiste told us all about her."

"Tanya Baptiste?" He seems confused.

"The woman you've been working with."

"Never heard of her." He thinks a moment, then scowls. "What's she look like?" When Belle gives him a thumbnail description, he says, "Tina Beaulieu. One of the people I trusted in Canada. If there's an operative for the other side, it's probably her."

"So, what about Catie?" Belle asks. "Who is she?"

"Not a person. An acronym. CATIE stands for Canadian-American Transcontinental International Extension."

"Is that the network of natural gas pipelines? Tanya or Tina or whatever her name is told us about it."

"Natural gas? That pipeline's got nothing to do with natural gas. It's about something more precious. The wars of the future."

"What are you talking about?"

Lou looks at her, at them all, as if it should be obvious. "Water," he says.

Belle is wiping old blood from around the leg wound with water from the sink. Cork can see that it was a clean through-and-through shot and doesn't appear to have hit a bone or pierced an artery. Still, the man's probably lost a lot of blood and the wound is clearly infected. With the water he's been sipping and with Belle's comforting, Lou Morriseau is coming around, but it's a struggle.

Stephen is holding up the map that he and Belle found.

"I sent that," Lou says, grimacing as Belle tends to him. "Afraid they would get to me before I could let anyone know. Mailed it from a post office before I hit Freedom Road. You got the thumb drive, too, right?"

"Here." Stephen pulls it from his pants pocket. "'Kill Catie' isn't much to go on. You scrawled it as one word and we had a hell of a time trying to decipher it."

"It is one word, along with the number. The pass code for opening the thumb drive."

"We tried that," Belle says. "It didn't work."

"Let me see." Lou studies the scrawl on the map. "Christ, I screwed it up. There should have been a zero before the five. Killcatie 0-5-slash-1-0. Kill CATIE May tenth. Sorry. Wasn't thinking too clearly, okay?"

"Understandable," Anton says. "But what's with the spiderweb of pipelines on the map?"

Lou Morriseau takes a while, breathes deeply several times, continuing to muster his strength. "We know better than most people about the government stealing our water. But this is on a continental scale, Anton. Those lines, they represent a network of pipelines that will siphon water from dozens of sources in northern Canada—Great Bear Lake, Great Slave Lake, Lake Athabasca, Reindeer Lake, a host of others. The pipelines will funnel it across the whole continent, throughout Canada and into the States for irrigation and industry. They'll pipe it to ports where it will be shipped out like oil. So much of the world is thirsty. Water is going to drive the whole geopolitical landscape soon, and Canada is one of the world's largest sources of fresh water."

"But there are treaties regulating access to water," Belle points out.

"Which they've gotten around before. Shoal Lake's a perfect example. Water usage here is governed under the Boundary Waters Treaty of 1909, which prohibits the level of siphoning Winnipeg needed for its own water supply. But when push came to shove, the governments found a way to give them what they needed. If you look at CATIE, waiver after waiver has already been granted at all levels, local, provincial, and federal. It's been written into legislation, included in convoluted riders. Easements for the pipelines have already been agreed to. The groundwork has been laid, billions of dollars invested." His explanation is interrupted by a fit of coughing. Belle lets him sip from the tin cup again, and after a minute of ragged breathing, he goes on. "They've been at this secretly and successfully for a very long time. Agribusiness, industry, banks, governments on both sides of the border. Only thing that can stop it now is a public uproar. For the past six months, I've been working with the women in Now We Speak to get the evidence we need to go public."

"Now We Speak?" Anton says. "Never heard of them."

"I know them," Belle says. "Organized a few years ago by indigenous women in the middle provinces. They've aimed at rallying First Nations people against dismantling laws that protect the environment. They're very good with social media and reaching out to even the most remote reserves."

"Contacted them about what I was discovering. They encouraged me to continue gathering information so that eventually we could expose this conspiracy."

"Why didn't you tell me?" Belle says.

"Or any of us?" Anton adds.

"Needed to keep it as quiet as possible. The government is always watching."

"What happened?"

"Set up a meeting to deliver the documents on that thumb drive. Photocopies of the originals are in my briefcase there." He nods toward the leather satchel on the table. "Memoranda, communications between businesses and governments—federal, provincial, local—all related to CATIE. Been sifting through thousands of documents for the past six months, gathering them."

"The proof?"

"Enough to pull back the curtain they've been hiding behind. If we can get all this out in the open, maybe we can get enough people angry and CATIE can be stopped. We need those documents to show that it's not just Indian conspiracy nonsense."

"This meeting you set up, I'm assuming it didn't go well," Cork says.

Lou squeezes his eyes shut and his face contorts. Cork wonders if he's feeling real pain now or just recalling something painful. "Was at a remote cabin belongs to one of the women from Now We Speak. We've met there before. Deep in the woods north of Winnipeg. Five-mile hike from the road. Impossible to find unless you know the way. Or we thought it was impossible."

"Maybe Tanya Baptiste told them," Belle says.

Lou shakes his head. "Might have known about the meeting, but she wasn't in on it, had no idea where the cabin was. My guess? Somebody tracked us. The others covered for me while I got away. But, as you can see, not unscathed. Afraid they may have killed everyone I left behind. Knew if I tried to cross the border, they'd be watching for me. Came here instead. On the way, I managed to mail off the map and that thumb drive. And buy a few eats." He pauses, thinks for a moment, then asks, "What day is this?" When Belle tells him, a look of relief comes into his face. "There's still time."

"Time for what?" Belle asks.

"Three days from now, May tenth, they're going to hold a conference at a remote retreat near Banff. Representatives from all parties involved will be there to finalize much of CATIE, sign accords. Like I said, we wanted to get word of all this to the media with the hope of ambushing them, getting everything out into the open, splashed across headlines. The only thing that can stop this now is public outcry."

"Why haven't you called?" Belle says.

"Afraid my phone calls were being monitored. Out here on Anger Bay, no service anyway. Thought as soon as I could travel, I'd get word out somehow. But—" He taps his infected leg.

WILLIAM KENT KRUEGER

"You could have talked to Edgar or anyone here, asked for their help," Anton says.

"Wanted to keep them out of this. Wanted to keep you all out of it. Safe. After they shot me—and probably killed the others—was afraid there's no limit to what they might do to the people I care about. Besides, I somehow managed to misplace the keys to my Jeep. Tried to walk to the island yesterday but couldn't even make it out the door."

"So, you were just going to wait and what? Die here?" Belle says angrily.

Lou lays his head back wearily against the cabin wall. "Like I said, not thinking clearly."

"We need to get you to a doctor fast," Anton says.

"And before Tanya or whoever she is brings those goons here," Cork adds.

"It may be too late." Stephen is standing at the front window. "Headlights, Dad."

"How many?" Cork asks.

"One vehicle."

Anton turns the flame of the kerosene lamp to a low flicker, and the cabin plunges into near dark. He takes a position at the window next to Stephen. Cork joins them, and they watch as the vehicle, a dark SUV, comes slowly along the narrow track through the trees. It stops behind Lou's Cherokee. The headlights die. The driver's door opens. A man gets out, a vague shape in the last of the twilight. He approaches the cabin slowly. He's cradling a weapon, a rifle. He stands looking at the cabin window, as if he can see Cork and the others there in the dark. Then he steps to the door and knocks.

Cork readies his rifle and nods to Anton, who opens the door.

"Lay down your weapon," Cork orders when the man steps in. "And put your hands in the air."

The man bends, lays his rifle on the floor, and straightens up with his hands raised above his head.

Stephen turns up the flame of the kerosene lamp, illuminating the visitor.

"Who are you?" Cork demands.

When the man speaks, his face is an oval of calm. "My name is Prophet."

PART TWENTY-FIVE

THE WOLF

CHAPTER 48

He had arrived in Bena in the late afternoon, as long shadows of the pines had begun to stretch across the road. He'd stopped at a place called the Big Winnie Resort and General Store and asked for directions to the Morriseau home. He'd parked in front of a tidy little house, mounted the porch steps, and stood in the gold light of the descending sun. When the door opened to his knock, he said to the woman who answered, "*Boozhoo*. I need your help."

And he told her his name.

Her face had been hard and her eyes full of suspicion as she scrutinized this stranger at her door. Then, as if she had seen something in him that put her doubt to rest, she softened and her eyes changed. Her husband called out from somewhere behind her, "Who is it?"

She replied, "He says his name is Prophet."

Now, as LeLoup crosses into Canada, he reckons he's less than an hour behind the Morriseaus, the O'Connors, and Tanya Baptiste.

He has directions to both the house on the island and the cabin on Fox Creek, along with a hand-drawn map, given to him by Vernon Morriseau. Morriseau had tried to insist that he go, too, but Le-Loup told him it was best he stay with Minnie.

"These people are the kind that will find and torture a family if it will get them what they want. God willing, they still don't have that. You need to remain here, and until you hear from me or your children, don't open your door to anyone you don't know. You have a rifle?"

"For deer hunting," Morriseau had replied.

"Keep it handy and loaded."

Although the road north is serpentine, LeLoup keeps the SUV he's taken from Fredricks in Aurora well over the speed limit, trying to cut the distance between him and the others. Cut, too, the distance between him and Kimball, because the man is a jackal and won't stop until he's sunk his teeth into his prey. Kimball will have help. His team in Minnesota has been decimated, but Kimball has others at his beck and call. The people backing him have armies.

As he speeds along, LeLoup thinks about his first meeting with Kimball. They were both in the Canadian military, posted in Kandahar, Afghanistan. LeLoup was halfway into his tour of duty when he was summoned to Kimball's office. The interview lasted one minute.

"You have a knack for tracking," Kimball said. "True?"

LeLoup was surprised that a man of Kimball's rank would know about the ability of one of his very junior officers. "True, sir."

"How?"

"I left school at sixteen and spent the next three years in the Northwest Territories learning to hunt, sir."

"Hunt what?"

"Mostly big game, sir. Deer, bear, moose, caribou, musk ox."

"No wolves?"

"I'm Wolf Clan, sir. I don't hunt my brothers."

"But you've hunted humans, I've been told."

"I sometimes helped out the RCMP."

"Because you had a reputation."

"Word got around, sir."

"Word has got around here, too. I'm creating a special unit to track and kill targeted Taliban fighters who've fled into the mountains. I need people who can follow them regardless of the terrain. Can you do that?"

"I can, sir."

And he did, until his tour of duty ended. Then came his second meeting with Kimball.

He was working as a hunting guide for a wilderness operation out of Yellowknife when Kimball knocked on the door of his rented apartment above a beauty salon.

"Sir?" LeLoup said, taken completely by surprise.

"No longer in the military. No need for *sir* now."

He let the man in and fixed them both tea, and Kimball laid out his proposition.

"Private security company?" LeLoup said. "Mercenaries, you mean."

"A word with pejorative connotations. We provide armed security for people who need protection."

"Like who?"

"At the moment, I need a man like you in Sierra Leone. Do you know where that is?"

"The west coast of Africa. What do you need a man like me for?"

"The government is fighting a war against rebels who want control of the diamond fields."

"The government can't do this themselves?"

"Their army is a little on the untrained side."

"And you've been helping with the training?"

"Exactly. But I need someone with your particular skill set."

"To track down the rebels."

"And train others how to do that as well."

"I like tracking bear and moose."

"And living above a beauty salon? How would you like to own a cabin on Great Slave Lake? Or anywhere else for that matter?"

"Bought with mercenary money?"

"Money earned legitimately in the protection of those who can't protect themselves."

That was often not the case, but once LeLoup signed on, it became easier and easier to ignore the gray areas of the job. And there were long periods between assignments when the money allowed him the freedom to live in the cabin he bought on Great Slave Lake and every morning wake to the knowledge that he was embraced by one of the most beautiful wildernesses in the world, light-years from the humiliations of the residential school of his youth, from the dirt of the city, from the senseless tug-of-war between tainted governments and equally tainted rebels and greedy cartels.

But even then, walking alone in the woods that had become home to him, he heard the whisper of something more, something that kept him from the peace he thought he'd purchased.

For ten miles, he negotiates the rugged dirt track leading toward Shoal Lake. He plans to head to the house on the island first, thinking it might be the more comfortable option for refuge. Vernon Morriseau cautioned him that the way to the cabin on Fox Creek is easy to miss if you aren't watching, so LeLoup, as he nears the island, does just that. He spots the turnoff, two slight depressions that could be tire tracks, barely discernible between the trees, then drives on.

A couple of hundred yards shy of the bridge on Morriseau's crudely drawn map, he brakes to a stop. In the dim twilight, he sees a blockade created by two black SUVs. Nothing is going onto the island or escaping from it. Although he can't see the man, he knows Kimball is there, can feel his presence in the same way he was able to sense a hiding enemy in the mountains of Afghanistan or the jungles of Sierra Leone or Colombia.

He turns, backtracks to the cutoff for the cabin, and follows the narrow corridor through the woods to its end. He sees a light in the cabin and a Jeep Cherokee parked out front. As he approaches in his SUV, the cabin goes dark. He pulls up beside the Cherokee, kills the engine, and steps out, bringing with him his Weatherby MeatEater. He walks toward the cabin, pauses, and stares at the darkened window beside the door, aware that he is being watched. He steps to the door and knocks.

CHAPTER 49

"My name is Prophet."

LeLoup has laid down his Weatherby and put his hands in the air, as instructed. The flame on the kerosene lantern has been turned up, and in the light, he can see all those gathered in the cabin. Most of them are Native.

The man looking nearly dead on the bunk is Lou Morriseau. In preparation for Kimball's mission, LeLoup memorized the faces of both the man and his wife. The young woman sitting with him is Belle Morriseau, and the man who opened the door is her brother Anton. LeLoup was shown their photographs at the home in Bena. The white man who ordered him to lay down his weapon is, he guesses, the Mide woman's husband, Cork. The young man, who clearly has Native blood in him, must be O'Connor's son, Stephen.

"You're the one from the woods," O'Connor says.

"One of them," LeLoup acknowledges.

"My wife tells me you're a different man now," O'Connor says skeptically.

"This time I'm here to help. You've been tracked."

"We know," Anton Morriseau says.

LeLoup looks at the man on the bed. "The Cherokee out front? Yours?"

Lou Morriseau nods.

"Then the rest of you must have come by—boat?"

None of them offer a reply, but LeLoup understands. Why should they trust him?

"The man who's tracked you here is named Kimball. If he finds you, he'll make certain that no one else does. Ever. That's after he's gotten from you whatever it is you have that he wants. Then he'll erase every bit of evidence that he was ever here and that you were ever here."

"People on the island know we're here," Belle says.

"And who will listen to them?" LeLoup says. "Governments, all of them, make people disappear. How long does the echo of those who go missing last? It doesn't matter that anyone knows you're here. What matters is that no one will be able to discover where you've gone. You need to go before Kimball and his people come here looking for you."

"They don't know about the cabin," Belle says.

"I wouldn't count on that." It's O'Connor's son who speaks. "Tanya."

Whoever that is, LeLoup can see that it's a name with a profound and dark impact. "You need to take the Jeep and get away now."

"No keys," Lou Morriseau says in a dead voice.

"Then we'll take my vehicle," LeLoup says.

O'Connor hesitates, studies LeLoup's face, their eyes meeting for a long moment. Then he nods. "Let's go."

"Help me, Anton," Belle says. Together, she and her brother help Lou to stand. He nearly crumples when he tries to put weight on his wounded, infected leg, but the strength of the others keeps him from falling. They hobble together toward the door.

"Okay if I get my rifle?" LeLoup asks.

O'Connor nods. "Take it."

"My satchel," Lou Morriseau says.

Stephen grabs it as they pass the table. O'Connor opens the door and gestures for LeLoup to go first. The others follow him into the gathering dark.

They're halfway to LeLoup's SUV when two sets of headlights appear a hundred yards down the track through the woods.

"Edgar?" Belle says hopefully.

"Those are xenon headlights," LeLoup says. "I'm guessing not standard equipment for any vehicles on the reserve. It's Kimball."

"What do we do?" Belle asks.

"You take the boat, all of you," LeLoup replies. "I'll hold them off."

"If we stick together, we might be able to hold them off," Anton Morriseau says.

LeLoup shakes his head. "If you stay, people will die. Take the boat and the outcome will be different."

"What about you?" Belle says.

"I've dealt with Kimball before. I'll handle him."

"How do we know we can trust you?" Stephen O'Connor says.

"Your friend Henry Meloux would ask, what does your heart tell you?"

In the looming dark, the older O'Connor studies LeLoup. "*Migwech*," he finally offers.

"Take my briefcase, Prophet," Lou Morriseau says. "It's what they're after."

"No, Lou," Belle says.

"Everything in there is on the thumb drive. Maybe if this Kimball gets what he wants, he won't do anything drastic."

"You don't know Kimball," LeLoup says. "But maybe it will buy you more time."

He takes the satchel, then watches as the others disappear around the side of the cabin, heading through the birch trees toward the lakeshore.

He returns alone to the cabin, sets the satchel on the table, and lowers the flame of the kerosene lantern to a bare flicker. He stands at the front window as the headlights near. He doesn't fear this confrontation with his former commander. There is a calm inside him more profound than any he has ever known. The path he is on, he understands, is the path that was always meant for him, and it will take him where he was always meant to be.

The SUVs pull up behind Lou Morriseau's Cherokee and the SUV LeLoup came in, blocking any hope of escape. The doors open and four men exit from each of the vehicles, eight in all, armed with rifles. They wear dark-shaded clothing, prepared to blend into the night. LeLoup is dressed in the camo he wore in the Boundary Waters days ago. He can smell the faint aroma of the smoke from the last campfire, the one he shared with the two Mides, and there is comfort in that primal scent.

He watches the operatives spread out, flanking the sides of the cabin, covering any escape he might attempt. Those who remain in front of the cabin use the Cherokee as cover. It's clear that Kimball is preparing for a firefight.

"You inside the cabin! Lou Morriseau! This is the police. Come out with your hands up!"

It's Kimball's voice. LeLoup makes no reply. Time is what he's playing for here.

"We know you're in there, Morriseau! Come out or we'll use force to bring you out!"

LeLoup slips to a side window, sees that one of the operatives there is working his way toward the cabin. He fires a shot through the window, aimed not to kill, just to warn. Then he moves to the window on the other side and does the same. There's no returned fire. LeLoup understands that Kimball doesn't want to take any chances killing Lou Morriseau before the man has given him what he came for.

"All we want are the papers! Hand them over and we'll leave here quietly!"

LeLoup thinks about one of the missions Kimball recruited him for in Colombia years ago. After FARC demobilized, a remnant group had taken a Canadian nun hostage for ransom, and Kimball brought in LeLoup to find her and her captors. It was the dry season, and LeLoup had no trouble tracking the group to a small compound, a collection of shacks, really, on the bank of a river backwater near the border with Venezuela. Kimball and the team had entered the compound at night and extracted the woman without firing a shot. As soon as she was safely away, however, Kimball commenced a firefight that decimated the small group of former guerrillas. LeLoup hadn't participated in that part of the operation. Tracking was all he'd been hired to do. But he'd led Kimball there, and although the guerrillas were not people he particularly cared about, he could see no reason for the slaughter, and felt a gnawing sense of responsibility. When he'd questioned Kimball later about the necessity of the killing, the man had replied, "A rabid dog will continue to bite until you kill it, no? How were those people any different?"

LeLoup suspects that to Kimball, Lou Morriseau is simply another rabid dog.

The shot comes through the front window, showering glass across the wood floor. One shot, that's all.

"Just a warning, Morriseau! There's plenty more where that came from! We're not leaving until we have those papers!"

LeLoup pitches his voice high. "I've made copies and sent them to the newspapers."

"If that's true, then there's no reason not to give us what we've asked for!"

"I don't have the papers with me."

"Fine! Just let us come in and look!"

"One man, no weapon."

There's a period of quiet, then Kimball calls back, "Deal!"

"What's your name?"

"What does it matter?"

"Say your name."

"Yeats!"

LeLoup smiles. Whenever Kimball uses a pseudonym, he always chooses a poet.

"Come ahead, Yeats. But only you."

The man leaves the cover of the parked vehicles and walks toward the cabin. It's too dark to see him clearly. If it is Kimball, he will have a weapon on him, maybe a Sig P365 in an ankle holster or a knife tucked somewhere. It will come out the moment LeLoup's attention is directed elsewhere.

"Stop," LeLoup orders when the man is near the door. He can see now that it isn't Kimball. "Turn around and go back the way you came." As the man turns to follow the instructions, LeLoup calls out, "This time make sure it's you, Yeats."

Half a minute later, one of the men walks to the cabin. From the way he limps, LeLoup is certain that this time it's Kimball. "Open the door and enter."

Kimball steps inside.

"Close the door behind you." When Kimball has complied, LeLoup says in his normal voice, "How's the leg?"

He can tell by the long pause in responding that he's taken Kimball by surprise. But the man's voice, when he answers, is as cool as iced tea. "The old man, he somehow flipped you."

"He just helped me see who I really am."

In the ghost of illumination the tiny kerosene flame offers, they eye each other.

"And who are you, LeLoup?"

"Prophet."

"Of things to come?"

"Of the next few moments anyway."

"So, what now, Prophet?"

"We wait."

"Where has Morriseau gone?"

"To safety."

"There's no such place. If I don't get him, there are others who will."

"Not before the world knows the truth, whatever it is."

Kimball gives a bark of a laugh. "You think that will end this? There's far too much at stake."

"If the information Lou Morriseau has can be written off so easily, why all the efforts to find him? No, Kimball, I smell fear."

"Then we're done here."

"Not quite. Why don't you just have a seat?"

"I believe I'll walk out that door instead."

"I don't think so. Remember McHugh."

"Shoot me and it will be in cold blood. Would you do that?"

"Do you want to take that risk?"

"You've always been a strange one, LeLoup, but something I've always known about you is that you don't really have the heart for killing. Not in cold blood anyway."

"Try to walk out the door, and we'll both find out if that's true."

Kimball's eyes are locked on LeLoup's face as if trying to see through to the man's thoughts. In the next moment, whether he will test LeLoup becomes a moot point.

The window shatters and something hits the floor. Although LeLoup can't see the smoke, he senses the tear gas immediately and covers his face with the crook of his arm. Kimball is already out the door. LeLoup has no option but to follow.

Outside, he's tackled immediately, and bodies pin him to the ground. Blow after blow is delivered to his head until he drops into a black that is very near unconsciousness. But not quite. He can feel himself rolled to his stomach, arms pinned against his back, wrists bound with a plastic restraint.

"Get him up," he hears Kimball order.

He's hauled to his feet and supported as he finds his footing and his senses return. Someone shines a flashlight into his eyes, blinding him. Behind the light Kimball speaks. "Where has he gone?"

"I told you. To safety."

The blow comes to his solar plexus, knocking the air out of him, and he struggles to breathe.

"How'd he get past us?"

"Just smarter than you, I guess."

Another blow that would double him over if he weren't being held so tight.

"Whoever you are now, Prophet or just the pathetic remains of a man, it's time you disappeared. Then we'll find Morriseau and he'll disappear, too."

"You don't need to go after him. What you're looking for is in the cabin. The satchel on the table."

Kimball leaves and comes back a minute later. "Why did he leave this behind?"

"Because his life is precious to him. And I promised him I would see that you didn't get it."

"And yet here it is."

"Can't say I didn't try."

"We'll still get Morriseau," Kimball says. "I don't like loose ends. Bring him."

The light swings away from his eyes, and it takes a few moments for LeLoup's vision to adjust again to the dark. He's shoved toward the SUVs parked behind the Cherokee.

He's always known the end would be death. It's the same for every living thing. But all his life, he's believed that his death would mean nothing, and this, more than death itself, is what has always troubled him. But the old Mide finally opened his eyes to the true nature of the journey he's been on his whole life, and if this death is the one that has always awaited him, there is a reason.

They are at the vehicles when lights appear on the lane through the woods, a long train of more than a dozen sets of headlights. Truck engines growl like a pack of hungry wolves. The train stops at the edge of the small clearing where the cabin sits on the bank of Fox Creek. The squeals of truck doors opening on hinges is followed by the *pop, pop, pop* of those doors closing. An army of silhouettes gathers in the glare of the headlights.

"All we want is Prophet."

LeLoup recognizes the voice of Cork O'Connor.

"He's in our custody," Kimball says.

"Custody of who?" This time it's Anton Morriseau who speaks.

"The authorized representatives of the Crown," Kimball declares.

"Bullshit." This is a voice LeLoup doesn't recognize. "We are the authorized representatives of the Kekekozibii First Nation Anishinaabeg. You are on sovereign tribal land. Here, we give the orders."

There is a sound like a hundred castanets tapping nearly in unison, a sound LeLoup recognizes as the chambering of rounds and the racking of slugs in dozens of rifles and shotguns.

"Mr. Authorized Representative of the Crown, it would be a good idea to hand over this man and lay down your weapons. Then you can all go on your way peacefully," the voice says.

LeLoup has been with Kimball on many missions, both in and out of uniform, and has often seen him act with cruelty rather than necessity. He knows that Kimball hates to lose. The man stands unmoving, his face ice white in the glare of the headlights and his eyes burning with a silvery fire. LeLoup is concerned that the man might still be considering a firefight, one that he can't win and that may cost the lives of a lot of good people.

"Morriseau's gone, Kimball," LeLoup says. "You've got what you came for. Mission accomplished."

For a long moment, Kimball makes no reply. He studies the large gathering that confronts him, assessing all the fire-power they hold. Finally, he says to his men, "Lay down your weapons."

Kimball's people comply. Several men from the reserve emerge from behind the headlights and walk among them, collecting the firearms.

"Over here, Prophet," Cork O'Connor says.

Although Kimball has ordered his men to disarm, as LeLoup walks toward the gathering silhouetted in the headlights, he half expects a bullet in his back. But he crosses the neutral ground without incident, and on the other side, Anton Morriseau cuts the plastic restraint that binds his wrists.

"Tanya!" O'Connor calls out. "Step into the light!"

A woman emerges from behind the safety of one of the SUVs and enters the illumination of the headlights. O'Connor pulls his cell phone from his jacket and snaps a picture.

"We know that Tanya Baptiste isn't your real name, but no matter," O'Connor says. "We're going to make sure that the photo I just took gets circulated among all the reserves in Canada. Good luck in the future pretending to be anything other than who and what you are."

The man who seems to be in charge says to Kimball, "Mr. so-called Representative of the Crown, have your people back away from their vehicles."

Kimball gives the order: "Do as he says."

When Kimball and his operatives have distanced themselves, the man in charge says, "The tires, guys. All of them."

Several armed men move around the SUVs, putting a bullet in every tire. Then they rejoin the others.

"It's probably a good idea to stay here the night," the man in charge says. "You never know what might be waiting for you on these back roads in the dark."

The people around LeLoup begin to return to their vehicles.

Anton Morriseau touches LeLoup's arm. "Come with us, Prophet."

He's led to a truck and gets in with Morriseau and O'Connor. All the vehicles maneuver U-turns, then head back the way they came.

"The others?" LeLoup asks. "Your son and Lou Morriseau and his sister?"

"On their way to a hospital the other side of the border," O'Connor tells him. "By the time we returned on the boat, a friend of Anton, a man named Edgar Green, had rallied his people."

"You heard Edgar back there at the cabin," Morriseau says. "He was the one giving Kimball all the grief."

"One of Edgar's friends loaned Belle a Jeep. We thought it was best that they get started while we came to give you a hand," O'Connor concludes.

LeLoup shakes his head. "Kimball will see to it that they're picked up at the border checkpoint."

"Don't worry," Anton Morriseau assures him. "My brother knows a few unofficial ways to get across."

At the junction of Freedom Road, Morriseau pulls to a stop. Another truck draws up and stops beside him. A man gets out and steps to the window Morriseau has lowered.

"*Chi migwech*, Edgar," Morriseau says.

"Haven't felt this pumped in a long time, Anton." LeLoup

recognizes the voice of the man he now knows as Edgar Green. "This will be a story we'll be telling on the island for a good long while. Thanks, O'Connor, for all you've done. And, Prophet, we're in your debt. *Migwech*."

"Means 'thank you,'" Morriseau tells LeLoup.

"And how do you say goodbye?" LeLoup asks.

"There's no word for goodbye in our language," Morriseau says. "The closest we come is *minawaa giga-waabamin*. Means 'see you later.'"

"*Minawaa giga-waabamin*," LeLoup says.

Edgar Green smiles. "Anton, get your ass in gear before that bunch of jackasses back at Fox Creek decide to try something else."

Morriseau starts for the junction of the Trans-Canada Highway, and from there toward home in Minnesota.

LeLoup has been on many missions in the company of many men, but he has never felt the kind of companionship that overwhelms him in this moment. As they rumble along Freedom Road with the dark woods embracing them on all sides and the eyes of countless stars watching them from above, he whispers to all the spirits that he understands surround them, "*Migwech*."

To which O'Connor adds quietly, "Amen."

PART TWENTY-SIX

STEPHEN

CHAPTER 50

Belle is behind the wheel of the borrowed Jeep Compass. As they pass the dark track that leads to Fox Creek, Stephen peers through the trees. He hopes that the man who calls himself Prophet and those who've gone to his aid can hold the intruders at the old cabin long enough for Belle to get the Jeep clear of interference. If they make it to the other side of the border, he believes, they'll be safe.

Lou Morriseau lies across the backseat. Stephen and Belle talk little. It's been a journey, one that has brought more than its share of challenges. Still, sitting next to Belle, studying her face in the glow from the dashboard, Stephen knows that he wouldn't trade this day or the two before it for anything. He's never met a more remarkable woman.

They hit the junction of the Trans-Canada Highway and drive west a dozen miles. At the turnoff for East Braintree, they head south and are on the serpentine road back toward Minnesota. Stephen finally allows himself to breathe freely.

Near the border, Belle slows and finds the turnoff to the back road they followed when they crossed into Canada illegally that afternoon.

"Wait," Stephen says. "Tanya knows about this road. They might be watching it."

"There's another," Lou says weakly from the backseat. "In fact, several. See if you can get Anton on the phone. If they've left the reserve, he may have service by now. Let him know we're taking the bog road."

"The bog road?" Belle repeats.

"Just tell him. He'll know what it means."

Belle tries the call, connects, and because of the concern about their calls being monitored, she says simply, "Bog road."

Anton replies, "Ten-four."

When the call is ended, Lou says, "Turn around."

They backtrack a couple of miles, and Lou directs Belle onto a dirt lane that heads west into thick woods. They follow the lane another mile and turn south along vague tire tracks down a narrow passage as ill-defined as the one that led to the cabin on Fox Creek.

"There are bogs everywhere, Belle. Take it slow," Lou says. "One misstep, and we could end up sinking out of sight."

For the next hour, they proceed at a snail's pace. The road snakes through marshland. In places, the trees and underbrush crowd against the Jeep so close that the branches scrape along the sides of the vehicle with sounds like fingernails dragged across blackboards. Whenever Belle is in doubt about the way, Lou lifts himself up from where he lies and guides her.

"Watch it, Belle!" Stephen barks.

She brakes immediately, and just in time. She was about to plunge the Jeep into a black morass.

She draws a deep breath. "I think I'd rather take my chances with the Border Patrol."

"You're doing fine, Sis," Lou says. "Just keep it slow and easy."

Belle cuts hard to the right, following a track barely discernible in the headlights. They proceed another hundred yards and are again moving down a tight corridor lined with trees when their way is blocked by a fallen log.

"Damn," Lou says.

Stephen hears the absolute exhaustion in his voice, as if this is the final blow.

"Relax. We'll clear it," Stephen assures him. "Come on, Belle."

It's a tamarack, a bog tree, long dead. In the Jeep headlights, Stephen can see where the trunk has rotted out near the base and a strong wind must finally have toppled it.

"We'll never move this thing," Belle says. "We need a chain saw."

"Let's see what's in the Jeep."

In the cargo space, they find an assortment of tools, a hatchet among them.

"Better than nothing," Stephen says.

"It'll take hours to hack through the tree trunk. Lou—" She looks toward the rear seat, but her brother has once again laid himself down.

"Do you have a better suggestion?" Stephen says quietly.

Belle shakes her head.

"Then let's get to it."

Stephen has seen sharper edges on a butter knife. The blade cuts poorly into the wood. He hacks away until his arm feels ready to drop off, then Belle takes over. For nearly an hour, they work at the cutting, taking turns. They've almost hacked through when Stephen stops, his arm raised high for the next blow. He slowly lowers the hatchet.

"What is it?" Belle asks.

"Listen."

She cocks her head, then says, "Oh, God, no."

It's the *whack, whack, whack* of helicopter blades, nearing.

"There," Stephen says and points back the way they've come.

A few hundred yards behind them, a searchlight is probing the narrow track they've followed.

"Kill the headlights, Belle," Stephen says.

She rushes to the Jeep and the headlights die. Stephen joins her.

"What is it?" Lou asks as he lifts himself slowly in the rear seat.

"A helicopter," Belle says. "Looking for us."

"How far to the border?" Stephen asks.

"I don't know." Lou sounds like a man ready for the grave. "I'm not sure where we are now."

"If we can just make it to the border," Belle begins.

Lou shakes his head. "The border's not going to stop these people. You two go on. Make sure that thumb drive gets into the right hands."

"What about you?"

"I'll stay with the Jeep, delay them as long as I can."

"You're in no condition—" Belle begins.

"Just do it. What's in there is more important. I've worked too hard to have it all fall apart now. Stay on this track through the bogs and you'll come to a road eventually, dirt but a real one. It'll cut east, connect you to the main highway into Roseau."

"Lou—" Belle tries again.

"For God's sake, just go."

"He's right, Belle," Stephen says. "We need to move."

"Turn the headlights back on," Lou says.

Stephen gives him a questioning look.

"A moth to flame. I want to draw them to me."

Stephen turns on the headlights, leaves the Jeep, and makes his way over the fallen tamarack, Belle following behind. The night is dark, moonless. They both use the flashlight apps on their cell phones to see their way. Stephen hopes that Lou's right and the headlights will be what the chopper zeroes in on. They hurry, jogging, glancing back often. They see the spotlight sweeping, sweeping, then it pauses.

"They've got him," Belle says and stops running.

"We can't help him," Stephen tells her. "If you love him, you'll do as he asks, get these documents into the right hands."

He can hear her sobs as she turns, and they start again together, heading away at a run.

CHAPTER 51

It's the dead of night in a place where bogs abound, and Stephen is exhausted. Belle, too. They walk now, have walked for hours it seems. They're on the dirt road Lou Morriseau spoke of before they abandoned him, the one that will take them to the main highway into Roseau. The batteries of both their cell phones have been drained and can no longer light the way. But there's another light source that illuminates the road and the woods around them. The aurora borealis is aflame, a brilliant curtain that drifts and dances across the sky, firing the landscape with a bright kaleidoscope of color. Under other circumstances, Stephen would be sitting and admiring the display. As it is, he's just grateful for the light it sheds.

They haven't spoken for a while. The exhaustion is part of it. But Stephen also senses that Belle is trying to come to terms with what Lou asked of her. It was a sacrifice for them both, brother and sister, and Stephen just hopes to God that what the thumb drive holds is worth the price.

"I thought he was pulling away from us, ashamed of his heritage," Belle says at last. "And all along, he was doing something important to help."

"You couldn't have known."

"But you did. Your vision of him fighting the Windigo. I should have trusted him."

"He could have shared his secret with you."

"Right, and we could all be dead now. These people, they're animals."

"Just human beings not listening to the best part of their hearts."

"You sound almost forgiving." There's acid in her voice.

"I know a man whose heart is so large it can offer forgiveness to anyone. He gives me hope, for myself and even for people like those who are after us."

"You're talking about Henry Meloux."

"I saw him dead, Belle. Another of my visions. It broke my heart. Henry knew about the vision, knew what I saw, and he opened his heart to it."

"But he's not dead, is he?"

"As far as we know. He's still out there in the woods."

"You're thinking maybe he's out there to die?"

"To accept the end of his journey. Maybe."

"Doesn't it make you sad?"

"If it's his time, I'll miss him and I'll grieve. And then I'll move on. It's what Henry would want."

"Like I should move on, whatever happens to Lou?"

"That wasn't where I was going, but it's something to think about." Stephen lets a few moments of quiet pass, then says, "I've been thinking. If I go to the university next fall, is there any chance you might still be in the Twin Cities?"

"I have to be there for my bar exam." She lets a few moments pass. "I could probably stick around for a while."

Their conversation is cut short when two sets of headlights appear suddenly on the dirt road. The lights swing around a bend fifty yards ahead where the trees are thick enough to have created a blind. There's no time for Stephen and Belle to run. They stand frozen in the headlights, blinded by the glare, beneath a sky exploding with color.

The vehicles stop. Doors open. Stephen tenses, anticipating the worst. That all the efforts will have been in vain. That all the sacrifices have been for nothing. He puts an arm around Belle, and she does the same for him as they await their fate.

"Belle, oh, my God, Belle!"

It's Minnie Morriseau's voice. She comes out of the glare of the headlights. Belle separates herself from Stephen, and mother and daughter share a long embrace.

"You okay, Stephen?" Vernon Morriseau steps before him, puts a hand on his shoulder.

"You're a sight for sore eyes," Stephen says. "What are you doing here?"

"We got a call from Anton hours ago. He told us you were taking Lou to the medical clinic in Roseau. We were on our way there. Then we got another call from him, directing us here."

"What about Lou?"

"He's been airlifted to the Roseau clinic."

"Airlifted?" Stephen says. "That helicopter wasn't the enemy?"

"Roseau County Sheriff's Office. Anton and that sheriff of yours in Tamarack County did some calling."

A man in the uniform of the Roseau County Sheriff's Office walks up beside Vernon Morriseau. "Stephen O'Connor? Belle Morriseau?"

"Yes," Stephen says.

"You'll need to come with me, folks. There's quite a bit of sorting out to be done."

PART TWENTY-SEVEN

RAINY

CHAPTER 52

She gets the call late in the night, but she hasn't been asleep. She's been sitting on the sofa in the living room, trying to calm her spirit. That afternoon, a man lost his life in her home. Although she's cleaned up the mess of that carnage, cleaned it after Marsha Dross's people had done their necessary work, cleaned it before little Waaboo could see any indication of the violation, she's still unnerved. She understands that after such violence, her own spirit needs cleansing.

"Cork? You're all right?"

"On my way home."

"And Stephen?" she asks.

Jenny and Daniel, dressed in their robes, come down the stairs from their bedroom and sit down, flanking her on either side.

"He's safe."

"You found Lou Morriseau?"

"Yes, but he's got a nasty leg wound. Anton called in some favors with local law enforcement in Roseau and Marsha Dross made some calls, too. Lou's been airlifted to a clinic. How are you doing?"

"Holding up. But I'll be better when you and Stephen are home."

"Soon," Cork says.

"What about Prophet?"

"We dropped him off just this side of the border. He said he wasn't ready to deal with the U.S. authorities yet. He may be gone for good."

"LeLoup is gone, but I have a different sense about Prophet. We'll see. How are you, love?"

"Tired. And my ribs are killing me. Aside from that, pretty good."

"When will we see you?"

"I'll meet Stephen in Bena and we'll come back together. Home by morning. Love you," he says just before he ends the call.

"And I love you."

As she explains the situation to Jenny and Daniel, Waaboo drifts down the stairs. He crawls onto his mother's lap. "I dreamed about Baa-baa and Stephen."

"Dreamed what?" Jenny asks.

"They were in a storm and then the sun came out."

"The sun is out," Rainy tells him.

Waaboo looks toward the window. Outside night still holds fast. "No it isn't."

Rainy smiles and strokes her grandson's hair. "In so many important ways, Little Rabbit, it is."

PART TWENTY-EIGHT

TOGETHER

CHAPTER 53

They wait on Crow Point. It's been days, and Henry Meloux still hasn't returned from the great wilderness. Others from the Iron Lake Reservation have joined them, some coming at sunrise, leaving at sunset, returning in the morning. Others pitch tents and settle in for a vigil that lasts around the clock. There have been suggestions that they should mount a search for the ancient and beloved Mide, but Rainy has resisted this. In their last parting, Henry made it clear to her that this journey, wherever it led him, was his alone.

Belle and Anton delivered the thumb drive safely to the women of Now We Speak. The meeting at the isolated retreat near Banff, ambushed by the media exactly as Lou Morriseau had hoped, was a debacle for those parties involved. A storm of protest has already arisen across the continent, and the governments of Canada and the United States, both of whom disavowed any knowledge of this clandestine plot, have pledged full and public investigations. There's skepticism even among those on Crow Point that CATIE can be stopped. Yet Belle continues to offer her mantra: The arc of the moral universe is long, but it bends toward justice.

Lou and Dolores Morriseau check in regularly from the hospital in Roseau. Belle, who is among those keeping vigil on Crow Point, tells Stephen that Lou and Dolores are like a couple of newlyweds.

Stephen has built a fire in the ring where Henry has often held ceremonies. He and Belle and others keep the flames burning night and day, offering tobacco and prayers.

LeLoup, the man they have all begun to refer to as Prophet, hasn't been seen or heard from since he crossed the border with Cork and Anton Morriseau.

Cork and Rainy are among those who've pitched a tent. Belle, too. Stephen sleeps under the stars. Jenny and Daniel rotate in the vigil, driving from town, sometimes with Waaboo in tow. Everyone who comes to Crow Point brings food to share.

The waiting is difficult. Cork has said it feels like the unquiet calm before a battle or bad news. Rainy chooses to think of it as the challenge of hope. Although Stephen doesn't tell anyone this, his vision of Henry lying dead is with him constantly, and he can't help but think of this time as preparation for acceptance of the inevitable. He often walks with Belle and feels great comfort in her companionship. He still hasn't kissed her. The circumstances feel wrong for that kind of exchange. But it is always on his mind.

Then one morning Prophet crosses the meadow following the path from the double-trunk birch. He walks in the gold of morning light. Rainy and Cork stand together, watching him come. He stops in front of them, unshoulders the pack he's brought, and lays it on the dewy grass.

"I've come to learn," he says.

Rainy welcomes him and he joins the others who wait for the old man.

*   *   *

Ten days have passed. The gathering on Crow Point has shrunk to a few. There is talk of a ceremony of some kind, not a burial ceremony because there's no body to bury, but some way in which to celebrate the long and beautiful life of Henry Meloux. It's Stephen who speaks most powerfully against it.

"Henry always said we need to listen. If he was gone, wouldn't the spirits of the woods speak of that? Wouldn't we have heard?" He looks to Rainy and Prophet, then to his father.

And Cork is again reminded of Meloux's encouragement to silence all the voices in his head and listen. He tries, but what he hears is his own heart telling him he can't let go of his old friend and mentor, not yet.

So, they wait some more, those who refuse to abandon hope.

And finally one night, as they are gathered around the fire that Stephen and Belle have kept burning, their hope is rewarded.

The fire has dwindled, the flames are low. Above, the moon is full, a brilliant circle, an eye set in the dark face of night. They have all been silent, gazing into the dying fire, alone with their thoughts. It's Rainy who lifts her eyes and sees him.

"Uncle Henry," she says, her voice faltering.

They do not move. They've been waiting for him for what seems like forever, but now his appearance is so sudden and unexpected that the surprise has stunned them.

At last, Cork says with a note of censure, "We've been worried, Henry."

The old man gives his shoulders a little shrug. "If that is what you choose to do with your time, blind fox."

"We've all been worried," Rainy says.

"I did not mean to cause you concern. I only wanted to be certain."

"Of what?" Rainy asks.

"That it was not yet my time. For that, I had to listen long and deep." He offers them all a gentle smile. "I confess I am grateful. It is good to be alive."

He adds wood to the flames so that the fire blazes back to life, sending smoke and embers upward toward the bright eye of the watching moon. Then he sits among them, glowing in the firelight. And they, too, are grateful. Grateful beyond words.

AUTHOR'S NOTE

The parts of this story that concern the situation of the Anishinaabeg of the Shoal Lake Forty Reserve, which straddles Manitoba and Ontario, are based almost entirely in fact. In 1919, a water diversion project channeled freshwater from Shoal Lake to Winnipeg and, in the process, devastated the community's burial ground, isolated the Native people on a man-made island, and caused catastrophic freshwater problems for nearly a century. Although I've altered a few recent developments for the sake of the story, the greed for water at the heart of this history is all too true.

CATIE is fictional, but the idea of continental redistribution of water is not. In North America, one of the grandest plans of all was the North American Water and Power Alliance (NAWAPA). First proposed in the 1950s, the concept was a massive rechanneling of water from Alaska and Canada to the lower forty-eight states. The scheme involved approximately 370 construction projects and the creation of a five-hundred-mile-long reservoir in what is known as the Rocky Mountain Trench, which would have totally inundated the Canadian cities of Banff and Jasper. The idea had a grand reception at first, but the cost—estimated in 1964 to be in excess of $300 billion—was ultimately deemed prohibitive and the ecological impact too momentous.

In 2015, NASA satellite data revealed that twenty-one of the world's largest thirty-seven aquifers have been severely depleted. Water scarcity has already caused human suffering and migrations on a massive scale. Water is now being called the next gold. As the supply of freshwater continues to dwindle and both greed and necessity begin to rule our thinking, it's neither difficult to believe that new technology will give rise to additional schemes for continental redistribution nor inconceivable that nations will go to war for control of this precious commodity.